Warnings flashed  **Eden's head...**

This wasn't wrong, it _____ regret this," she murmu___. ___-___. Then, catching Armand's face in her hands, she kissed him.

It was a dizzying experience. Wrong, because kissing him made her feel more alive than she had in months. Maybe years. He explored her mouth with a thoroughness that scorched her blood and had her knees threatening to buckle. For a moment, the garden actually did feel magical. And sexual.

"No...Armand, wait." She made an effort to pull away. "I shouldn't have, you know, done that."

"Ah, but you did." His lips curved against hers. "And you had to know I wouldn't refuse."

Dear Harlequin Intrigue Reader,

It's the most wonderful time of the year! And we have six breathtaking books this month that will make the season even brighter....

THE LANDRY BROTHERS are back! We can't think of a better way to kick off our December lineup than with this long-anticipated new installment in Kelsey Roberts's popular series about seven rascally brothers, born and bred in Montana. In *Bedside Manner*, chaos rips through the town of Jasper when Dr. Chance Landry finds himself framed for murder...and targeted for love! Check back this April for the next title, *Chasing Secrets*. Also this month, watch for *Protector S.O.S.* by Susan Kearney. This HEROES INC. story spotlights an elite operative and his ex-lover who maneuver stormy waters— and a smoldering attraction—as they race to neutralize a dangerous hostage situation.

The adrenaline keeps on pumping with *Agent-in-Charge* by Leigh Riker, a fast-paced mystery. You'll be bewitched by this month's ECLIPSE selection—*Eden's Shadow* by veteran author Jenna Ryan. This tantalizing gothic unravels a shadowy mystery and casts a magical spell over an enamored duo. And the excitement doesn't stop there! Jessica Andersen returns to the lineup with her riveting new medical thriller, *Body Search*, about two hot-blooded doctors who are stranded together in a windswept coastal town and work around the clock to combat a deadly outbreak.

Finally this month, watch for *Secret Defender* by Debbi Rawlins— a provocative woman-in-jeopardy tale featuring an iron-willed hero who will stop at nothing to protect a headstrong heiress...even kidnap her for her own good.

Best wishes for a joyous holiday season from all of us at Harlequin Intrigue.

Sincerely,

Denise O'Sullivan
Senior Editor, Harlequin Intrigue

EDEN'S SHADOW
JENNA RYAN

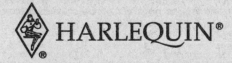

HARLEQUIN®

TORONTO • NEW YORK • LONDON
AMSTERDAM • PARIS • SYDNEY • HAMBURG
STOCKHOLM • ATHENS • TOKYO • MILAN • MADRID
PRAGUE • WARSAW • BUDAPEST • AUCKLAND

ISBN 0-373-22816-3

EDEN'S SHADOW

Copyright © 2004 by Jacqueline Goff

www.eHarlequin.com

Printed in U.S.A.

ABOUT THE AUTHOR

Jenna Ryan loves creating dark-haired heroes, heroines with strength, and good murder mysteries. Ever since she was young, she had an extremely active imagination. She considered various careers over the years and dabbled in several of them, until the day her sister Kathy suggested she put her imagination to work and write a book. She enjoys working with intriguing characters and feels she is at her best writing romantic suspense. When people ask her how she writes, she tells them by instinct. Clearly it's worked, since she's received numerous awards from *Romantic Times* magazine. She lives in Canada and travels as much as she can when she's not writing.

Books by Jenna Ryan

HARLEQUIN INTRIGUE

88—CAST IN WAX
99—SUSPENDED ANIMATION
118—CLOAK AND DAGGER
138—CARNIVAL
145—SOUTHERN CROSS
173—MASQUERADE
189—ILLUSIONS
205—PUPPETS
221—BITTERSWEET LEGACY
239—THE VISITOR
251—MIDNIGHT MASQUE
265—WHEN NIGHT FALLS
364—BELLADONNA

393—SWEET REVENGE
450—THE WOMAN IN BLACK
488—THE ARMS OF THE LAW
543—THE STROKE OF
    MIDNIGHT
816—EDEN'S SHADOW

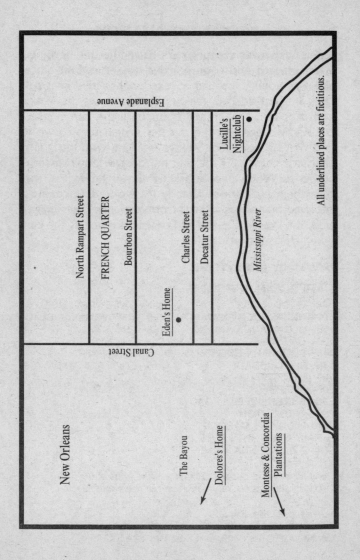

New Orleans

North Rampart Street

FRENCH QUARTER

Bourbon Street

Charles Street

Decatur Street

Esplanade Avenue

Canal Street

Eden's Home

Lucille's Nightclub

Mississippi River

The Bayou

Dolores's Home

Montesse & Concordia Plantations

All underlined places are fictitious.

CAST OF CHARACTERS

Eden Bennett—Adopted as a child, she is a ringer for her natural sister—and next in line for the family curse.

Armand LaMorte—A dark and mysterious police detective. He has many secrets to keep.

Lisa Mayne—One of three birth sisters. She discovers her natural father—then is accused of murdering him.

Mary Tamblyn—Youngest of the sisters. Her interests are entirely self-centered.

Maxwell Burgoyne—Biological father to Eden, Lisa and Mary. Did the family curse kill him?

Lucille Chaney—Eden, Lisa and Mary's birth mother. She has a shady past.

Dolores Boyer—Lucille's mother. She knows more than she should about many things.

Robert Weir—Maxwell's business partner. He appeared to gain nothing by Maxwell's death.

Dali Kafkha—A voodoo queen who believes in curses.

Limping Man—Is he part of the curse, or merely biding his time?

In memory of Catherine (Kay) Goff:

You gave me life.
You gave me love.
You believed in me.
You were the perfect mom.

I love you…

Prologue

Voodoo child with Carib blood,
And eyes of green. This is foreseen:
The eldest born to eldest grown,
My pain shall bear. Believe. Beware.
For deeds long past *chère* child will reap,
My vengeance curse, of death—or worse.

The woman's name was Eva Dumont and she wrote the curse in blood. Her blood and that of the man who was her father.

He had left her mother for another woman. He would pay for that betrayal, as would his offspring.

Her shadow, her curse, would fall from generation to generation. Not one of that tainted line would escape her voodoo spell.

Chapter One

"Mind you don't make the fillings too white, dear. I don't want to glow in the dark when I smile."

"I'll match your natural color," Eden Bennett promised, "X-ray that upper molar again, and we'll go from there."

"So long as it doesn't exceed thirty dollars." The old woman cleared her throat, then asked, "It won't, will it?"

"Twenty-eight thirty-seven, cleaning included. Open for me now, okay, and try not to swallow."

The old woman snagged her wrist before Eden could position the wedge. "You'll be gentle, won't you? My roots are as weak as my ankles these days."

Nothing wrong with her grip, though, Eden noted. She patted one bony shoulder. "I work on my grandmother's teeth, Cornelia, and her roots are three years older than yours."

Reassured, the woman relaxed into the padded dental chair. She didn't watch the television Eden had mounted to distract her more squeamish patients, but rather kept her eyes fixed on Eden and her fingers curled tightly in her lap.

She was a sweet old woman, poor as Eden's patients tended to be on Tuesday afternoons and evenings, but more trusting than many who ventured into her French Quarter office.

Since Cornelia wouldn't let anyone else do the cleaning, Eden had sent her dental assistant home forty minutes ago. With luck, she'd missed the deluge that was currently making a river of the streets and sidewalks outside.

Eden was just touching her drill to one of Cornelia's seven remaining teeth when the examination room door burst open. If she hadn't learned from one of the best, Cornelia's tooth count would have been down to six.

"Eden, you have to—" The woman on the threshold halted. "You're still working? Do you know what time it is?"

"It's 8:27, Mary—" Eden pulled her mask down "—p.m. I won't be finished until after nine, and no, I don't have any extra twenties in my purse."

"I didn't come looking for money." Mary offered Cornelia a perfunctory smile. "Mary Tamblyn. I'm Eden's sister. I didn't realize patients came here quite this late. Myself, I can't deal with pain at night."

Not easily ruffled, Eden motioned at the door. "There's coffee if you want to wait."

"But..." Mary's look of annoyance changed to one of resignation. "Oh, all right, but it's important this time, Eden, or I wouldn't be here."

She really wouldn't, Eden thought after coaxing Cornelia's mouth open again. Mary liked the French Quarter well enough, but going to a dentist's office instead of searching out a freaky party? No way. She must want more than money.

"Your sister doesn't dress like you, does she, dear? Or look a great deal like you, either. So much blond hair..." Cornelia spoke around the wedge. "She has nice teeth, though. Are they all her own?"

"All but one. An ex-boyfriend knocked out her left incisor a year ago."

Cornelia made a clucking sound. "Bad relationship?"

"Misdirected racquetball." Eden replaced her mask and picked up her drill. "Mary isn't big on sports, or men who play them these days. Okay, no more stalling. Open, and I'll have you patched up in no time."

"Will it hurt? I think I can still feel part of my gum."

"Cornelia, I gave you enough novocaine to keep you numb until breakfast. I'll go slow. You can pinch my left arm if you feel anything."

EDEN KEPT HER MIND on her work and off Mary for the next forty-five minutes. By nine-fifteen, Cornelia was scraped, filled, filed and X-rayed. She handed Eden three tens at the door, squeezed her hand and told her to keep the change. Eden watched her climb into her brother's 1965 Buick Wildcat and tried not to think about how a man with cataracts managed to drive at night in a downpour.

Mary came up beside her. "Those two should be using public transportation."

Eden winced as Cornelia's brother ran the right tires up over the curb. "They only have to go twelve blocks."

"Huh. Big spender, too—tipped you a whole dollar plus change. Thirty bucks—man, you never give me deals like that."

"You don't live on a fixed income and have two sons who bleed you for what little pension money you receive." Eden tucked the bills into the pocket of her pants, stretched as she walked to the rack and removed her lab coat. "So what's the deal? Did you sell a bunch of pictures and you want me to spring for the champagne?"

Mary stared after the disappearing Buick. "They're photographs, not pictures, and no, I didn't. God, I hope I don't end up like them one day." Turning her head, she ran her gaze up and down her sister's body. "Or you, either, for that matter."

Eden made a quick check of her face and hair in the waiting room mirror. "What's wrong with how I look?" Other than maybe a little washed out under the bright lights.

Mary shrugged. "Nothing. You're gorgeous. Every man I date says so. But…" Her expression grew mysterious, and Eden sighed. She recognized the sign.

"'For deeds long past, *chère* child will reap, my vengeance curse, of death—or worse.'"

Eden, who'd taken a moment to release her dark hair from its ponytail, gave her head a shake and her shoulders a roll. "Why do you love that old rhyme so much? You don't believe in family curses any more than I do."

"I know. But then it doesn't apply to me, does it? I'm the youngest in our patchwork family." Mary's leather pants and jacket creaked as she headed for the door. "Let's blow this spooky tooth palace. Something's happened, and you're the only one who can make it right."

"I have to clean…" Eden started for the examination room, but Mary grabbed her arm. "I'm not being dramatic, Eden. This is big, or at least it could be, and it doesn't involve you lending me money. It's about Lisa."

Something tightened in Eden's stomach. Mary wouldn't hesitate to plead her own cause, but she seldom championed anyone else's. And she never looked rattled.

"What about Lisa?" she asked. "Is she sick? Hurt? In trouble?"

"The last thing." Loosening her grip, Mary made a disgruntled sound.

"Okay, look, our middle sister, who pored over the records of every adoption agency in the city, found you, found me and brought us all together ten years ago, was questioned by two cops. They came to the house tonight. They were asking her questions about a man named Maxwell Burgoyne."

"Someone she's dating?" No, that couldn't be right, Eden realized. Lisa didn't date. She waved the question aside before Mary could respond. "Never mind. Just tell me who he is."

"You want it straight?"

"Please."

"Maxwell Burgoyne is our biological father—as in the unknown X chromosome that forms half the link between us."

Stunned, Eden stared at her. "Lisa found our natural father? I thought he was dead."

Mary's red lips curved into a sardonic smile. "He is dead, Eden, deader than Dickens's ghostly doornail. The thing is, he only got that way two nights ago. Maxwell Burgoyne was murdered in a plantation cemetery seventeen miles outside of New Orleans. And according to the city's finest, Lisa was quite likely the last person to see him alive."

THEY WENT TO EDEN'S French Quarter walk-up. It was ten minutes from her office on foot, less than three in Mary's zippy black sports car.

Lisa had given her the car as a gift two years ago—or so Mary claimed. Eden had a feeling this gift, like so many others, had been bestowed out of guilt rather than generosity.

Not that Lisa wasn't generous. She loved to give. She donated to several charities that Eden knew of and spent hours every week trying to entice Eden to move in with her and Mary. She would buy them a three-story house in the Garden District, large enough that they could all have private suites.

"I can afford it," she'd told Eden only last month. "You know I hit the adoption jackpot, and now that my mother and father are both gone, their money's just sitting there, waiting to be spent."

"But not on us," Eden had countered. "Take a Mediterranean cruise, Lisa. Meet men. Flirt, dance, do something that doesn't involve soil, fertilizer and root rot."

"I love my garden, and I don't know how to flirt." She'd started to take Eden's hand, but stopped herself as she invariably did. "I inherited a lot of money, Eden, more than Mary knows about or could ever finagle out of me."

"Invest it then—and I don't mean in a bigger house."

"You don't want to move, do you?"

"Not really. I like my place."

"It's very nice, but it's so small. You can't spread out or grow bushes or even many herbs. I know you're used to tiny spaces because of where you lived in San Francisco…"

Which had nothing to do with anything as far as Eden was concerned. Amused, she'd replied, "I grew up in suburbia, Lisa, not the backwoods. My parents left their hippie groove before I finished grade school. My mother actually went back to college and got her degree in philosophy."

"And now she's a professor at LSU," Lisa supplied.

"Was." Eden had propped her chin in her hands and tried to figure out how many different kinds of flowers were in the vase on Lisa's kitchen table. "She accepted a position at Florida State last fall, remember?"

"She moved away?"

For a moment, Lisa had appeared confused. That quality of losing her bearings had puzzled Eden ever since they'd met ten years ago. Mary called them day trips. Eden wondered if there might not be more to it than that.

She was thinking about Lisa as she unlocked the wrought-iron gate at street level and climbed the outer stairs to her apartment. Her sister had actually located their biological father. The why of it aside, Eden gave her credit for persistence. By all accounts, including that of their natural mother, the man had died years ago.

"It feels like a thousand degrees," Mary complained. She'd removed her jacket and now wore only a faux-leather halter top with her tight pants and spiky heels. "Lisa could be in trouble up to her big green eyeballs, and—" Her own eyes widened. "Why on earth are your windows closed?"

"Because Amorin would jump out onto the porch. Then she'd dig up the courtyard garden or get hit by a car, and I don't want either of those things happening to my cat, that's why my windows are closed. The ceiling fans are on. But talk to me about Lisa, Mary. What did the police want from her?"

The question had a surly edge, Eden realized. Her experience with the New Orleans force as a whole hadn't been good. With one member in particular, it had proved disastrous.

But that was a memory for another time—maybe twenty years from now.

It took three shoves, a kick and two thumps with her fist to open her apartment door. Thunder rumbled on the river, and for a moment after she touched the light switch, Eden thought the power was going to fail.

"Just what we need in Hemingway Central," Mary muttered at her elbow. "A candlelight vigil." At a look from Eden, she kicked off her shoes. "Yeah, I know, cut the chitchat. What can I say? There's background stuff, I suppose, but we both know whatever went down in that plantation grave-yard, Lisa didn't hit Burgoyne on the head and take off."

Eden tried a second light. It flickered but stayed on. "Is she a suspect?"

Mary fussed with her hair. "She's a person of interest at this point because, like I said, she's the last person the cops know of who saw the guy alive. But that's today, Eden. What happens if they can't find anyone to pin his death on? It'll come back to Lisa—or it could. Okay, we'd be talking circumstantial evidence, but Lisa says she didn't think much of the guy the first time she met him, and I don't get the impression she was any more enamored after the second meeting. She doesn't have an alibi for the time of the murder, either, and I can't give her one because I was out with friends."

Eden struggled to digest everything as she turned on her temperamental air conditioner. "She met this man twice?"

"That's what she says. I didn't hear about either meeting until the cops showed up tonight. Anyway, my point is this. You know a few cops, right?"

"Don't start," Eden warned.

Mary tapped impatient fingernails on the tabletop. "Forget the past, will you? You do know some cops. You could get information."

Eden could be stubborn, too. "Mary, the only cops I knew have either quit or been reassigned."

"What about that prosecution lawyer you dated last year?"

"You want me to ask him to spy for us?"

"If necessary, yes. Look, I don't think you're clueing in here. This little scenario has the potential to go very bad, very fast."

Circumstantial evidence…

Eden rubbed her temples. It was still hot in here. She really needed a new air conditioner. "Back up a little," she suggested. "Did Lisa go to this plantation with—what was his name?"

"Burgoyne, Maxwell. She says no. They had dinner near Chalmette, or started to. He said something that ticked her off—which couldn't have been easy since she's virtually untickable—and she left. He followed her out. They got into their respective cars and drove away. Lisa went home. Maxwell went to the auction preview. Less than an hour later, someone slammed him on the head, and it was lights out for Mr. B.''

Unimpressed, Eden kicked her sister's feet off the chair where she'd propped them. "Maxwell Burgoyne was a person, Mary, and he was murdered. You could try for a little compassion.''

"Why? Because he was our father?''

"Oh, no." Eden swung around to face her. "No way was some stranger my father. You want to talk science and procreation, fine, but my dad, my real dad, had a ponytail until I was thirteen, which he cut off so I wouldn't get bugged because he and my mother were going to chaperon my first spring dance.''

Because that same real dad had also died of cancer five years ago and Eden still cried when she thought about him, she halted her tirade there and forced her mind back to Lisa.

"Do the police have a murder weapon?" she asked after a pause.

Mary started to put her feet up again, caught Eden's expression and shrugged. "I get the impression no. I think the sticking point is that several people in the restaurant where they ate heard Maxwell laughing—and not in a nice way, if you know what I mean. That's why Lisa got upset and took off. You know how lame she is at hiding her feelings.''

"What did Maxwell do, professionally?''

"Businessman, big time.''

Eden leaned on the kitchen counter and stroked her white cat. "Powerful people tend to cultivate enemies," she mused.

Mary snorted. "What was that you said about compassion? Oh hell, I hear a cell. Is it mine or yours?''

"Must be yours. My ring tone doesn't sound like bad disco.''

"It's Beethoven." Mary dug the phone out of her shoulder bag. "What is it? I'm busy.''

If she hadn't seen it happen, Eden wouldn't have believed

it was possible. Within five seconds, the blood had drained from Mary's face, leaving her pasty white and gaping.

She hissed into the phone. "You can't be serious. When? Are you sure?" She closed her eyes, groaned. "This can't be happening." Jamming two fingers into her temple, she breathed hard. "Okay, let me think, let me think." Her eyes opened, slid to the window, then slowly, very slowly traveled to Eden's face. "A lineup," she murmured. The fingers she'd been pushing into her temple pointed at Eden. "Hey—yeah, it could work. It really could… What? Oh sure, I know the precinct. Thanks, Dev. No, just lock up and go home."

"Who was…?" Eden began, but Mary had already ended the call, grabbed her hand and started dragging her toward the bedroom.

Eden yanked free. "Are you crazy? Who was that?"

"A neighbor. The cops came again. Lisa's been taken in for further questioning."

A streak of lightning over the old city caused the power to flutter for several seconds. Eden rubbed her wrist.

"Go on. I know there's worse to come."

"They have a witness."

"Someone saw Lisa murder Maxwell Burgoyne?"

"Apparently."

"That's ridiculous."

"No, that's New Orleans." Thunder shook the foundations of the old building. Mary's eyes glittered. "You know the justice system, Eden. All it takes is one bad cop. He wants Lisa guilty, bam, she's guilty."

"It's hardly that simple, Mary." And Eden didn't want to go there in any case. "What's your point?"

"Look at you, Eden." Planting both hands on her shoulders, Mary propelled her to a plantation mirror in the hall. "Look at your face. Look at your hair—dark, thick, long. Green, green eyes. Gorgeous features."

Eden saw it coming. She might be a step behind, but only a baby step.

"You and Lisa are ringers for each other." Her sister sounded both triumphant and relieved.

Eden resisted the idea. "Mary, we're not…"

"To a stranger, you are." She caught Eden's glare and shrugged. "Well, okay, you're close enough, or you will be once I fix your hair and you put on a pair of jeans and a pink T-shirt." She frowned. "I think that's what Lisa was wearing today. Pink or peach."

"I don't have a pink T-shirt."

"Close'll do, Eden." Exasperated, Mary tugged and twisted until Eden's hair was wrapped in a messy bun. She found a pencil on the hall table and stuck it though the knot to secure it. Then she stood back. "It'll work." She spun Eden around. "You have to do this, okay? Lisa's our sister, and we both know whoever he or she is, this witness is lying. Lisa doesn't even swat flies. She wouldn't hit a man on the head and kill him."

"Mary…"

"Please, please tell me you don't have an alibi for Sunday night."

"I don't need one."

"Stop being difficult. What did you do on Sunday?"

For Lisa's sake, Eden relented. "I had dinner with Dolores at her place."

Dolores Boyer was their natural grandmother and the only family member Lisa, Mary and Eden all got along with. She made her home north of New Orleans in the bayou and only came to the city when she absolutely had to.

"That's perfect." Mary arranged strands of loose hair around her sister's face. "She'll go along with you when she realizes what's at stake." She stopped styling. "You were alone, right?"

"Yes." Eden removed the pencil. "Look, Mary…"

"There's no look. Our neighbor specifically said the word lineup. You have to be in it."

Eden studied her reflection. Lightning forked through the night sky, threatening the power once again. But even though the lights trembled and faded and the hall was poorly lit, she saw Lisa's features in her own.

Struck dead in a graveyard, Mary had said. No way had Lisa done that. But there was a witness…

"Must've been drunk," she decided. With a sigh, she took the pencil from her sister, wound her hair back up and headed for the bedroom.

"Where are you going?" Mary demanded.

"I have an old red T-shirt somewhere. I also have to phone Dolores and tell her about Sunday night." The lights popped off then on. "Look, let's get this done while I'm still feeling halfway sane."

For some reason, the words Mary had recited earlier ran through her head.

"'…For deeds long past, *chère* child will reáp, my vengeance curse, of death—or worse.'"

It was a family curse, Dolores had told them, passed through her to their birth mother Lucille, then on to Lucille's eldest child. In the para-scientific world, that made Eden the target of its voodoo wrath.

And for the first time since she'd heard it ten years ago, the malice behind it made Eden shiver.

ARMAND LAMORTE stood in the shadows on the glass side of a two-way mirror and regarded the assortment of women behind it.

Without looking away, he spoke to the officer who'd just entered, a veteran cop with a gimpy leg and a ratty clipboard. "What's the woman's last name, Al?"

"Mayne, Lisa. She's twenty-eight. Owns two big garden supply shops and a catering company in the city. You know the family?"

"I've heard of them. She inherited well."

"Every dime of the old family money. She was the sole heir, adopted at twenty-two months. She has two blood sisters but no siblings in the legal sense."

"The three were split up?"

"At a young age. Don't know the story there." Al flipped through the wad of papers on his clipboard. "I do know the other two weren't as lucky moneywise. The youngest crapped out totally. Her old man lost his job and turned to alcohol. Her ma died when she was ten."

Armand's gaze settled on the most striking of the women behind the glass. She wore a snug fitting red T-shirt that ended just above the waistband of her equally snug jeans.

Al followed Armand's gaze. "That's Eden Bennett, one of the sisters. She's older than the suspect by a year."

Armand half smiled. "I met her ex once."

"Then you'll know she's not a fan of cops or cop stations. She called in a favor and got herself into the lineup. I've seen the pair of them close up. There's a strong resemblance."

"That should confuse your witness nicely."

"You don't have to sound amused," Al grumbled. "I'm stuck with the paperwork on this one, and trust me, between Burgoyne and his holdings, a tardy witness, no murder weapon and now a doppelganger tossed into the mix, I'll be filling out reports for the next six months."

Armand kept his eyes on Eden. "You think Lisa Mayne hit him?"

"Personally? No. Poison's a woman's weapon."

Armand's lips curved. "Some would call that a sexist remark."

"I'm sixty-two and deskbound. I'm entitled. I told you, I've seen the woman. In my jaundiced opinion, she wouldn't have bludgeoned the guy."

"Maybe she has a Jekyll and Hyde personality."

"Not from what I saw. A little off in space, maybe, but hey, she's rich."

Armand couldn't resist a grin. "You need to get out more."

"What I need is for Parker to get his butt in gear. He's handling the witness. Name's Robert Weir. He looks like a librarian."

"Credible?"

"On the surface. Says he freaked when he saw Burgoyne get hit. Did I mention they were business partners?"

"Burgoyne and the witness?" Armand regarded Eden through half-lidded eyes while he rolled that tidbit over. "What's Weir's story?"

"He panicked when he saw the murder, took off and hid out at home for two days."

"Didn't want to get involved?"

"Something like that. He told us up-front he wasn't fond of his late partner."

Armand slid his gaze sideways. "So if the surviving partner had no love for the dead one, where do you read the words *credible witness*?"

"We have no priors on the guy, in fact no charges of any kind. Three parking and two speeding tickets in the past fifteen years, all paid in full. He has an ex and a kid, a daughter. No problem there. He's on the books for child support, and there haven't been any gripes from his former wife, so he must be coming through. He has a condo in the Warehouse District and he went to Tulane."

"Your alma mater."

Al's expression grew pensive. "I wanted to be a pro running back in those days."

Armand ran his eyes over Eden's legs. He'd bet a month's pay they were the longest in the room. "There's no security in pro sports, Al. You're better off here."

"Uh-huh. And while we're on the subject, you're here to-night because…?"

"Why else? I missed your smiling face."

Al snorted. "I haven't smiled since that bullet shattered my kneecap three years ago. You got nothing better to do, go hunt up Parker and tell him to get in here with that witness."

She didn't paint her fingernails, Armand noted. And he could see the green of her eyes from here. "You need to slow down, Al, lay back." He smiled. "Take a vacation."

"Love to. You wanna do my job while I'm gone?"

"Sorry, already booked."

"That's what they all say." His head came up. "Is that Parker's voice?" He paused on his way out. "You gonna leer at Lisa Mayne's sister all night or check out that waterfront hotel you mentioned earlier... Is that you, Parker?" He raised his voice before Armand could answer. "We're in 5C," he called. "Later, Mandy."

Armand nodded. Eden had a look of alertness about her that he found intriguing. She wouldn't miss a trick—which would make her extremely difficult to deceive.

A smile curved on his lips even as his eyes lingered on Eden's face. He pushed off from the wall. He had his work cut out for him.

Chapter Two

It took the better part of three hours to straighten things out. If you could call them straightened. Eden's neck and shoulder muscles felt knotted, and she could still hear one of the women in the lineup crunching hard candy.

Lisa had been dazed throughout the ordeal. She still was. Eden watched her through a glass room divider from her seat in the corridor. She was talking to a bald police officer with shiny brown pants and a paunch.

At least it was quiet here, she thought. And on the murky side of dark.

Resting her head against the wall, she closed her eyes. They hadn't seen the witness or learned his name. All Eden knew was that a man had come forward after a two-day delay and announced that he could identify Maxwell Burgoyne's murderer.

Eden also knew that thanks to her presence in the lineup he'd been unable to make good on his promise.

"Your sister's a fortunate woman."

The voice came from the shadowy region to her right. When she opened her eyes, she saw a tall, male silhouette lounging against one of the archway frames.

His hair, she noticed, skimmed his shoulders. While he appeared relaxed, she heard New Orleans in his voice and recognized the predator behind it. Whether she'd met him here or on a California beach, she'd have pegged him as a cop right off.

"Not in the mood to chat?" he asked when she didn't respond.

Because it wasn't in her nature to be rude, she murmured, "Lost in thought, I guess. It's been a long day. I suppose she is fortunate, yes."

Because he lingered in the shadows, she couldn't make out his features. Except his mouth. She could see that clearly enough. "You're Eden Bennett," he said. "And, like your sister, you have no alibi for the night Maxwell Burgoyne was killed."

"Exactly. No alibi, no way for your witness to be sure which one of us he thinks he saw, no charges pending against either of us at this point."

"There will be a thorough investigation, you understand that."

Eden drew her brows together. "We're counting on it, Detective…"

"LaMorte," he obliged. "Armand."

"Are you involved in this investigation?"

"I'd be crazy to be here at this hour if I weren't, don't you think?"

"Maybe. You look like a night shift kind of person to me."

"Uh-huh. Do you believe your sister's innocent?"

The question didn't faze her, but Eden still wished she could see him better. "Absolutely. The only things Lisa's ever killed are aphids, and not many of those."

"She's a gardener." He smiled at her speculative expression. "It's in the report. She says she was home and working in her garden when the victim was struck. Do you like gardens, Eden?"

"I appreciate them." She glanced at Lisa, saw the strain on her features and gave an inward sigh. "Will this take much longer?"

"I doubt it. You're the oldest, aren't you?"

"I'm twenty-nine," she told him. "Lisa's twenty-eight.

Mary's twenty-six. We were raised by three different sets of parents.''

"Did you know Maxwell as children?''

"We never even knew of him. Lisa located our birth mother, Lucille Chaney, six months before she contacted me. That was ten years ago. Lucille said she put us up for adoption when her husband died.''

"No money to raise you?''

"Among other things. Wasn't this information in that report of yours, Detective LaMorte?''

"Some of it was. You can call me Armand.''

"Thanks, but I prefer Detective.''

He shrugged. "We'll be seeing a lot of each other in the coming weeks, Eden.''

His words almost sent a chill down her spine. But Lisa wasn't guilty, and Eden could hold her own with any cop, even one with a slow, sexy smile, long dark hair and—she had a fatalistic instinct about the last thing—dark eyes that were going to make her think things she shouldn't.

"Why do I sense you want to slap me?'' he asked in amusement.

"It's been a long day. I'm tired.''

"You don't like cops, do you?''

Now, finally, he moved—out of the deepest shadows and into the light.

Damn, she thought with a sigh. He had a face to match his voice and his smile. He also had those dark eyes she'd imagined and, for a split second, a glint inside them that made her nerves jitter.

"I was married to a cop once. It didn't work out. He looked a little like you.'' Right down to the stubble, she thought and found herself smiling at the irony of the situation. "We divorced three years ago. I'm over it.''

"Over the unpleasantness or the man?''

"Both. Our split wasn't unpleasant, just…'' Disappointing, she reflected. "Strained,'' she said.

He didn't believe her, but it didn't matter, or at least it

shouldn't. Yes, she would see him during the course of the investigation, but she could keep her distance as well as any other woman. Better, since seeing him would remind her again and again of what she'd been through once and had no desire to go through a second time.

The smile that hovered on his lips suggested he knew exactly what she was thinking. "I met your husband, Eden. Our paths crossed once on a rather involved drug bust." He shrugged. "I used to work in Vice."

Eden stood. "Then you'll understand my reasons for saying good night."

Instead of backing off, he moved closer. "You can't avoid me."

She was exhausted, out of her element, and in no mood to play games with him. "I don't have to avoid you, Detective. You're involved in an investigation which I have no choice but to endure. I don't waste time worrying about things I can't change."

He cocked his head. "What about your sisters? Can they cope as well as you?"

Oh, he was dangerously attractive all right. She glanced through the glass door. "Lisa's stronger than she looks. As for Mary…" She flicked a hand. "She's not on the hook for a crime. She'll be fine."

"She's at Pascoe's as we speak."

Eden recognized the name of the trendy Caribbean lounge. "There you go, then," she said. "Mary's coping as always."

"You call drinking martinis at 1:00 a.m. coping?"

Eden found it interesting that his amusement didn't annoy her. "It's her way, Detective, not mine." She switched gears to inquire, "This witness of yours, is he by any chance connected to Maxwell Burgoyne?"

Armand's expression told her nothing, and of course he'd discovered another shadow in which to conceal himself. That the shadow happened to be less than a foot from where Eden stood didn't improve her mood.

"Before the lineup, one of our computer artists put together a composite based on the witness's description of the murderer. That picture could be of you or your sister.''

"Which proves…?"

"Nothing on its own.'' His lashes lowered. "Tell me, is your sister right-handed or left?''

"Right. Why?''

"You signed your name with your left hand tonight.''

"I sign with my left, but I promise you, I can inflict pain with either. You're not very subtle, Detective LaMorte. I take it Maxwell Burgoyne was struck by a right-handed person.''

He didn't answer, and a second later the door across the hall opened.

Lisa emerged looking edgy and drawn. "Thanks for waiting, Eden.'' The blackness under her eyes had grown more pronounced. "Lieutenant Owen says we can leave.'' She rubbed her forehead. "Who were you talking to when I came out?''

Eden glanced back. Somehow, it didn't surprise her that Armand had vanished. "A man, a detective on the case. He asks questions, but doesn't answer many.'' She regarded Lisa. "Are you all right?''

"I want to get out of here.''

Eden checked out the shadows one last time. "They're so elusive,'' she said softly.

Lisa blinked. "What?''

Unsure what to make of the entire bizarre encounter, Eden shook her head. "I'm either incredibly perceptive, or—'' she released a weary breath "—I'm headed for a whole lot of trouble.''

ARMAND WATCHED HER GO. She was more than he'd anticipated and not like her sister at all.

He had his cell phone out and the number punched. As she left the building with Lisa, he pressed the button to make the call.

"Is it done then?'' his father demanded over a static-filled line.

"For the moment.'' Armand took care not to lose his cover

of darkness. Eden owned a sporty, black car, similar to both her sisters', and she had the sexiest walk of any woman in New Orleans.

"Are you napping, Detective LaMorte?"

He smiled a little. "Observing. How did you know it was me?"

"Who else would phone so late? You understand your job?"

Armand's gaze hardened. "I only need to be told once. Are you sure this is how you want it to be? It's more complicated than you thought."

"There we agree," his father said. "But more complicated doesn't mean we can walk away. You made me a promise, and I mean to hold you to it."

"I'll keep my word." Armand followed Eden's movements as she disengaged her alarm. "They're leaving now, probably to pick up their other sister."

"You sound displeased. You should be happy."

"Why, because Maxwell Burgoyne is dead? I'm supposed to extract justice for death, not applaud it."

"We both know what kind of snake Maxwell Burgoyne was while he lived. Now he's gone, and I need your help, father to son. Don't disappoint me."

"Have I ever?"

"In the important ways, no. Just remember what's at stake here, and if you have to, lock your conscience away. It'll only be a burden to you in this case."

This case, Armand thought as he disconnected. This skewed and twisted case into which he had been plunged with next to no warning.

Like it or not, however, he was in deep and stuck there. Whether that would prove to be good or bad depended entirely on how the victim's murder was viewed.

"STOP AT LUCILLE'S CLUB," Lisa pleaded with Eden. "She's part of our lives. We should tell her what's happening."

"I didn't drink enough if I'm hearing this." From the back,

Mary used her knee to poke Lisa's seat. "Although she conveniently neglected to mention it to us, Lucille was married to Maxwell Burgoyne. She knows he's dead. The rest of it has nothing to do with her."

Lisa faced her sister. "Why do you hate her so much? Because she runs a nightclub?"

"No, because nightclub's just a polite name for the business she really runs."

Nonconfrontational by nature, Lisa appealed to Eden. "Can you talk to her, please? Oh, and turn left here."

Eden had fought this battle with herself back at the police station. "Ten minutes, Mary," she said. "You can wait in the car." Which was the last thing Mary would do.

Lucille's club, called Nona, was situated on the fringe of the Vieux Carre. The sign over the door didn't flash or shine so the club didn't appeal to the masses. That was exactly as Lucille wanted it. Her other business ventures—and she had more than a few, Eden had discovered over the years—did that. Nona was understated and personal. It was also the place where Lucille could be found six nights out of seven.

"I still haven't figured out how someone as cool as Dolores could have given birth to a tarantula," Mary muttered. "Too bad the family curse didn't strike Lucille."

"It couldn't. She wasn't the oldest," Lisa reminded. "Lucille's brother died from the curse twenty years ago. He drove off a cliff or something."

Mary folded her arms. "Yeah, well, Dolores has a few things to answer for if you ask me."

"Like what?"

Eden glanced in the rearview mirror for the fifth time in two minutes and saw Mary roll her eyes. "Like why she never mentioned that Lucille's ex-husband—"

"Our biological father," Mary inserted.

"Was alive," Eden finished. "Lucille lied, Lisa, and Dolores went along with her."

But Lisa was always ready to defend other people. "Of

course Lucille lied. You'd have lied, too, in her position. You didn't meet Maxwell. He was—awful.''

It was a huge comment coming from Lisa.

Bright headlights in the rearview mirror diverted Eden's attention. She noticed a faint blue tinge around the edges. Was someone following them? Out loud, she asked, "Awful how? Was he obnoxious, abrasive, sloppy, rude?"

"He wasn't sloppy." Lisa indicated the curb lane. "There's a parking spot. He was obnoxious and rude, and I didn't like him at all. I'm sure you heard, I met him twice.''

Eden wedged her car between two monster SUVs. "Why a second meeting if he was so bad?"

"Because after our first disastrous outing last Wednesday, I figured I must have misjudged him. No one could be that horrible. So I called and asked if we could have dinner somewhere. I wanted to try again.''

"But you hadn't misjudged him."

"If I did, it was on the generous side." Lisa's shoulders twitched. "I don't want to go into detail. Just believe me when I say he had a mean tongue.''

"Ah, so that's why he hooked up with Lucille. Like seeks out like." Mary made a face as she read the sign above the door. "I hate this place, but at least Mommy Dearest keeps a well-stocked bar. Defend her all you like, Lisa, I still have a bone to pick with—" She stopped, frowned and backtracked. "Wait a minute, he was rich, right? Eden, didn't I tell you earlier that Maxwell Burgoyne was loaded?"

"You said big-time businessman. Lisa said horrible." Eden used her remote to lock the car doors. "I wouldn't get my hopes up if I were you.''

"He might have left us something in his will," Mary persisted. "You know, a conscience thing."

Lisa shook her head. "Maxwell didn't have a conscience, Mary. There won't be any guilt money."

"Oh, well, screw him then. Or him if the opportunity arises." Mary poked the front door open with her fingertips. "I smell raspberries.''

Eden looked up. The rain clouds had moved downriver but no stars shone overhead. The air felt heavy, almost suffocating. Cars rolled past on Canal even this late at night. She heard a saxophone down the street and the repeated *zot* of someone's bug zapper.

Everything seemed normal. So why, she wondered, couldn't she shake the image of those stupid blue-tinted headlights in her rearview mirror—or the face of a cop who preferred shadow to light?

"Losing it," she decided and followed her sisters inside. "Hey, Ty."

"Hey back at'cha." Lucille's six-foot-six rail-thin assistant waved a ring-covered hand at the rear of the building. "She's up in her office if you're looking."

"Bring bourbon," Mary called over her shoulder.

Ty ignored her. "Bad day?" he asked Eden.

"Okay day, not great night." She squinted through palm fronds, people and tables to a trio of women on a small raised stage. "Is it blues week?"

"Winding down now, sugar. Got a reggae band booked tomorrow. Tell your chippy little sister, Lucille still keeps a good bar upstairs."

Eden grinned. "Mary doesn't really have a chip on her shoulder, Ty. She took a method acting course last year and hasn't realized it's over yet."

Ty chuckled and moved on. Eden headed for the stairwell.

Lucille's preference ran to freeze-dried palms, rattan furniture and dim lighting. Blues music drifted out of the private rooms, and the air did in fact smell like raspberries.

Because she'd done her first filling at seven-thirty that morning, Eden's head felt as fuzzy as the lights. She'd crossed, she reflected, into that weird realm between consciousness and sleep.

The wall beside her was lined with oil paintings, most of them abstract, and every one as dark and mysterious as Armand LaMorte.

"Hell." With a sigh, Eden started up.

"Hell, is it? And I thought you liked my place."

Her heart lurched. Pushing a fist into her ribs, Eden breathed out and turned. "I don't need a coronary to make this night a bust, Lucille. Don't you creak when you walk?"

Lucille, a tall, fine-boned woman with straight, dark hair, a thick fringe of bangs and bloodred fingernails, gave Eden's cheek a pat. "You were creaking enough for both of us, love. What are you doing here so late?"

Eden relaxed. "Lisa wants to talk to you."

"I heard the story."

"The whole thing?"

"Most of it. There was a police officer here tonight, an old friend. We chatted. He left twenty minutes ago."

For some reason, Armand's face flashed in Eden's head. She pushed it out and asked, "Is this cop a regular friend?"

"Yes, but I'd appreciate it if you wouldn't use that word around Mary. Since my potpourri now contains a hint of poison, I'll assume she's upstairs with Lisa."

Humor crept into Eden's tone. "Wanna run?"

"It's tempting." Lucille plastered on a smile. "I'll settle for letting you lead the way—in case she's conned Lisa into buying her a gun."

Gun, cop, Armand LaMorte. The circle drew her in, as did all the problems Eden saw looming before her. Why couldn't Mary look like Lisa instead of her?

Barbs flew the moment they entered Lucille's office. Eden ignored them and drank in the atmosphere to distract herself.

The decor was Haitian with an abundance of ebony wood. Eden zeroed in on the sofa and dropped onto it. Five minutes passed before it occurred to her that Lisa had vanished.

"She made a beeline for the lower balcony." Mary gestured at a large outer terrace. "Digging helps her deal. She told me to fill Lucille in. Now that's done, where's the key to the liquor cabinet?"

Lucille's brows elevated. "You don't seem concerned about Lisa's state of mind, Mary. Since when can't she speak for herself?"

"She asked, I complied. Who am I to psychoanalyze her? She's dealing, okay?"

"By digging in my club garden at 2:00 a.m.?"

"Digging's what she does." Annoyed, Mary paced. "Why am I talking, Eden, and you're not?"

"I'm too tired to talk." She wasn't even sure she could open her eyes now that she'd closed them. "I see disembodied teeth smiling at me. I think I have an extraction at nine-thirty tomorrow morning." She forced her eyelids halfway up. "Lucille, why didn't you tell us about Maxwell?"

"Because he was a dreadful man. Not bad from birth, but he became that way over the years. For you to have known him would have served no purpose."

Mary prowled the room. "You'd never know she grew up in the bayou, would you, Eden? Bottom line, the guy was a creep."

"Did Dolores know about him?" Stupid question. Dolores knew everything about everyone in her life.

"She agreed you shouldn't meet him."

"But you must have realized Lisa would track him down eventually."

"I thought Lisa had put that obsession behind her. I had no idea she planned to hire a private investigator to search for him. I wouldn't have expected her to bother."

"Well, no, seeing as you lied to us so convincingly." Mary tugged on the armoire door. "You remember the tale, Lucille. Our natural father sailed off to the South Pacific with a team of scientists and their ship went down, blah, blah, blah."

Curious now, Eden asked, "What made Lisa look for Maxwell, Mary?"

"Hey, I just found out about the P.I. thing myself. I have no idea what middle sis was thinking or why. Maybe the ship going down sounded hokey to her. It might have to me if I'd cared enough to think about it. I'd say you should ask Lisa, but she's out of talk mode at the moment. As soon as we came in here, she got that 'I need to get my hands in dirt' look in her eyes and took off out the balcony door. Can we go now, Eden?''

"As soon as my muscles reconnect to my brain. Have you spoken to Dolores yet, Lucille?''

"Briefly. She said you didn't have dinner with her last Sunday. That's very generous of you. Unwise perhaps, but generous.''

Guilt niggled as Eden recalled her resistance to the police lineup. "It was Mary's idea.''

"And a selfless one, I'm sure.''

Lucille's mocking smile brought a scowl to Mary's lips. "Extraction tomorrow, Eden. Let's go.'' She slid her hip sack over one bare shoulder. "Oh, by the way, Lucille, in case no one's told you, you look like hell.''

"I've been on a diet.'' Lucille regarded Eden from her oversized office chair. "Why are you staring at my armoire? Is someone lurking in the shadows?''

"No, only shadows.'' And a face Eden couldn't erase from her mind no matter how hard she tried. She brought her gaze around. "Who might have wanted him dead?''

"A better question would be, who wouldn't? Anyone he knew could be on the list.''

Eden didn't buy that. "Few people would resort to murder, Lucille. Nasty phone calls, maybe, but killing's a drastic last step. The list can't be long.''

Lucille shrugged. "How long does it need to be? Would there be twenty names on it? Easily. Thirty? I'd say yes. As many as fifty? Possibly. Disgruntled employees have been known to commit horrific crimes. Push the right button and a mind, already badly strained, snaps.''

Eden conceded the point. And yet... "How many disgruntled workers do you figure would look like Lisa and me?''

"Ah, yes.'' Lucille sat back. "The witness.''

Mary snorted. "For witness, read real murderer.''

"I'm sure the police have considered the possibility, Mary. At any rate, Eden has rendered his testimony useless, so it'll be back to basics for now.''

Mary made a sound like a growl. "I'm getting Lisa."

When she was gone, Eden stood. It was either that or curl up on Lucille's sofa for the night. "Is Dolores okay about Sunday then? She didn't sound happy when I called."

Lucille rose as well. "She's fine with it, Eden, but I'll warn you now, she's on a tear about the family curse."

Eden tipped her head back to ease the tension in her neck. "Tell her I'll watch my back." She glanced at the terrace. "Is Mary shouting at me?"

"Such a loving sister. Eden, wait." Lucille wrapped a hand around her wrist. "I want you to promise me you'll let the police handle this."

"Why?"

"Because I know you. You don't trust them. You have a stubborn streak, and you love Lisa almost as much as the family you grew up with."

No, she didn't. She wanted to, but she didn't—which was undoubtedly the reason she'd gone along with Mary's scheme. Guilt was an amazing weapon, as effective as it was destructive.

"Talk to me about this tomorrow, okay?" Eden headed for the terrace door. "My brain's processing on low right now. I need sleep and time to think."

She heard Mary outside, ordering Lisa to forget about Lucille's flowers and worry about what really mattered.

"Don't let Mary bamboozle you, Eden," Lucille warned. "Lisa's freedom is imperative to her, but not for reasons of love. It's all about money. Mary might not control the bank account, but she controls the next best thing—Lisa herself."

Setting a hand on the door frame, Eden glanced back. Mary was right, Lucille did look like hell. "She doesn't control Lisa, Lucille. Plays on her emotions, yes, and there's no question she loves money, but I think she also cares deep down."

Lucille's gaze strayed to the river. "Mary is Maxwell's daughter, his blood by birth. Circumstances fashion much of who and what we ultimately become, but sometimes bad blood just plain wins out. I'll leave it at that. Good night, *chère*."

Eden hesitated a moment longer, but couldn't think of anything to say. She did marvel, though, at how quickly a person's life could go from simple to complicated. One incomplete dinner, one man dead, one nightmare commenced.

She only wished that a large part of that nightmare didn't involve a dark-eyed police detective.

THIRTY MINUTES PASSED before Lucille did anything more than stare at the flashes of lightning still visible on the river. The club would be empty now except for the tables behind the back rooms. Mary didn't know about those. None of them did.

There were other things they didn't know, some important, some not.

She shifted her attention to the wall safe, the most cleverly hidden of the three she'd installed when the club opened. There were bankbooks inside, as well as stock certificates and money. There was also an unmarked envelope.

"No!" She shook her head. "No."

Touching a sore patch in the crook of her elbow, she moved to her desk. It was late to be phoning people, but then again, not everyone who lived and breathed could be called people. Some were vultures. Others were vermin. And at least one person she knew of—the only one still alive—could more appropriately be called a serpent.

Chapter Three

Eden hadn't made it through dental college without a great deal of self-discipline. She regrouped on the drive home and told herself she would hold together until the investigation into Maxwell Burgoyne's death was behind her.

She spied bluish headlights twice in her rearview mirror before she dropped Mary and Lisa off, but not again after that. Determined, she put the sightings down to imagination and tried to concentrate on molar extractions until she reached her apartment.

Someone close by was humming a song. The voice slid through the darkness like a vapor. Listening was almost as effective as yoga for mental relaxation.

Armand LaMorte's face hovered on the edge of her mind. It was 2:30 a.m. If she went straight to bed, she could squeeze in six hours of sleep. A good dentist could drill and fill just fine with six hours under her belt. Of course, that precluded any worry time for Lisa, and she absolutely could not let herself delve into the paradox that was Maxwell Burgoyne.

He was an X chromosome, she reminded herself as she unlocked the gate, nothing more. Well, except he was also dead, and that was both unfortunate and problematic.

With the exception of the distant singer, the complex was silent. If she listened hard, she could hear remnants of thunder, but the rain had long since departed. Only the humidity remained, air so heavy with moisture she might have been walking underwater.

Street lamps guided her. Her neighbors were either asleep or out. Two of them had left New Orleans for the summer.

Eden gave the front door a bump with her hip while she twisted on the key. To her surprise, it opened. She switched on the table lamp and, picking up her mail, headed for the kitchen to check Amorin's food dish.

"Bills and junk. What else is new?" She tossed the envelopes on the staircase and called, "I'm home, Ammie."

The sound of shattering glass halted her.

Before she could call Amorin again, a man hurtled out of the darkness. He knocked her sideways with his shoulder and kept running. In his haste, he slipped on the wooden floor, collided with the hall table and sent her lamp crashing to the ground.

Once the initial jolt subsided, Eden scrambled to her feet and rushed after him.

He couldn't open the door. The knob kept slipping out of his hands. He resorted to kicking it and grunting like a pig.

Eden caught him easily— at least she caught his shirt. "You broke my lamp..." she began, but got no further. The door burst open and both of them were flung backward into the wall.

The intruder's elbow plunged into her ribs. Panicked, he took off in search of an alternate exit. Eden knew he hadn't found one when she heard a thump followed by a howl of pain.

Careful not to get kicked by flailing feet, she eased her arm up the wall and located the light switch. When she saw the man pinned on his stomach, she breathed out a disbelieving, "This night can't be happening," and sank back to the floor. "What," she demanded with as much energy as she could muster, "are you doing here, Detective LaMorte?"

Armand had his right knee lodged in the intruder's back, and his wrists held fast. He didn't answer right away, and she didn't repeat the question. "You're an idiot, Kenny," she said instead. "One of these days, someone's going to forget how nice your mother is and press charges."

In the process of handcuffing his prisoner, Armand stared at her. "You know this guy?"

"I know his mother. She lives across the courtyard. I only know Kenny in passing."

Armand flipped the intruder over and studied his face. "How old are you? Sixteen? Seventeen?"

The young man swore at him.

"He looks sixteen," Eden agreed. "He acts five. He's really twenty-one."

"Drugs?"

"For some reason he's convinced I keep a supply of pain-killers here. This is the fourth time in two months he's broken in while I've been out. Before that, he was…" She stopped as the reality of the situation struck her. "Wait a minute, it's two-thirty in the morning. What are you doing in my home, or anywhere near it for that matter?"

Wincing, she climbed to her feet.

Armand immediately abandoned his prisoner. "Are you hurt?"

"No." She didn't want him to touch her. However, he did, and in doing so, pinned her as effectively as he had Kenny.

"Don't move," he said. His fingers slid over her ribs with aggravating thoroughness. "You might have broken something."

"I'm fine." It took a huge effort not to grind her teeth. "Really." She stopped his probing hands with her own. "I'd know if anything was broken. But thank you."

"Going blind here," Kenny wailed from the floor. "Light's too bright."

"Close your eyes," Eden suggested. She concentrated on her own breathing. Why did sexy cops always have stubble? She nodded at the floor. "Worry about him, Armand. He's photosensitive."

He didn't back off. "You could have a fracture and not know it."

"Doctor first thing tomorrow—today—whatever. I promise." When he ran his hands along her rib cage one last time and made her shiver, Eden finally took the initiative and stepped out of reach. "You haven't answered my question, Detective."

A smile curved his lips. "You called me Armand a minute ago."

"I was in shock." Because Kenny was whimpering, she took pity on him and dimmed the lights. Big mistake, she realized. It bathed the hallway in shadows and gave Armand back that air of mystery she'd been endeavoring to block out all evening.

He was taller than her and very lean. His hair fell past the collar of his shirt, curling just enough to make her fingers long to run through it.

Not going there, she promised herself and, tucking her hands behind her back, leaned against the stairwell wall.

"Why are you here?" she asked again.

He crouched to inspect Kenny's eyes. "I had questions. When I realized you weren't home, I waited."

Disengaging her left hand, Eden massaged her aching ribs. "So you were on the street while Kenny was ransacking my apartment?"

"The plan was to ask questions, Eden, not anticipate a break and enter."

"Fell asleep, huh?"

He sent her a wary look and didn't respond.

Eden breathed in and out, decided it didn't hurt too much, then stopped and raised her head. Where was Amorin?

"You can't manhandle me," Kenny snarled. "I'll say you did if you jerk me around."

"I'll say he didn't if you've let my cat out," Eden retorted. "Where is she, Kenny?"

"Is she small and white?" Armand asked.

Eden followed his gaze—and pretty much gave up on the night. Her cat sat on the stairs, watching the scene below through unblinking eyes.

Setting Kenny aside, Armand reached up a finger to stroke the cat's chest. "You don't look much like Eden, do you, sweetheart?"

"We both scratch," Eden remarked with mild asperity. "And, if necessary, bite."

"Are you going to bite me?" he asked the cat.

Amorin stared for several more seconds, then rubbed her head against his hand.

"Like seeks out like." Eden echoed Mary's earlier sentiment. Exasperated, she glanced at Armand's prisoner who was now on his feet. "For God's sake, Kenny, make up your mind. Either whimper or snarl, but choose one and stick to it."

Armand gave him a shove. "Do you want to press charges?"

"No, take him home and let his mother deal with him."

She felt Armand's eyes on her face. "I still have questions, Eden."

"You won't get coherent answers at this time of the morning, Detective. Kenny's mother lives across the courtyard. It's the patio with the rose arbor."

"Are you sure you're all right?"

"I'm not hurt if that's what you mean." There was another lamp beside her, but for some reason Eden didn't turn it on. "Lisa's innocent. If you're a good cop, you'll prove that."

He held Kenny back as he bridged a portion of the gap between them. Even with the AC unit off and the air swirling like dark liquid around them, Eden felt the heat of his skin.

"What if I can't prove it?" he countered softly.

She kept her head up and her eyes on his. "If you can't," she said, "then I will."

"WE MADE IT THROUGH the salad course, and one drink. Maxwell ordered a glass of bourbon, and I had iced tea. He went to the men's room while we were eating. Maybe he made a phone call then, but he didn't call anyone from the table. He made me uncomfortable with the things he said. He swore a lot, and he had a loud voice, so everyone around us heard him.

The cruder he got, the more I wanted to leave. I guess he knew that, because he laughed at me. Finally I was so embarrassed, I put my money on the table and left. He must have paid his part of the bill, too, because I'm told he came out right after me. Maybe people thought we were together, but we weren't, Eden. I came straight home. He went on to Concordia, the plantation where the auction was going to be held…''

Eden recognized the name. She'd dated a boy in high school whose grandfather had worked there.

"It had a lopsided roof," she said out loud in her office.

Her dental assistant, Phoebe, smiled. "You're thinking about Concordia, am I right?"

Eden examined an X ray. "Made the morning paper, huh?"

"The whole gruesome tale. Murder at Concordia. Witness on-scene. No charges made. Police have spoken to the last person known to have seen the victim alive, one Elizabeth Jocelyn Mayne of Lanyon-Mayne fame. You okay there, Henry?" She patted the arm of their eleven-year-old patient whose eyes were glued to the overhead television. Spider-Man had him all the way.

Eden smiled. "If his eyes get any bigger, they'll pop right out of his skull." She returned to her work. "I didn't read the article, Phoebe. How detailed was it?"

"Not so much. It mostly described the guy who died. Don't get offended, okay, but I thought it was kind of cool in a morbid sort of way. I've never known anyone who was associated with anyone who was associated with a dead man. And a dead man with clout to boot."

"So you've heard of Maxwell Burgoyne?"

"Not specifically, but they listed several of his holdings. I recognized about six of them. MamaDees Molasses and MamaDees Golden, Brown and Demerara Sugar, the LoBo record label, the FM radio station and the Pro-Max line of tools. They also mentioned a factory that makes hand-painted tiles, but I think it's out of state. The guy had major bucks."

"He also had a heart condition," Roland, their receptionist, called through the open door. "He took pills for it."

"His heart didn't kill him, Roland," Eden pointed out.

"No, something metal did that." He shook a folded newspaper. "It says there were flecks of rust found in the head wound."

"Are you hearing any of this, Henry?" Eden asked.

The boy's eyes remained on the screen. He wore headphones in any case, but she wanted to be sure. The topic of murder wasn't likely to rate high on his parents' list of suitable dental office conversations.

Never one to linger on a topic, Phoebe began talking about her daughters, and Eden was able to finish her work in silence.

She'd been toying with an idea all day, but she didn't know if it was a good one or not. What she wanted to do was drive out to Concordia where Maxwell had died. What she should do, however, was drive over to Lisa and Mary's place and coax Lisa into going through the story again. She'd gone over it on the phone earlier today, but Lisa had been preoccupied. She'd been using her trowel as they'd talked.

"Mary talked about doing a photo shoot tonight, north of here," Lisa had remarked. "It involves the last rays of light. Some magazine in Massachusetts that wants to do a spread on vampires and witches. She says they've got the witch part covered, but they're looking for ruins where vampires might live, or unlive, or whatever it is vampires do."

"You sound down, Lisa. Do you want to go out to Dolores's for dinner?"

"No." Lisa had been firm. "I'm not ready for Dolores yet. She's the second closest person I know to a witch, and she'll make me relive the whole nightmare again. The police have already asked me a million questions. I can't tell them anything, and it's frustrating. I mean, I didn't like the man, Eden, but I swear I didn't hit him. How many ways can I say it so they'll understand?"

Eden understood. After all, she'd had a cop waiting outside her apartment last night with questions. True, he hadn't been able to ask them, but only because he'd been sidetracked by an addict looking for painkillers. And then she'd been tied up at work today and she'd told Roland not to disturb her with anything except emergency calls.

Her conversation with Lisa played on while she finished Henry's fillings, gave him the lollipop her young patients expected and stretched her cramped arm and back muscles.

"I wanted to talk to Lucille, Eden, I really did. But when we got there last night, suddenly I couldn't face her. Mary thinks I'm flipping out, but I'm not. It's just easier for me when I'm in a garden. Mine mostly, but any garden will do. I love the elements. They're magical. You mix earth, water and light, a little seed, and suddenly, there's life. Plants don't ask questions, they simply exist and, with the proper care, thrive. I can't imagine my life without them."

That much Eden had realized the day she'd met Lisa. "Can I ask one more question?" she'd pressed.

"Why did I go looking for our natural father ten years after Lucille told us he was dead?"

"Right."

"I heard her talking one night out at Dolores's. I'd walked in from the road. They didn't know I was there. I was passing under the window when Dolores up and asked Lucille what she would do if we ever learned the truth. Lucille wanted to know what truth, and Dolores said about our biological father being alive. I was stunned, Eden, so stunned I couldn't go in. I turned around, drove home and went straight to my garden to think. The next day, I hired a private investigator. It took him eleven weeks. He started with Lucille and worked backward until he came up with a name."

"Maxwell Burgoyne." Eden thought for a minute. She'd never understood Lisa's need to discover her birth relatives. "Maybe you should have left it alone, Lisa," she'd said, "for all our sakes…"

Lisa hadn't, however, and the rest couldn't be undone with a wish.

Wishing also wouldn't help Eden avoid Armand LaMorte for much longer. Roland said he'd called an hour ago. He'd tried again while she'd been ushering Henry out the door.

There would be no more reprieves, she thought, glancing at the wall clock. Avoidance was in her hands now. If she was fast and lucky, she could make it home unobserved. Then she'd be free to do—well, whatever seemed most appropriate.

Her cell phone rang as she was unlocking her car. The display read Mary so she answered.

Her sister sounded testy. "Lisa said you wanted to talk to me, Eden."

With her free hand, Eden unfastened her hair. "Don't start with me, Mary. I got less than four hours of sleep last night, and I had to pull a mouthful of teeth this morning. Do you know how difficult that is?"

"I know it's gross."

"The before picture kind of was. The after will be good in a few days. Where are you right now?"

"En route to Montesse House. And don't say it's dangerous there. That's the whole point of my trip."

"Vampires, huh?"

"Feel flattered, Eden. Lisa told me you two had a long chat this morning. All I've gotten from her today is the brush."

"Your battery's dying," Eden said. "Look, I'm going home for a few minutes. I'll pick up some food and bring it to Montesse, okay?"

Mary's response was lost in a blank spot which Eden took as a yes.

Twenty minutes later, she'd changed into drab army pants and a white T-shirt, ignored her answering machine, left a message for Lisa, fed Amorin and purchased dinner. Dusk had begun to settle by the time she reached the outskirts of the city. She noticed black clouds stacked in an angry bunch to the north and wondered if Mary's battery had in fact been dying. An electrical storm might have disrupted the signal.

For highway driving, she turned her headlights on full and mapped out the route to Montesse in her head. She needed to leave the highway, and the road leading to the Mississippi was anything but smooth. This trip would be hard on her tires.

Her phone rang again a mile past the plantation exit. With

no other cars in sight and the potholes readily visible in the thickening twilight, she read the screen, smiled and answered. "Hey, Dolores."

"Don't you hey me, pretty girl. You lied to the police. I'm not happy about that, not one bit."

"No surprise there."

"Lisa would hit herself on the head before anyone else. What were you thinking doing such a thing, putting your life in danger?"

"Why am I in danger?"

"What do you call a family curse if not dangerous?"

Silly, but Eden wasn't about to say that to someone she loved. Instead she replied with patience, "The curse has no bearing on this, Dolores. It's a—" Breaking off, she regarded her rearview mirror. There was a car with blue-tinted headlights behind her, she was sure of it.

"You still there?" Dolores demanded. "What's going on? Why'd you stop talking?"

"I thought..." She saw nothing now, no car or headlights, in fact, no movement at all. "It's okay, I guess. I just have this weird feeling I'm being followed. I see pale blue lights behind me, and I freak. Then they vanish, and I realize I'm jumping at shadows." Which was, she reflected with a sigh, a word she really hadn't needed to use. "Tell me, Dolores, have you spoken to a Detective LaMorte yet?"

"It's possible. I've spoken to many police officers today. Told them all I didn't make gumbo for you and me on Sunday night, no sir. Why ask me about one in particular?"

"I have a feeling he's going to be a pain."

"Maybe he'll catch the killer quick and leave us with only the curse to worry about."

"I'm not worried, Dolores."

"Then I'll have to worry twice as hard, won't I? You don't do me any favors with your unbelieving attitude, Eden. Who raised you makes no difference. It's the blood in your veins that counts."

"Boyer blood."

"No, my blood. I wasn't born a Boyer. That curse took away my brother who was a year older than me. He had no children, so the focus shifted—and if you say it must be a smart curse, I'll put you over my knee next time I see you."

"I believe you." Eden bumped through a rut and bit her tongue. "Ouch."

"You're driving too fast like always."

"How do you know I'm driving?"

"I hear the engine."

"Over the stereo?"

"Music's too loud, too."

Suspicious, Eden demanded, "Did Mary or Lisa call you tonight?"

"No, and I don't expect they will. When trouble comes, Mary either gets drunk or finds a man to distract her. You, you decide you're fine and go about your business, oblivious. Lisa buries herself and her problems in her garden."

The criticism stung. "I'm not oblivious, Dolores."

"You want to be. You try to be. You wriggle and squirm, and only when you're slapped in the face with an unpleasant thing do you acknowledge it exists. Where're you driving to, anyway?"

Eden's first impulse was to sulk and not respond. Her second was to retaliate. Her third was to take it on the chin—sort of. "Montesse House," she answered, then waited because she knew that wouldn't sit well.

"You're going out there alone, at night?" Dolores uttered a colorful curse of her own. "Are you a crazy girl? That place is falling apart. It's haunted by three ghosts, did you know that? Haunted and decaying from the foundation up."

Eden looked back, saw nothing and felt a stab of contrition because Dolores sounded so upset.

"Mary's there," she explained. "That's why I'm going. I won't explore the house. I know it's in bad shape. It was a wreck ten years ago when I saw it for the first time."

"I should never have told you about it," Dolores moaned. "Three teenage girls gonna get all kinds of ideas about a tale like that. Still, the oldest girl has sense—or so I thought. Next thing I know, you're traipsing off together to search for ghosts just because I said the curse was placed on our family by the original owners.'' Annoyance gave way to exasperation. ''Why is Mary there? She keeping a still we don't know about?''

''She's taking pictures.''

''In the dark?''

''It won't be dark for another hour.'' Although that could change, Eden realized. Between the black clouds, a road lined with moss-shrouded live oaks and only a patch of blue left to the west, it was a bit like driving into a witch's cauldron. ''It reminds me of a vampire's lair out here.'' She heard Dolores's hand smacking her knee.

''You're after vampires?''

''Mainly the atmosphere. It's Mary's deal, Dolores, not mine. I need to talk to her away from Lisa. Something's…'' She tried to think of how to put it. ''Something's wrong. Lisa's not herself. I can't say what it is exactly, but she feels off to me.''

Dolores's tone softened. ''This is a difficult time for her. Lisa won't meet a problem head-on, and dirt holds no answers.''

Eden laughed. ''You didn't sleep last night, did you?''

The old woman chuckled. ''That was bad, wasn't it? Yes, I am tired. But mostly I'm worried. Not so much about Lisa. She didn't bludgeon Maxwell Burgoyne. It's you and the curse, Eden. I've had dreams lately, bad dreams, about death and pain. I see zombielike creatures and hear old voodoo chants. I see shadows as dark as night and inside them, people whose faces I can't make out. But they're after you, and they're close.''

Her ominous tone more than her words sent a shiver down Eden's spine. Then she caught a flash of pale blue light in her side mirror and swore.

''What's that you said?'' Dolores demanded.

''Someone's close to me all right,'' Eden told her. ''But

he's no zombie. This person drives a car, and he's a lousy tail. I'll call you later, okay? I promise, this isn't related to the curse,'' she added before she pushed End.

The headlights disappeared among the trees, but as far as Eden knew the road wound without deviation down to Montesse and stopped there. Unless he turned around, her tail would wind up directly behind her.

She spied the crumbling roof first, followed by the white-washed columns. Four of eight remained intact. The others had broken into large pieces. Several of those pieces had been hauled away by scavengers searching for remnants of a Civil War house.

In truth, Montesse had its roots in an era prior to the war. It had been dismantled piece by piece in France and brought to North America by ship in the late seventeenth century. The Dumont family servants had taken apart, transported and reconstructed the building under the keen eye of their matriarch, Therese Dumont. However, as Dolores told the story, it was Therese's daughter Eva who'd actually placed the curse—on her father and the woman she'd considered to be the cause of her family's destruction.

Eden braked at the end of the road where it opened to an overgrown clearing. Leaving the engine running, she waited for the source of the headlights to appear. When it didn't, she tapped her fingers on the steering wheel and debated her next move. She could go back and search the road, keep waiting in her car, or find Mary and do what she'd come to do in the first place. Choosing the latter, she drove on until a fallen sycamore prevented her from getting any closer.

There was no sign of Mary's car and only river sounds audible as she slid from her seat.

Dolores insisted Montesse was haunted. Given its gloomy appearance beneath a canopy of purple-black clouds and shadows long enough to conceal a bevy of vampires, Eden had no trouble believing in the possibility. Not that she actually did believe, but if she had and if they were to manifest themselves anywhere, here would be the perfect spot.

A chorus of distant bullfrogs accompanied her as she picked her way around the ruined building. She liked the Quarter better, she decided. Noise, light and color were friendly things. Solitude, peppered with thoughts of zombies, curses and voodoo queens was downright creepy, even for a resolved non-believer.

She spent the better part of forty minutes tramping around the grounds. As a last resort, she slogged through bushes and weeds to the riverbank. A sluggish current carried the water past a shore far too wild now to accommodate a boat dock.

Although she didn't find Mary, Eden did locate her sister's car. It was parked on a back driveway that must have led to Montesse from one of the other highway exits.

"At least I know you're here," she said, nursing a scratch on her arm. "That's something."

Aware of the deepening twilight and the fact that she hadn't brought her flashlight, she headed back to the house. Mary's voice resounded eerily in her head.

Voodoo child with Carib blood, and eyes of green. This is foreseen...

Through Dolores, Eden had inherited Haitian blood. But not, she promised herself, a mystical Haitian mindset. She and Lisa had been born with green eyes.

The eldest born to eldest grown, my pain shall bear. Believe. Beware.

Dolores had been the eldest grown, and of course Eden was the eldest born—but that meant nothing. Curses had no place in the twenty-first century.

For deeds long past, chère *child will reap, my vengeance curse, of death—or worse.*

Worse than death was a prospect Eden preferred not to consider, at least not as it pertained to the supernatural. But she had to admit, it was difficult to ignore a thing when you had a sister and grandmother who were forever bringing it up.

Determined not to dwell on such an unpleasant subject, Eden trudged through the mini jungle that had once been Therese Dumont's prized garden to the back terrace. Gravel and broken concrete crunched underfoot the closer she drew to the old house. She spotted a beam of light—or possibly the flash of a camera—upstairs, and called to her sister. Receiving no answer, she tried again in a less patient tone.

"Are you up there, Mary?"

She heard a sound like stone grinding against stone and attempted to pinpoint it. She was standing beneath a wide protrusion that had once been the second-story gallery. It would have wrapped around the entire house and, in the back at least, allowed for a spectacular view of the river. Eden felt certain the sound she'd heard had come from the upper wall.

When the air stilled and the sound didn't repeat, she gave up. Absolutely nothing moved, not even the deadhead flowers hanging by a thread to their stems.

One last time, she tipped her head back and called to her sister.

To her surprise, she heard what might have been an answer. Something echoed inside the house.

That meant she'd have to break her promise to Dolores—probably her neck as well. Pushing aside a tangle of vines, she backtracked through the garden.

An old pergola hung at a precarious angle above her. Like everything else, it was choked with weeds, many of them dead, all of them clinging. Thorns snagged her pants, making her grateful she'd worn a pair of old hikers.

A granite cross and a cracked marble headstone lay across the path. Eden didn't see a raised plot, which probably meant someone had tried to make off with the stone, failed and wound up abandoning it. She looked, but couldn't read the writing in the poor light. Respectful of its significance, she stepped over the stone and continued on toward the terrace.

Three wide steps appeared through the dense foliage. Lisa, she mused, would love to get her green thumbs on a place like this.

Eden yanked down one last vine and spotted the bottom step. Scratched, but glad to be out of the maze, she muttered, "Vampires live in cellars by day, Mary, not second-story bedrooms. Even fly-by-night magazine editors can tell the difference between a bed in a crumbling master suite and a coffin in the basement.''

A train rolled past across the river. The whistle reached her over the croaking bullfrogs.

She looked back at the fallen headstone and for a moment was tempted to get her flashlight. If the stone was Eva Dumont's, she could tell Dolores...

''No.'' She stopped the thought flat. The past was the past, over and done. No matter what Dolores believed, there were no such things as ghosts. And even if there were, if she didn't hurt them, why should they bother her?

The grinding noise reached her again. Tilting her head back, Eden glimpsed a rectangular object above. Then she spied a blur of motion and felt a pair of strong arms wrap themselves around her. She saw dark hair and a flurry of leaves and felt her body leave the ground. A second later, she landed on her back on the garden path.

Stunned, she watched as a large white planter crashed onto the very spot where she'd been standing.

Chapter Four

It took Eden a long, startled moment to regain her breath and her bearings. When she was able to roll over, she found herself staring into the face of Armand LaMorte.

He'd managed through some bizarre midair twist to land beneath her and at the same time give her a full terrifying view of what had almost happened. While part of her was grateful, another part wanted to know what the hell was going on.

Strangely calm, she said, "Should I bother to ask?"

He narrowed his eyes at the upper balcony. "You ask. I'll find out."

Eden realized she was still lying on top of him. Pressing her palms into his shoulders, she pushed up, but he caught her before she could escape.

"Did you hit your head?"

She touched a sore spot above her left eye. "On yours, I think."

Crouching, he used his thumb and forefinger to trap her chin and tip her head back. "Am I clear or a blur?"

All too clear, she thought and let her own hand fall into her lap. "I can see you, Armand. What happened?"

"Good question. If you're not hurt, I'll find us a good answer."

"Don't move," he called as he disappeared through an ancient set of double doors.

After a moment, her gaze slid to the side. There, not ten

feet in front of her, was all that remained of a rectangular concrete planter. She'd noticed it on the gallery wall when she'd stepped over the headstone in the garden.

But weren't those pony walls as wide as the steps below? It should have taken a small earthquake to move the thing. The inside had been filled with dirt and weeds, so it must have weighed several hundred pounds.

"Eden?" Mary appeared around the side of the house. "What was that crash...?" She appeared shocked when she spied the wreckage. "Whoa. Well, that sure wasn't here a few minutes ago. Are you okay?"

"If alive qualifies as okay, then yes." Eden let Mary pull her to her feet, felt the ground wobble and rested her spine against one of the pergola supports. It would pass, she promised herself. She hadn't hit the ground that hard. "As a point of interest," she asked, "did a gorgeous man in a black shirt and jeans fly past you a minute ago?"

"I was trying to get into the cellar," Mary replied. "And I haven't had a sniff of a gorgeous man since the weekend. The only person other than me who's here is B.J."

Eden closed her eyes. "And B.J. is...?"

"Mostly grunts and muscles. I met him at a party and figured he could help me arrange the vampire scene so to speak. I'd have mentioned him on the phone, but you hung up." She nudged a fragment of the fallen planter with the toe of her boot. "Did this thing almost flatten you?"

"Almost."

"You have good reflexes, Eden."

"I have a tail."

Mary eased away from both her sister and the rubble. "What you have, babe, is a curse." Her arms twitched. "Man, I'm so glad I'm the youngest."

Eden left the pergola. The ground had stopped moving, but her head throbbed down to her shoulders. "When did you lose your muscle man?"

"Twenty, twenty-five minutes ago. He saw a spider."

Eden's gaze rose to the second story. "How strong is he?"

Mary flexed her bare arm. "He's got biceps like Popeye and a vocabulary to match. But, hey, you need a tree felled or a door ripped off its hinges, he's your—" She stopped. "Wait a minute, you're not thinking... My God!" she exclaimed. "You are thinking."

"Not very well yet, but Mary, planters as big and heavy as this one don't just fall. It was pushed, or levered or something. I heard a grinding sound right before it came down. And don't talk to me about vindictive ghosts. I went through that with Dolores earlier."

Mary sniffed. "Did you go through the curse, too?"

Eden released a heavy breath. "There's no curse, okay? People move heavy objects, voodoo rhymes don't."

Mary skirted the dirt mound. "Go ahead and deny, Eden. Dolores will insist it was the curse. Think about it. Even if she does live in the swamp, she's an educated woman. True, her mind's a little left of center, but you don't get a degree from Loyola unless it's deserved. So, there you are, an intelligent woman believes."

"This is a pointless conversation." Eden returned to the path to view the upper level. She didn't see a flashlight beam anywhere—assuming Armand had been carrying a flashlight. Pushing on her temples with her fingers, she murmured, "I should have gone to Concordia."

"You should go into hiding."

"It's a thought," Eden agreed, but her reasons had more to do with a certain dark-haired cop than the family curse.

Mary snapped restless fingers. "I wonder if B.J. went back to the car." Joining Eden on the path, she tapped her sister's shoulder. "Uh, about this gorgeous guy you mentioned... You did say gorgeous, right?"

Had she? On her knees, Eden brushed dirt from the marble headstone. "Maybe," she conceded. "I didn't mean to." Because it was too dark now to make out the worn letters, she abandoned her task and measured the distance between the veranda and the gallery by eye. "That wall up there is at least two feet wide, wouldn't you say?"

"No idea. I was in and out like Speedy Gonzales. I don't need to bump into a ghost with a bone to pick over something one of my ancestors did."

Eden let it go. Where was Armand, and why hadn't he come onto the gallery? "I'll bet you drive a car with tinted headlights," she accused under her breath.

"You're acting a little weird, Eden," Mary remarked.

Eden heard nerves beneath her sister's irritation and lowered her gaze. "Someone in a car with blue-tinted headlights followed me out here tonight."

"Okay, I'll buy that. Just don't go S.L. on me." At Eden's uncomprehending expression, Mary clarified, "Spooky Lisa. She has moments lately of, you know, going off to Mars. She's done it before, it's just that since Maxwell died, one wrong word and, bam, she's in a funk."

Not a prolonged one, but Eden knew what Mary meant. She'd seen them, too, those moments when Lisa appeared to put the world around her on hold.

Maybe in the end that's all there was to Lisa's sudden standoffishness. A major disappointment had led to the death of their natural father and a near murder charge. Who wouldn't react to something so dreadful? One thing was certain, funk or not, Lisa simply wasn't capable of committing the kind of violent act that had ended Maxwell Burgoyne's life.

"This could be cool." Dismissing her sister's problems, Mary returned to the terrace.

Eden had to squint to see her. She was only twenty feet away, but darkness had pretty much settled. In fact, the shadows had grown so thick under the balcony that little more than Mary's silver belt buckle remained visible.

"Coffin dirt," Mary declared. The buckle dipped as she did. "I've lost the light, but you could hold a beam on it. We'll make a body impression, spread the chunks of cement around."

Eden called up to the gallery, "Armand, are you there?"

Mary's heels clopped on the terrace tiles as she rearranged

the fallen planter. "I'm no good at this. Stop shouting, Eden, and help me here. It's incredibly... Ahh!"

Her sentence ended on a yelp. Her belt buckle vanished.

And a pair of hands seized Eden from behind...

EDEN'S REACTION was instinctive. She rammed both elbows into the stomach of the person holding her. She heard a muffled "Oomph," and felt the hands on her shoulders tighten.

A man growled in warning, but he was cut off by the *click* of a trigger being drawn back.

"Let her go. Do it slowly, and move away. Now."

Eden recognized Armand's voice.

Whoever he was talking to released her slowly as instructed. The moment she was free, Eden spun—and did an immediate double take. A more superstitious person might have mistaken the man for a troll.

Deciding that Armand was the lesser of two evils, she backed across the uneven ground to his side. She found herself strangely fascinated by the man whose hairy arms and bushy beard appeared to be the color of a ripe tomato. "Something happened to Mary right before he grabbed me," she said.

A break in the clouds allowed a three-quarter moon to illuminate the area. Eden started for the steps. The man opened his mouth, took a second look at Armand's Magnum and promptly closed it.

"No problem here," Mary called before Eden reached the terrace. "Don't everyone rush to my rescue at once. I only tripped and gave myself a concussion."

"Stay where you are," Armand told her.

The redhead was downright squat, muscular to the max, but shorter than Eden's height of five-eight by a couple of inches. Even so, his torso looked broader than a tree trunk and with arms like his, he could undoubtedly lift the front end of her car.

"Are you B.J.?" Eden asked.

"Bobby John Finnegan." His gaze was fixed on the gun

barrel aimed at his throat. "I heard voices. Reckoned one of 'em might be Mary's."

"Where did you come from?"

"Front of the house." He pointed. "I used the driveway on account of I don't like walking in tall weeds."

"Afraid you'll fall into Middle Earth?" Armand suggested.

"Snakes like weeds. I don't like snakes."

Mary strode over, probing the back of her head. "So, Eden, is this your gorgeous guy?"

Vague amusement sparked Armand's eyes, but he kept his gun on B.J. "Do you know this man?" he asked her.

Mary shrugged. "We came here together. I didn't know he had crawly-phobia." She studied Armand's features. "I guess you are sort of gorgeous, although it's hard to tell in the dark with a weapon pointed in the general direction of my face."

Armand tucked the gun into his shoulder holster. "Have you been inside the house?"

He directed his question at B.J. who appeared horrified by the thought. "Are you nuts? It's bug central in there. I was looking for Mary. Saw you." He nodded at Eden. "You were exploring down by the river and around those old shacks out back. Heard you call her name, so I knew you were looking for her, too. I'd have hollered, but you mighta wanted me to check out the shacks, and that wasn't happening in this lifetime."

"My hero," Mary sneered. "Okay, I'm out of here, vampires be damned."

Her cranky tone brought a smile to Eden's lips. She gestured at the tangled garden. "Do you want Armand to walk you to your car?"

"My camera bag's on the terrace." Mary still sounded irked. "I brought a big flashlight. And B.J.'s got a second one stuck to his belt."

"He can go, right?" Eden asked Armand.

"To New Orleans, yeah. We'll have a chat at his place tomorrow."

B.J. glanced at the holstered gun. "Sure, no problem. You, uh, need my address?"

"It'd help."

B.J. gave him the necessary information, cringed when Mary started along the garden path, then squared his shoulders and followed.

Arms folded, Eden stared at Armand and waited for him to speak.

"Go ahead," she prompted when he didn't. "I'm open to any and all explanations. Come up with a good one and I might even believe it."

"Let me see your head."

She slapped a palm against his chest to hold him off. "We've done this already, Detective. No more touching. You saved me from a falling planter and stopped B.J. from crushing my bones to powder. I'm honestly grateful for those things, but I still want to know why you followed me home last night and out here tonight."

"I didn't." Smiling a little, he plucked a leaf from her hair. "You look a lot like your sister, Eden, but somehow your beauty's more intriguing to me. Why is that?"

She smiled back. "Because I have a brother who taught me how to box in the third grade and at the same time knock a man's front teeth out if he makes me mad by not answering my questions, maybe?"

Armand chuckled. "You fix teeth. You're not likely to knock them out."

"I can do both if you're up for a spar. I keep a pair of bag mitts in my trunk, and you know where my New Orleans office is. Why did you follow me?"

"I told you, I didn't." He snagged another leaf. "You have incredible eyes, do you know that?"

Torn between laughing and punching him, she opted for poking him in the chest. "Car, pal. Yours. Now."

His mouth curved. "You don't trust me, do you?"

Eyes as dark as his should not, she thought with a sigh, be legal. "I want to see your headlights, Armand."

"There must be something more interesting I could show you."

Her brows went up. "Maxwell Burgoyne's murderer would work."

His breath stirred the hair on her forehead, that's how close he'd gotten to her. "Say more personal, then."

She wasn't up to playing games with him. But neither was she about to back down. "Where are you parked?"

"Near the fallen sycamore."

She kept wanting to stare at his mouth. She forced her eyes upward instead. "I thought you didn't follow me."

"I parked beside you. That isn't following."

"And you knew where I was because…?"

He trapped a strand of her hair between his fingers and stroked it with his thumb. "Maybe I'm telepathic, Eden. My mother claimed to be."

Although she was fascinated by his face, Eden held tight to her train of thought. "My grandmother believes in an old family curse, Armand. I'm a DDS. I believe in science and sometimes in karma. I'm not big on telepathy, and no matter how many times you try to distract me, I still want to see your headlights."

He studied her through his lashes. His gaze lingered just a little too long on her lips.

Not good, she decided and stepped back. She planted her hand once again on his chest and this time locked her elbow. "I want—"

"Yes, I know." His eyes glinted. "Headlights. Explanations. Remember, you've been avoiding my questions all day as well."

The more distance she put between them, the more in control Eden felt. She started toward the front of the house. "I had a full schedule when I began my day, and I squeezed in two emergency reconstructions at lunch. I assume—" she glanced backward at the eerie silhouette that was Montesse House "—there was no sign of anyone inside."

"No sign I could detect, but someone could have been there. I saw footprints, inside and out. Leaves, too, and litter."

For the first time since the planter had fallen, Eden allowed uncertainty to creep in. "It wasn't an accident," she said without thinking. "I heard the base move."

Armand surprised her by nodding. "There was no reason for it to fall, and coincidence is a thing I seldom accept." Catching her easily, he draped an arm over her shoulder and pointed. "There it is, behind your car as promised."

Eden halted. "You drive an SUV?"

He smiled. "You make it sound like a crime."

It had been a car behind her, a darker, late-model car, she was sure of that. Biting her lip, she shrugged off his arm and headed for the front of the vehicle. "Would you mind turning on your headlights?"

"I can think of better things to do, Eden." But he opened the door and switched them on.

She stared at the twin beams until her eyes stung, then turned away in frustration. Not even a little blue. "Okay, you didn't follow me, at least not in a way that I could see."

"Not in any way." Clearly intrigued, he watched her pace. "Obviously you don't like my headlights. Are you going to tell me why, or should I guess?"

She stopped in front of him. "I saw headlights with a faint blue tinge when I dropped Mary and Lisa off last night. I saw the same thing on the plantation road tonight. I thought it was you tailing me."

He considered that for several seconds, then wrapped his fingers around her wrist to prevent her from moving away. "I called Lisa," he said without embellishment.

It took Eden a moment to understand. When she did, she closed her eyes. "I did, too—before I came to Montesse."

"You left a message telling her where you were going. She told me how to find you. Still…" He arched a brow. "I prefer the idea of telepathy."

She sighed. "I was wrong last night, Armand. You don't

remind me of my ex-husband at all. But you're still a cop, and that makes you off-limits as far as I'm concerned."

"Ah, but I have a job to do, Eden. I can't be off-limits until it's finished."

"Someone pushed that planter from the wall tonight. Maybe someone who's angry at me for inserting myself into that police lineup. Mary believes your witness is bogus. I think I'm starting to agree with her."

"The witness has been checked out. He's clean." Armand moved a shoulder. "That doesn't mean we won't be keeping one eye on him."

When the tingling threatened to spread to the rest of her body, Eden withdrew her hand. "Find out if he has blue headlights," she suggested, "and go from there." She made a point of not rubbing her wrist on the leg of her pants. "Can you tell me his name?"

"I can tell you he knew the victim."

It was something, she supposed. "What do you think of all this, Armand?" She gestured at the house, then back toward New Orleans. "A planter that couldn't have fallen on its own, a man who couldn't possibly have seen either Lisa or me bludgeon anyone, headlights behind me—"

"A drug addict in your home last night."

She loosened up enough to laugh. "That's the one thing here I do understand. As for the rest..."

Spreading her fingers, she backed away, from her thoughts and from him. She could set it all aside tonight because she was shaken and confused. But what about tomorrow?

ARMAND WANTED A CIGARETTE. Didn't have one—he'd given in to his father's nagging and quit seven years ago—but the craving remained and it was strong. That the craving had its roots in something totally unrelated to tobacco was a given; however, if he could lie to Eden, he could lie to himself. For now.

The ground behind him crunched. Armand recognized the

plodding gait and didn't turn. "She left two minutes ago," he said, his eyes still on the road Eden had taken.

"You sound mad. Are you mad, because I did what I was supposed to do."

"Did you?"

"I tried my best. I can't help it if my timing was off. I'm not quick on my feet." Gravel and twigs crunched again as the man shifted his weight. "Aren't you going to say something?"

He really wanted that cigarette, Armand reflected. "I'll follow her home."

"That's it? That's all you have to say?"

"For the moment." As he opened the door of his Explorer, Armand sent the man a deceptively calm look. "Although you might want to think about getting yourself a car with regular headlights."

Chapter Five

Eden's head buzzed. It didn't hurt anymore, but there were so many thoughts running around inside it, she couldn't hold on to any of them for more than thirty seconds.

"Whoa, yeah, that's more like it." Her patient, a pale, thin actor with black hair and red fingernails, probed his incisors with a partly frozen tongue. "Cool tips."

"Uh-huh." Eden removed her gloves. "You want them any pointier, Denis, you talk to a cosmetic surgeon."

"You are a cosmetic surgeon, Doc."

"No, I have a soft spot for starving actors. When does your play open?"

"Two weeks. I'm the hip vampire, live in a cool crypt. Sets are mediocre, but the acting'll make up for it. Can I, you know, do an I-owe-you till next month? I mean, I could scrounge some cash from Mary if you need it now."

"Mary'd just scrounge it from Lisa," Eden said as she organized his X rays. "Roland knows the deal, Denis. You can sign on the way out."

Denis ogled himself in the mirror. "Truly wicked work. Hey, Roland, check out the new fangs..."

Eden smiled, but only until she caught a glimpse of her own reflection, then her thoughts veered toward Lisa, cemetery plots and murder. Voodoo curses, too, she added, recalling the dream she'd had last night, but that was irrelevant and the least of her problems right now.

Phoebe popped her head into the examination room. "I stuck a couple of those new procaine samples in your purse, Eden. The information's attached. The stuff's supposed to do an instant freeze job. Oh, and Mary called while you were with Denis. Detective LaMorte left a message on their machine. He's going over to see Lisa tonight."

"Means Mary wants to bail, and I'm supposed to run interference for Lisa."

"If I were you, I'd bail with her. Lisa's a big girl, Eden. She can handle the police."

"I know, but I want to talk to her anyway. The least I can do is be there when Detective LaMorte does his grilling thing."

Phoebe grinned. "Mary described your detective to me, honey. The word *gorgeous* came up more than once."

"Did she also mention annoying, sly, evasive and suspicious?"

"No, but better and better. Is he single?"

"Don't know. Don't care."

"Really." Phoebe's eyes twinkled. "How refreshingly unbelievable."

Releasing her hair, Eden tucked it behind her ears. She'd had the strangest dreams last night of kissing Armand instead of leaving him at Montesse and of some woman chanting in the dark. Eden had awakened hot and panting—and with the creepiest sense of déjà vu she'd ever experienced.

She tried not to sound irritated when she said, "There's no curse."

Phoebe's brows went up. "Interesting jump. From cop to curse."

"No curse."

"You keep saying it, honey, but you were born here. Voodoo shops on the street corners, psychics stacked to the rafters and so much old Cajun magic that even scientists have stopped trying to explain it away. Skeptic or not, you gotta believe somewhere down inside."

Eden scowled. "You want me to believe I'm marked for death by a spiteful Creole witch?"

"No, I want you to take care. Think of yourself. Mary does it all the time."

"Mary doesn't look like Lisa. She gets to be out of this mess. I'm stuck in the middle of it."

Phoebe came in to cup her cheek. "There's no mess, Eden. That witness you told me about at lunch is lying, simple as that. He didn't see squat the night Maxwell Burgoyne died. And by the way—" she gave a quick pinch before strolling to the door "—little sister looks more like you and Lisa than you think. It's called a family resemblance. And wouldn't Mary just love to hear that? Do her fangs still come out when she sees Lucille?"

"Just say the name."

Phoebe clucked her tongue. "Not good, really not good. Mary needs to lose that attitude before it eats up anything healthy living inside."

"She's only a little bitter, Phoeb."

"You'll have to prove it to me, I'm afraid."

"Can't right now." Eden shed her lab coat, smoothed the wrinkles from her ivory sundress and exchanged her working shoes for a pair of high-heeled sandals. "I want to talk Lisa into dinner before Detective LaMorte descends on her."

"Try the arboretum on Decatur," Phoebe suggested. "And good luck with the gorgeous cop."

THERE WAS NO SUCH THING as good luck where Armand was concerned. Eden had come to that depressing conclusion on the drive home last night. The best she could hope to do was shore up her defenses and, where possible, maintain maximum distance.

She parked in the driveway of the nineteenth-century Garden District house that had been built by Lisa's adoptive great-grandfather. It was a peculiar Victorian Gothic structure that set Eden's teeth on edge. The windows on the second and third

Eden's Shadow

floors speared upward like medieval arrows. The ones at ground level had a boxy look that always appeared to gape.

Trapped between angry and forlorn was Eden's take on the atmosphere. Even the resident ghost suffered from a split personality. She alternated between shrieks and moans, depending on her mood, or so Dolores had told Lisa. Eden preferred to believe the sounds were nothing that new pipes and a few well-placed nails wouldn't fix.

She knocked on the paneled door, waited then knocked again. She tried the knob and felt it turn. "Lisa?" she called into the foyer.

Of course her sister didn't answer. She'd be in her garden by now, up to her elbows in peat moss and mud.

Eden shivered when she stepped inside. No matter who decorated it, the place had a gloomy vibe. It screamed Old World horror and invariably felt shadowy—which was odd, really, since there were plants and flowers everywhere she looked. They spilled from stone boxes, metal urns and pots big enough to hold a corpse.

Lovely thought, that, Eden reflected crossing the Aubusson carpet at the foot of the staircase. She called Mary's name, but only as a token. When evening came, Mary went, and usually stayed out until dawn.

The wall beside her groaned. "Hey, Claudette," Eden said to the ghost. "Still can't figure out whether your husband went up or down, huh?"

From what she'd heard about the house's original owner, she'd have guessed down, but apparently his widow preferred to wait here rather than search there in the hope that he would somehow find his way back to her.

True or not, the story certainly fit the house.

As she made her way toward the terrace, Eden tried not to relive the dream she'd had last night. She knew it had been curse related, with a dose of Armand LaMorte thrown in for good measure.

She'd been outside, kneeling before a marble headstone. She'd smelled the swamp close by. A man had lurked in the shadows behind her. Armand perhaps? A woman had been chanting. Eden had seen fire and felt the heat of a sticky summer night. There'd been drums, too, in the background, pounding out an ancient native beat.

She'd run across Lisa at some point. Her sister had been surrounded by leafy plants and a host of weird-looking flowers. Her dress had been as green as her eyes, her feet bare, her arms dirty up to her elbows.

Things had happened in the dark, but nothing that Eden had retained. Her heart had been racing when she'd awakened, and in that moment before her eyes adjusted, she felt certain she'd seen a face in the shadows. A face that had become two faces before they'd dissolved into a blank, black wall.

"Forget about it," she ordered herself. "Curses and kisses make for freaky dreams." Her sigh had a frustrated edge. "Lisa?" she tried again.

As she passed through the kitchen door, she inhaled the smell of camellias and roses. The sun had dipped below the tree line, creating just enough murky patches to put a hitch in her stride.

Lisa's garden unnerved her, no question about it. Vines curled along the ground and wound up around wrought-iron arches. Laden trellises towered overhead. Somehow, too, the stillness inside the house always managed to bleed out into the backyard.

A shiver prickled Eden's spine. She stared at the canopy of green above. "It's like having ghosts for sisters. Where are you, Lisa?"

The greenhouse was a possibility. Lisa maintained two of them, and a potting shed.

As she walked, Eden noticed every chirping cricket, every buzz, and every rustle of leaves around her. But those were normal sounds. The snap of a twig to her right was not.

Eden wasn't foolish enough to think Lisa was playing games with her. She stopped, forced herself to breathe and listened.

She heard nothing.

"Who's there?" she demanded at length.

No one answered. Thirty seconds ticked by. She wasn't wrong. She couldn't stay here all night. With her eyes on the path, she moved forward.

By the time she reached the corner, Eden's heart was pounding, like the drums in her dream last night. But unlike her dream, when she peered into the shadows, the only thing she spied was a squirrel, staring at her through wary eyes.

As rattled as she'd been, Eden laughed. Creeped out by a rodent. She needed a vacation.

Amused at her overreaction, she tried to recall which of the greenhouses Lisa preferred. Since she had no idea, she tossed a mental coin and turned left.

Lisa wasn't there, but the space smelled wonderful. Harp music, piped in from the house, played a mystical tune through a series of six speakers. The melody had a haunting Irish lilt, so Eden assumed she was in the out-of-climate greenhouse.

Compared to the garden, which often gave her claustrophobia, this place contained a magical atmosphere. It took her to the British Isles and made her think of castles and dungeons, fairies and dragons.

"Right." She looked around. "Just what I need, more stuff that doesn't exist cluttering up my mind."

But she liked it and took a moment to wander through the rows of potted herbs.

She smelled lavender and thyme, a fragrance with a lemony undertone and, beneath all of it, a hint of licorice. The scents reminded her that she hadn't eaten since noon. She craved grilled chicken with spicy Cajun cornbread and for Lisa to talk to her while they ate. Not prattle on about how people, like plants, needed roots, but really talk for once, about a childhood she seldom spoke of, about how she'd felt when her parents had died and how she felt now with Maxwell dead and more than one person questioning her part in that.

As she drifted among the tables, Eden noted the tidy rows of shelves, well stocked with plant food, pest control products and various types of soil. Two rusty metal rods stood propped against a table leg. In a box under the herb pots, Eden spied a crate containing a dozen garden claws, a mallet, three crow-bars and a saw that looked like it came from the nineteenth century.

Curious, she bent for a closer look. She paused when her gaze came to rest on the curved end of the largest crowbar. There was a stain on the mottled paint, one that might easily be mistaken for blood.

"Yeah, right," she muttered, annoyed with herself. "Lots of chemicals are dark, Eden. Grease can be dark."

But the mark didn't look like grease or paint or anything else she recognized.

She reached out to pick it up—and heard the door open just as her fingers brushed the metal.

Like the footstep in the garden, this was a stealthy sound. Not Lisa, she judged and took a firm grip on the bar.

Adjusting her fingers, she leaned her shoulder against the table and waited. Nothing stirred. Her leg muscles began to cramp. Had someone come in, or was she being paranoid?

She recalled the planter at Montesse last night and decided she'd rather be paranoid than dead.

Using the bar as a brace, she craned her neck and peered over the plant pots. The door was open, so something had happened. She'd closed it behind her when she'd entered.

Clutching the iron bar, she stood. Slowly. No one and noth-ing stood between her and the door. Leaving was a thought, but what about Lisa? Was she safe, or was someone following both of them?

"Damn," Eden whispered.

"Is there a problem here?"

If jumping out of her skin had been possible, Eden would have done it. Instead, she shot forward five feet, spun and whipped the crowbar up.

She didn't say a word. She didn't have to. Her expression said it all.

Armand regarded her with a blend of confusion and humor. "Who did you think I was?"

She gnashed her teeth and didn't lower the crowbar. "Not Lisa."

"Ah." He smiled. "So anyone who's not Lisa gets threatened with an iron rod, is that it?"

Eden counted to steady her nerves. "Anyone who's not Lisa and opts to skulk around her garden uninvited deserves to be threatened."

He held her gaze. "Are you trying to tell me you didn't know I was coming here tonight?"

"No, I'm trying to remember how to breathe." She ran exasperated eyes over his blue shirt, jeans and boots. "How do you walk without making noise?" She recalled the footstep in the garden and shrugged. "Much noise."

"Practice. It works for all things."

She let the crowbar drop, started to shake her head, then realized she'd been pointing the stained end at him.

She wanted to toss it back under the table but leaned on it for a moment instead.

"Mission accomplished then?" she asked.

"Not quite." He regarded a column of blue flowers. "Is that monkshood?"

Eden frowned. "I'd have guessed bluebells myself."

"But then you don't garden, do you?"

"Not really, no. Do you?"

"Small-scale only."

Eden continued to study him. "What do you grow?"

"Depends on the season."

"Do you have a greenhouse?"

"No, just a plot of land beside my home."

"A house home?"

"Like that." He didn't blink. His eyes held hers as he advanced. "Why are you always wary around me, Eden?"

Finally she tossed the crowbar back under the table. "I was taught not to trust strangers."

"Or give in to fear?"

"I'm not afraid of you, Armand." Not physically anyway. "It's…" She started to say it was her own thoughts that scared

her, but thought better of it and shrugged. "I have other is-
sues."

"Like hating cops."

"Like lots of things." As soothing as it had been, now the
music hit a jarring note. "Look, if we have to fence, can we
do it away from Lisa's garden? It starts to feel like Hansel and
Gretel's forest after a while."

"Wart's woods," Armand corrected.

"Wart?" She stared. "King Arthur's Wart?"

A humorous brow rose.

"Sorry," she apologized. "You just don't strike me as the
fairy tale type."

Wrong thing to say. He moved closer, fixing her with those
incredible eyes. "You're pigeonholing me. I know almost as
many fairy tales as I do ghost stories. My mother read them
to me at bedtime."

"Does your mother live in New Orleans?"

Something flickered in his expression. "I grew up in the
bayou. My mother died when I was nine."

"I'm sorry," Eden said and meant it. "I'm very close to
my mother. I can't imagine losing her. How…you know."

He looked away. "She was murdered. My father found her
body in the swamp. She'd been missing for a week. People in
the area said she'd run off. We knew she hadn't."

Shocked, Eden asked, "Did they catch the person responsible?"

"Justice was served," he replied without elaboration. He
fingered the gold cross that rested in the hollow at the base of
her throat. "This is nice. Simple."

She thought her voice might desert her, but it didn't, not
even when he released the cross to stroke a lazy finger across
her collarbone. "Armand…" she began.

She should stop this, really should. But she was no longer
sure she wanted to.

Closing her eyes, she released a breath. It was crazy. She
was crazy. She raised her lashes and her head. "I'm going to

regret this," she murmured. "Big-time." Then catching his face in her hands, she set her mouth on his.

IT WAS A DIZZYING EXPERIENCE. Wrong, because she felt as if she'd tumbled off a cliff, but exciting, because kissing him made her feel more alive than she had in months. Maybe years.

It was Armand who took the kiss to another level, exploring her mouth with a thoroughness that scorched her blood and had her knees threatening to buckle. For a moment, the garden actually did feel magical. And sexual. Out of control.

Warnings flashed like neon signs in her head. This wasn't wrong, it was insanity.

"No... Armand, wait." She made an effort to pull away. "I shouldn't have, you know, done that."

"Ah, but you did." His lips curved against hers. "And you had to know I wouldn't refuse."

At that moment, Eden didn't know anything. Except she needed air. She set her gaze on a plant with drooping bell-shaped flowers and stepped back from temptation. Then, because she couldn't think of a single intelligent thing to say, she cast him a quick look from under her lashes, turned and exited the greenhouse.

A garden gnome's shovel snagged her hem five feet outside the door. She resisted an urge to tear the fabric free and instead worked it gently off the cracked concrete.

Round gray eyes, one of them badly damaged, stared at her with a hostile expression. It was a leprous little statue, not so much gnomelike on second look as troll. Like B.J., minus the tomato-red hair.

Lisa collected garden statues, most of them cast-offs, all of them ugly and in need of repair. Eden hadn't seen this one before, and the way it scowled at her, she felt like damaging its other eye.

Instead she wrapped her arms around her waist, stared at the path and called herself an idiot. Or, well, maybe not that bad, but she had to learn to say no and mean it, not cave in every time she got within range of Armand's aura.

"Eden?" The sound of Lisa's voice brought her head up and around. Her sister had dirt smeared on one cheek and both hands were caked with mud. "When did you get here? I didn't know you were coming."

"Mary phoned me."

Lisa rubbed her fingers together, dislodging clumps of dirt. "Does she think I need a baby-sitter?"

"More likely," Armand remarked from the doorway, "she wanted to warn Eden that I was coming to talk to you."

Lisa blinked. "And you are?" She frowned. "Were you in my greenhouse?"

She asked the question of Armand, but it was Eden who responded. "Only for a moment, Lisa. We didn't disturb anything." Except a crowbar she didn't want to think about. "Have you met Detective LaMorte?"

"No—yes—I'm not sure." She worked up a smile. "Have we met, Detective?"

"On the phone." He glanced at a garden figure which stood on a broken base. "Do you have some free time now, Ms. Mayne?"

"Lisa." She sounded weary but up to the challenge. "We can use the terrace. My geraniums need water." She shot a look at Eden. "You didn't disturb my shooting stars, did you?"

"I don't even know what they are, Lisa. All I saw were some herb pots, flowers that I'm told aren't bluebells and other ones shaped like bells that weren't blue."

"They're—" Lisa gave her head a shake. "Never mind, let's go. I'll answer your questions, Detective, but I can't imagine you'll be any closer to catching Maxwell's murderer when we're done."

Eden cast Armand a surreptitious glance. She wanted him to look perturbed, or at least a little ruffled. What he looked instead was preoccupied.

And for some reason she couldn't fathom, Eden found that more disturbing than his kiss.

TIME DRAGGED. Or flew. Speed of passage depended entirely on one's point of view. For the person with Eden Bennett uppermost in mind, it moved in fits and starts.

No doubt about it, she was posing a major problem. She'd done what any good sister would do under the circumstances, but now she was taking the matter to a new and unacceptable level. She was digging. Not in an obvious way, but the intention was written all over her face. She wanted truth—and that was a very serious problem.

In fact, it was downright dangerous, wasn't it? Because even without her meddling, so much could go wrong.

The falling planter hadn't worked; that meant something else would have to. Because one way or another, Eden's digging had to be stopped.

Chapter Six

"Evening, *mon ami.*"

Al looked up from his overflowing desk, blinking like a diver who'd surfaced to discover himself in another world.

"Oh, it's you." His vision cleared, and he scowled. "Why's it so dark?"

"Possibly because it's after eleven."

He gave a disbelieving snort. "I told Francine I'd be home by eight." He patted the blotter for his desk clock, found it and swore at the position of the hands. "Dammit, she'll have my hide. Where's the phone?"

"On the floor, between your wastepaper basket and a three-foot stack of files." Armand chuckled. "You need a better system, I think. What are you working on?"

"A backlog up to my armpits." Al sniffed. "Is that coffee I smell?"

Pushing off from the doorjamb, Armand handed him a large takeout cup he'd purchased down the street. "A gift in exchange for the results I know Benny rushed up here from the lab."

"Huh. You gave Benny wine didn't you, probably imported."

"I don't know him as well as I do you." Armand set a hip on the edge of Al's desk. "Which folder is Burgoyne's?"

Al slurped and closed blissful eyes. "This is my kind of bribe, Mandy. It's on the stack next to the keypad. Lab results

are on top. I'll save you time and tell you your blood sample
wasn't human. Lab figures bird, probably sparrow.''

A portion of Armand's tension abated. "A cat might've
killed it, and Lisa moved the corpse with the crowbar.''

"Works for me." Al took another long drink. "Did she
have much to say?''

Armand shrugged. "She answered my questions. I didn't
press for details.''

"Already done anyway." Al scratched his stubbly chin.
"Any impressions you'd care to pass on?''

"She's got baggage.''

"Uh-huh. And there's a person in or out of this room who
doesn't?''

Friend or not, Armand wasn't prepared to give him the reaction he so obviously wanted. "Most of us in or out deal,
unless you and Francine are having problems I don't know
about.''

"Just too many late nights and not enough sex. And speak-
ing of sex, how's the look-alike sibling?''

Armand recalled the feel of Eden's body pressed against his
when they'd kissed, of how she'd smelled—like wild roses—
and the taste of her mouth. He thought of all those things, then
he thought of his father and moved a noncommittal shoulder.

He extracted Maxwell Burgoyne's file from the stack. The
crime scene photos sat on top, grisly and graphic as such photos invariably were. His eyes went to a patch of ground behind
the corpse. "There," he said and laid the picture down to
point. "That's the spot.''

"Yeah, I noticed it. Ground's depressed and dry compared
to the surrounding area. Something's been removed.''

Armand considered the possibilities. "It had a rectangular
base. Could be a statue.''

"Makes sense, but the question is, did it go before or after
Burgoyne was hit?''

Armand shook his head. "We need to blow this up.''

"Lawson's gone for the night," Al motioned with his head.

"Use his computer, and leave me a copy. If whatever you're thinking pans out, you know the deal."

"Like it might ever change?"

A pair of bushy brows went up, "So how'd you say Lisa Mayne's sister's doing?"

Armand grinned just a bit and continued to study the photo. "She has a suspicion or two."

"S'at so." Leaning back in his chair, Al savored both his coffee and the opportunity to irritate an old friend. "Well now, she can join the club then, can't she? Because while I might love you like a brother, Mandy, I also know you well enough to figure you're not dealing straight with any of us on this one. Am I right, or am I wrong?"

Armand slid him a sideways look "You really want to know?"

Al screwed four knuckles into his midsection where an ulcer had burned for ten long years. "I don't like tightropes, old friend. There are people who depend on me and my paycheck. I gotta think of them before I do one too many favors."

Guilt niggled, but Armand squelched it by reaching into his pocket and pulling out a card. "Bonus, bribe or gift." He rose. "Call it what you will. The time and date are there for you. All you have to do is show up."

Years of training prevented Al's jaw from dropping, but his eyes popped more than a little.

Armand smiled. By the time his friend recovered enough to clear his throat and raise his head, he was gone.

TRY AS HE MIGHT, and he did his level best, Armand couldn't get Eden out of his mind. He kept visualizing her incredible legs, her smile—and the light of suspicion that glimmered in her green, green eyes.

As for kissing her, he knew better than to go near that one. He couldn't and do what he needed to do, what he'd promised to do. What he would do, no matter how attracted to her he might be.

Coupled with the blood sample he'd scraped from the crowbar in Lisa's greenhouse, he'd also managed to snap three pictures with his pocket camera. Eden's attention had been on Lisa. She hadn't noticed what he was doing. She'd sent him a mistrustful look as they'd walked toward the terrace, but he sensed it hadn't involved his actions outside the greenhouse so much as in.

He spent the majority of the night working on his computer and most of the following day asleep, trapped in a nightmare world of recurring dreams.

Voodoo had been on his mind for some time now. Not surprising really since his mother had been considered by many people to be a witch. Even his father had wondered about her, but only because he'd wanted her to use any means available to return to him after her death.

At 5:12 p.m., Armand rolled out of bed, unrested and edgy. He forced down a makeshift meal of pasta and grilled tomatoes and figured that would hold him until he reached the swamp and his father's jambalaya. Showered and dressed, with his hair still damp, he checked on the e-mail he'd sent near dawn, printed out the address he would need for the coming evening and headed for his Explorer.

New Orleans never slumbered, he thought as he drove through the city toward the Warehouse District. He smelled fresh baked bread, barbecued fish and flowers in the French Quarter. He saw bands of locals and tourists strolling and no less than five hookers trolling. He heard music, mostly drums and brass, but there were voices mixed in, smoky vocals that flowed out of the clubs and onto the streets and sidewalks.

He liked the colorful cafés with their living quarters a floor above. He admired the wrought-iron railings and the riot of perfumed greenery that spilled from hanging planters. The city whispered sex and secrets in a lazy, accepting sort of way. He knew the decadent southern belle boasted plenty of both, but he couldn't think of either one right now without drawing Eden into the mix.

So he sipped hot coffee while he waited at a traffic light

and listened to a zydeco musician create amazing Cajun-Creole rhythms on his washboard.

His waterfront destination had once been a paint factory. It boasted a full brick facade and mile-high windows. In its original state, Armand would have called it charming. With evening sunbeams streaming over the low-e glass and every brick on the street side sandblasted to death, he saw just another stack of condos that would drive any self-respecting ghost crazy and send if off to haunt the nearest plantation.

The tenant board outside gave nothing away. Armand pressed the number he'd been given, finished his coffee and wondered if anyone here had ever gone fishing in the bayou.

"Yes, who is it?"

Armand's smile had a mocking edge. He imagined his tone reflected it. "We talked on the phone thirty minutes ago. The courts will question such a memory if you've forgotten our appointment in so short a space of time."

The man made an uncertain sound. "Yes, of course. Police. Questions. Come in. Take the freight elevator to the fourth floor."

The industrial interior was as contrived as the revamped facade, but at least someone was playing Duke Ellington at full volume. Armand caught a whiff of must that reminded him of a crypt, and a smell like strong chili peppers. He'd rolled his sleeves up past his elbows and wore his gun in plain sight.

Robert Weir had the door open when he reached the upper floor. He watched his visitor approach. He had the typical bookish appearance of an accountant, but on closer inspection, more steel beneath it than one might expect.

Robert's clothes were drab—gray pants and a white shirt. His demeanor said meek and mild, but the expression in his eyes belied that exterior.

"I'm making tea." Robert showed Armand into the loft-style living area. "I have coffee, but it's instant."

"I'm fine." Armand bypassed a brown mohair sofa and

walked to the window, the best feature of the loft in his opinion. "You have an excellent view of the river."

"A surprising number of boats pass by each day." The kettle began to whistle. "Er, do you mind?"

Armand regarded the muddy water below and got right to the point. "Had your partner arranged to meet you at the auction preview the night he died?"

Robert answered from the kitchen. "We didn't talk about it, no. I went there of my own accord. Maxwell had a dinner engagement that night. With his daughter, I discovered later."

"The daughter you claimed to have seen murder him."

The click of teacup against saucer was punctuated by a short laugh. "You're certainly blunt, Detective LaMorte."

"And Maxwell Burgoyne wasn't?"

"Yes, but one learns how to handle deliberate crudeness over time. I was born in Dorset. That's in the south of England. My parents were teachers. They never raised their voices or their hands to me. We lived in a quiet village, but of course there were bullies there as well. When those bullies chose to torment me, my parents suggested I ignore them. I opted to discourage them instead." His eyes, possibly gray-blue behind a pair of wire-rimmed spectacles, gleamed. "I arranged it so a bucket of permanent black dye tipped onto their heads as they passed through a certain backyard gate."

Armand didn't smile, but he could picture the scene. "They never realized who'd done it?"

"No." Robert sipped his tea. "They never did."

"So you know how to handle a bully. Would you say that was a fair description of Maxwell Burgoyne?"

"I'd omit the *y*, but I daresay he was a mix of both. Not a stupid man by any means, but loud and unrefined. Maxwell liked to acquire things, objects of value if you will. Six times out of ten he made a profit from a quick turnover. Thus his penchant for estate auctions."

"You weren't equal partners, were you?"

"Not at all. I came on board at ninety-ten and remained

there until two years ago when my share rose to fifteen percent.''

''Why did you stay in?''

''Because fifteen percent of a sound corporation can amount to a handsome total.''

Something was missing, but since Robert hadn't come clean with any of the officers who'd questioned him to this point, Armand knew he was unlikely to do so now.

He returned his gaze to the river. ''That's a powerful tug,'' he remarked in a conversational tone.

Robert joined him, adjusted his glasses and squinted. ''Is that a tug out front?''

''You can't tell?''

''Well, I see the larger ship behind it, of course. Ah.''

Noting the beginnings of a flush, Armand carried on. ''You were what—thirty feet away from your partner when he was struck?''

Robert's sigh held a note of forbearance. ''Thirty-one point two feet to be precise. The distance has been established, Detective, and yes, there were a small number of branches obscuring my vision.''

''As well as Spanish moss.''

''That, too.''

''Yet you identified Lisa Mayne as the murderer.''

''I believed it was her.''

''Had you met her?''

''Not formally, but I knew her on sight. She came to our office complex two weeks ago. Gossip runs rampant in most places of business, and ours is no exception. Word spread like wildfire. We didn't speak, but I got a very good look at her.''

''You're sure it was her you saw and not her sister?''

Robert seemed nonplussed. ''That's what I heard. Maxwell's biological daughter had come to speak to him.''

''Eden Bennett is Maxwell's biological daughter.''

''Yes, but—I must have heard Lisa Mayne's name then, and that's how I put it together.''

"Heard her name," Armand repeated. "Through someone tuned in to the office grapevine?"

"Yes. Maxwell's receptionist was at lunch. So was Maxwell as it turned out."

"Did his daughter stay long?"

"Only a few minutes, but I remember the name Lisa Mayne, Detective. Or…" Another sigh. "Let's just say I assumed the name went with the woman. Perhaps it was mere speculation, and Lisa's name was circulating before anyone arrived at the office claiming to be Maxwell's child. It's a moot point in any case, isn't it? I couldn't differentiate between Lisa Mayne and Eden Bennett in the police lineup. Therefore, my testimony has been rendered invalid."

"For the moment," Armand agreed. "Details tend to crop up."

Robert nudged his glasses farther up on his nose. "What sort of details, Detective?"

He shrugged. "Someone might come forward, an unexpected person who, without realizing he or she can, will provide an alibi for either Ms. Mayne or Ms. Bennett."

Robert set his teacup on a chrome coffee table. "That would be unfortunate."

"You think so?"

"For a pair of sisters who appear to care for each other, yes, I do."

"But good in the sense that justice would be served."

"Well, yes, of course." Removing his spectacles, Robert polished them with a napkin. "I suppose you think my reaction is strange considering that I'm the person who came forward with regard to Maxwell's murder in the first place, but I promise you, it wasn't a decision I made lightly. I am nearsighted as you say, and I understood that shortcoming would be called into question. It was dark in the cemetery, even with the moon up. I truly believed I saw Lisa Mayne strike Maxwell. However, in retrospect, and also in light of the numerous interviews I've given recently, I realize that I might simply have transferred my knowledge of Maxwell's evening calendar from thought to conviction."

"That's very Freudian of you, Mr. Weir."

"I'm feeling rather Freudian these days, Detective LaMorte. Please believe me when I tell you I have nothing against either of my late partner's daughters—and before you ask, even less to gain by his death. Where Maxwell's shares in the corporation will go, I can't say because, to be perfectly honest, I don't know the answer myself. What I do know is that they won't be coming to me. In fact, my own position might be in jeopardy once the will is probated. A fifteen percent partner is, I'm afraid, all too easy to phase out."

Armand did smile at that remark, but there was a bitterness to it that only he understood.

He asked the rest of his questions more out of habit than necessity. He'd wanted to meet the man and get a feel for him. His story was already a matter of record.

His cell phone rang ten minutes later as he exited the warehouse. Not in the most receptive mood, he answered.

"Well?" was the first word out of his father's mouth. "Do you have a report?"

He had a headache if that counted. "I'm working on it. Are you home alone?"

"No and no. Leaving, though, lickety-split. Can you guess why?"

It wasn't hard. Armand's mood deteriorated further. "You want to lecture me, go ahead. I'm doing things my way for now."

"Your mama…"

"Leave her out of this." Armand stopped him cold. "Just do the lecture, and let me get on with my night."

"Get on with it where?"

"You tell me. Or I can make a call and find out for myself if you want to be difficult."

"You got that testy sound in your voice, Armand. I know you're hating every minute of this, but sometimes lying's the only way. Just you remember what a low-down snake Maxwell

Burgoyne was—and I'm insulting snakes with that comparison. Now I know the woman's pretty and smart, but that's none of your concern. You do what you have to for your daddy. I protected you as a boy, now I need you to return the favor.''

Armand could have recited the words with him. He listened instead, processed what he needed and finally ended the conversation.

No jambalaya tonight, he thought with mild regret. Then he summoned a vague smile and glanced north. That didn't mean the evening would be a complete bust.

Chapter Seven

"Swamps suck." Mary folded her arms across her chest in an ornery fashion. "I hate bugs and humidity and snakes and alligators. Dolores is cool and so are her beignets, but I always eat too many—and I don't see why I had to come with you anyway."

It was going to rain again, Eden thought. She felt a storm in the air, even though the sky showed no sign of cloud. Feeling cranky, she said, "This whole let's-mess-up-the-witness's testimony thing was your idea, Mary. If I have to listen to Dolores prattle on about a curse I refuse to believe in, the least you can do is help me put her mind back on Lisa where it belongs."

Mary studied her fingernails. "Lisa's fine, Eden, not chatty right now, but hanging in. I told you it wasn't blood on that stupid crowbar. Well, okay, it was." She brushed lint from her skirt. "But it came from a robin she found in her strawberry patch. The thing was dead and mangled, and she didn't want to touch it, so she used the crowbar to, you know, stuff it in a baggy for burying. All you had to do was ask her about it."

Not with Armand LaMorte sitting there like a cat waiting to pounce. "You know I couldn't," Eden replied with patience. "So I told you instead, because I knew you'd be your usual blunt self and do it for me." She studied the road. "Have they changed this intersection?"

"Possibly—if you can call dirt, potholes and half a crooked

sign an intersection.'' Mary sneered. "How can Dolores stand living in the back of beyond?"

"She likes reptiles—the sound of them at night, not crawling in her home.'' Out of habit, Eden glanced backward, but it was too early for headlights, and a bluish tint would be hard to spot with the sun's dying rays shining in the rear window.

Mary remained silent for several minutes while Eden wound her way through the tiny bayou town their grandmother had called home most of her life.

For her late husband's sake, Dolores had attempted to live in New Orleans once. She'd stuck it out for three years before coaxing him out of the city and back to the swamp. He'd made the commute every day until his death thirty-five years ago. By Eden's reckoning, that only amounted to twelve years of back and forth driving, but Mary saw it as twelve years that would have read like twelve decades. She figured the man had died to escape swamp life rather than of heart disease. Lisa merely mourned the fact that they'd never met him.

Drumming restless fingers on her arms, Mary blurted a sudden, "Who do you think killed Maxwell, Eden?"

Because her mind had been threatening to creep in Armand's direction, Eden welcomed the question. Or would have if there'd been a reasonable answer. "You know I never met him, Mary, let alone his associates.''

"Synonymous for enemies in Maxwell's case. Lisa said he was a jerk, and I believe her. Did you see his picture in the paper? Poor photography, I'll admit, but even allowing for that, he had a scary face.'' Mary made circles with her fingers and placed them around her eyes. Then she blew out her cheeks and bared her teeth. "I think he was supposed to be smiling in the shots I saw, but it looked more like a grimace. He had shiny skin, saggy jowls and a short, curly beard.''

"I didn't like his eyes.'' A shiver crawled down her spine as Eden recalled the grainy newsprint photo. "There was nothing in them. They looked pale and empty.''

"They were pale,'' Mary agreed. "Puke-green pale. There was a two-page spread on him in *City Scene Magazine*.''

Phoebe had showed Eden the article that morning. "His teeth were pointy, too," she said, "but I assume that was a trick of the light."

"Good thing you don't look like him, huh? Not," Mary added with a sniff, "that you're any better off taking after his ex." She went back to examining her nails. "So, of the people we know, who *do* you think did it?"

Eden blew down the front of her black tank top to cool her skin. "You want me to say Lucille, don't you?"

"She looks a lot like you and Lisa—or you look like her."

Something twisted in Eden's stomach, but she ignored it. "I'll go with the witness then. He and Maxwell were partners. People fall out, commit crimes, sometimes murder." Easing the car around a final bend, she bumped along the gravel road that led to Dolores's front door. In a more speculative tone, she mused, "I wonder what color his car headlights are?"

Beside her, Mary yelped and jumped upright in her seat. "What's she doing here?"

Eden spotted Lucille's late-model Lincoln and murmured a soft, "Perfect."

"Let me out." Mary wrenched on the door handle. "I'll hitchhike home. I can't be civilized to that woman twice in one week."

Eden hit the lock button before her sister toppled onto the road. "Think of it as a game of cat and mouse. Work on trapping her into a confession. I can't believe you wouldn't enjoy that."

"No way. This mouse is hitching a ride back to its city hole."

"Lucille's the mouse, Mary. Anyway, you can't hitch in three-inch heels, not in this ba—" She started to say backwater town, but changed it to, "Low traffic area. There aren't any sidewalks, and the potholes are as big as wading pools. Eat a beignet, and be glad you don't have to listen to Dolores forecasting your death."

"If you really were a voodoo child and you cared about me,

you'd use your powers to turn Lucille into a stick bug. She's starting to look like one with her stupid diets.''

''You were right before,'' Eden said. ''I shouldn't have dragged you out here.''

She still wasn't entirely sure why she had, but she suspected it involved Armand and the idea of using conversation as a diversion.

The man had haunted her dreams last night, although he'd been a shadowy figure who'd taken great care to remain outside the action unfolding around him.

Eden had seen Lucille's green eyes staring at her from inside a mirror that swished like swamp water.

''I am the vessel,'' was all she'd said, then she'd vanished, and Lisa had appeared holding two uprooted plants with spotted flowers and coarse leaves. She'd tossed the plants, flowers and all, into a steaming pot and muttered something in another language.

''He was a dreadful man,'' she'd added in a voice that hadn't quite been hers. ''He abandoned us. He abandoned her. He hurt her more than anyone will ever know. His betrayal was a knife stuck in her heart.''

Lucille had reappeared then and, in her unhurried way, extracted a bloody crowbar from her chest.

Eden had wanted to talk to both women, but Armand held her back. He'd actually placed a hand over her mouth when she'd tried to call out.

''Better to stay in the shadows for now, *chère,*'' he'd advised. ''Too many things remain unknown. Some of those that are can mislead, while others go unrecognized for now.''

Whatever that meant…

''I'm waiting in the car,'' Mary declared in a hot tone.

Eden's memory shattered. She twisted her hair into a ponytail to get it off her neck. ''Dolores has French wine to go with those beignets, you know.''

Mary considered that. ''Can I have your share?''

''Minus one glass.'' Eden slid out, sticky and hot. ''I hope it rains soon and clears the air. I feel as wet on dry land as I would if I were swimming in the bayou.''

"Oh, it'll rain," Mary predicted. "It'll be the great flood all over again, and we'll be stuck here with Lucille for forty days and forty nights. And just like Dolores's husband I'll freak, and my blood pressure will shoot up and I'll die and never get out of here."

Eden set her sunglasses on top of her head. "I promise not to bury you in the swamp."

As she spoke, she glanced toward the sinuous bayou. For the first time, she spied the outer edge of a long, black cloud-bank. "That looks ominous."

Mary trudged past her to the front porch, which was really the back porch because Dolores's big main windows all faced the swamp.

Colored bottles, crystals and carved wooden folk figures vied for space in an open cabinet beside the screen door. Because they were voodoo related, Eden chose not to examine them too closely. Not seeing made not believing easier somehow. But then, as it had done so often lately, the family curse whispered in her head.

Voodoo child with Carib blood, and eyes of green. This is foreseen...

Giving her shoulders an irritable roll, Eden shook the words away. When her gaze landed on a naked doll, a female with full breasts, dark hair and green marble eyes, she made an impatient sound. "What's the big deal about green eyes anyway?"

"No idea," Mary said. "Don't have 'em, don't want 'em."

"Sometimes you have them," Eden argued. "When you wear the right clothes."

"Only that one time when I played Maggie in *Cat on a Hot Tin Roof.* I had to wear a kelly green dress because the white chiffon had a brandy stain on it. The wig was wrong, too. It came from some eighties punk rock play, and it smelled like mothballs. My face was as green as my eyes that night. But normally—" she glared "—they're blue."

Eden let it go. She wanted to get away from the voodoo topic, the voodoo cupboard and most particularly the green-eyed voodoo doll. "Do you hear voices in the house?"

"I hear bugs and splashing water." Mary sent her an evil little smile. "You think maybe a gator got Lucille?" The smile vanished. "Why's she here anyway? She hates this place."

"But she loves her mother." Although Lucille seldom showed Dolores the kind of affection that Eden shared with her own mother. In fact, at times the relationship between Dolores and Lucille seemed downright confrontational.

Must be the magic, she reflected. Lucille had little regard for the supernatural, while Dolores reveled in it.

Setting relationships and the curse aside, Eden followed Mary along the brick path to a screened-in porch that over-looked the water.

Huge live oaks dripped Spanish moss almost to the ground. A gust of wind whipped fallen leaves around her ankles. The sun had set, and the bank of clouds was creeping closer. She heard a low peal of thunder as the rain approached.

Eden needed to talk to someone. She wondered if she would have come here tonight if her own mother hadn't been away on a two-week trip to Barbados. But out of country, out of touch was Alice Bennett's motto. She could be contacted in an emergency, but only through a series of phone calls that would take an hour to place. Then she'd be worried and prob-ably cut her trip short and—

Eden shook her head. Nowhere to go with that thought.

"Mud and bugs." Mary swatted a black fly. "I don't hear them, Eden, and I don't see Dolores's pickup. Maybe they went into—oh, damn." She hopped sideways on one foot. "I stepped on a beetle. They stink." Scraping her shoe on the edge of a brick, she grumbled, "You make one bone-headed suggestion about confusing a witness, and suddenly your life's a mess."

"Tell me about it." Eden avoided the squashed beetle and headed for the sun porch.

Mary continued to mutter. If nothing else, having her sister there kept Eden's mind from wandering into dangerous territory. You couldn't be with Mary and think about anyone except Mary.

Lucille's drawl reached her as she rounded a bush and descended three steps into the explosion of plant life that comprised Dolores's garden.

"You're lucky, really," Lucille remarked in her lazy southern fashion. "It's my ancestral genes that allow for that spark of hope."

Dolores snorted. "Don't waste that ancestral hooey on me. We both know how the lines come down. The curse can't help but get her, and the worst of it is, in the end, she'll be getting it from the selfsame person who started the thing."

"Some might call that karma," Lucille murmured. "Me, I call it bull. No witch who's been dead for more than two centuries is going to affect my destiny or that of the children I bore."

"Child," Dolores corrected. "Only one child you bore matters to Eva Dumont. Daughter cursed father and mistress, and so on down the line. Eldest born to eldest grown. I'm eldest grown. Eden's eldest born."

"And thus fated to die." Now Lucille sounded cross. "That's crazy talk, Maman, and you can't really believe it or you wouldn't be working so hard to—"

"What's going on?" Mary's voice behind Eden startled her. "Are they here or not?"

The conversation inside stopped the moment she spoke. Strangely enough, Eden had wanted them to continue. There was more to all of this than what Dolores had told them ten years ago.

Mary jabbed her in the ribs. "Come on. If we're going in, let's go. We can eat, drink lots in my case and get back to the city where beetles don't grow to the size of po-boys."

"Eden, Mary, is that you?" Dolores poked her head through a window. "Why're you lollygagging out there? Come in and talk. See your mama."

"There'd better be wine," Mary said tight-lipped.

More thunder rolled through the treetops. The yard had grown dark in the past five minutes. Eden felt the eerie transformation in her bones, and apparently Mary agreed.

"I keep expecting nasty little creatures to come hurtling out of the woods," she said with a shudder. "Why is that?"

"Because you're a ghoul at heart?"

Eden's attempt to lighten the mood failed. The moment Mary's gaze fell on Lucille, she marched straight to Dolores's wine rack and pulled out the biggest bottle she could find.

"Help yourself," Lucille said with a mocking smile. "The rest of us can share what's left in this carafe."

"Don't goad her, Lucille." But Dolores made a point of seating Mary as far away from her mother as was possible in the tiny living room.

Eden liked her grandmother's home, but spacious it wasn't. The dining room stood in a tiny alcove. It consisted of a round mahogany table, circled by six mismatched chairs. Only the living room furniture was new, and only because one of Dolores's friends had dropped a cigar on the sofa and burned a hole in the seat cushion. Still, it wasn't until a spring had popped through that she'd gone shopping.

For the most part, their grandmother surrounded herself with antiques. Some were valuable, most were not, but all were significant in some way.

As for Dolores, if this had been eighteenth century Europe, she could have been mistaken for a gypsy. At seventy-six, her black hair was liberally streaked with gray, and it curled down to her shoulders. She stood a ramrod straight five foot seven inches tall, favored flowy skirts and calf-high moccasins. Her jewelry, a mix of silver and onyx, was abundant and ran the gamut from loopy earrings and beaded bracelets to a pair of serpentine ankle chains she never removed.

As a rule, her brown eyes twinkled. Right now, they studied Eden as if trying to see inside her mind.

"You're worried," she said and, taking the wine bottle Mary had uncorked, splashed some into her empty teacup.

"Dolores…"

"No back talk. You drink this down, then tell us what's been happening since Maxwell died."

"Yeah, by the way, thanks for the warning about him." Mary retrieved the bottle and swept back to her seat. "You might have mentioned that our big, bad Daddy was alive and loaded."

"So you could what?" Lucille glanced at the gathering storm clouds. "Hit him up for a fatherly loan? He wouldn't have obliged you, I promise."

"A 'no' would have been better than what happened in the end, wouldn't it? Lisa's been camping out in her garden, and Eden's all steamed up over some hottie cop who's been following her around."

Lucille looked interested. "What would this hottie's name be?"

"Drink your wine, Mary," Eden warned before her sister could get going. "It's Detective Armand LaMorte, and I'm not steamed up over him. I don't trust him."

"But he is hot, yes?"

"Passable," Eden lied.

Thunder rattled the big windows. Through the largest of the three, she caught a glint of blue light. Not trusting that either, she endeavored to determine its source.

It hadn't come from the road, that was behind them. Maybe from the water, although this area of the swamp had so many rocks and shallow spots that boaters seldom used it.

"Something wrong?" Dolores asked as she continued to scour the tangle of moss and trees.

Ten seconds passed before Eden shook her head. "I guess not. I saw a light. All this curse stuff is making me jumpy."

"Good." Dolores's satisfied nod set Eden's teeth on edge.

"No, it's not good, it's bad. In fact it's downright crazy." Armand included. "I won't be frightened by a curse, Dolores. I'm worried about Lisa, that's why I came here tonight." Or part of it at least. "She won't talk to me—to either of us—about Maxwell Burgoyne."

"She didn't tell you what happened when they met?"

"Not about how she felt when he died, or the details of their meeting or what he said that made her hate him so much. It's like she's filling out a report when she talks about him. There's no emotion in her voice. Except, well—there really is. It's just not positive, and that's not Lisa."

"She's disappointed," Lucille remarked. "That's the reason I never told you about him and why Dolores and I agreed that, for all intents and purposes, he should be dead to you. Maxwell was a destroyer, Eden. He upset lives. Death hasn't changed that. He's gone and we're all in turmoil."

"We're in turmoil," Eden corrected, "because a witness said it was Lisa who killed him."

"Ah, yes." With her index finger, Dolores eased the teacup to Eden's lips. "Well-meaning Robert."

Eden almost choked. "You know him?"

"Maman." Lucille made a disapproving sound and sat back with her glass.

"You, too?" Eden was stunned. "Why didn't you tell us? It's that witness who—" She broke off midsentence. "You said Robert. What's his last name? What does he do?"

Dolores's bracelets clinked as she raised a hand for silence. "His name's Robert Weir, Eden, and he was Maxwell's business partner for many years. They were not friends."

Eden was still too incredulous to react properly, and with the exception of a small snigger, Mary had gone strangely silent. "How do you know this?" she demanded. Then a light blinked on, and she swung her gaze to Lucille's impassive face. "Your cop friend told you, didn't he?"

"He might have mentioned Robert's name."

Mary snorted. "Mentioned it, or traded it for a roll in the sack."

"Mary!" Dolores's tone was whip sharp. "You don't talk to your mother that way, not in my house."

"Fine." Bottle in hand, Mary stood. "I'll wait in the car then. Good hunting, Eden."

When she was gone, Dolores shook her head. "That girl

should be making her own way in life, not living off Lisa and running wild.''

Exasperated, Eden said, ''Mary's not the issue here, Dolores.''

The floor beneath them trembled. Thunder echoed over the bayou while forked lightning shot through the trees. The storm was all around them, yet the air remained perfectly still, and not a drop of rain had fallen.

''We'll need candles,'' Dolores predicted.

''You need to talk to me first,'' Eden countered. She refused to let the hurt and anger inside her show. ''I'll start. Robert Weir accused Lisa of murdering Maxwell because...''

HIDDEN IN THE GROWTH at the far end of the garden, a person with miniature binoculars watched the bayou house. Thunder rumbled overhead. The clouds were black now and heavy, alive with electricity.

Lightning storms were unnerving, always had been. But tonight was about focus, determination. She would get the message and know she'd gotten it before either of them left this swamp.

The rain would pose a problem when it fell. It needed to be done now.

A disposable lighter flicked in the gloom.

Within it glowed a pair of terrified green eyes.

Chapter Eight

Armand crouched in the bushes, and waited. Eden had been inside the house with her mother and grandmother for some time now. Long enough for the air to go still and the sky to turn unnaturally black.

He smelled damp earth, oleanders and the swamp behind him. But in his memory he smelled Eden. She wore a floral scent that made him think of the tropics and in particular of a boat trip he'd taken along the Amazon during his college years.

He glimpsed movement behind the largest of the three garden-facing windows, but nothing that indicated she was leaving. Mary had stomped out thirty minutes ago. She'd had a bottle of wine tucked in her arm and an undisguised smirk on her lips.

As he toyed with a twig, Armand pictured Mary's face. He let it melt into Eden's. No doubt about it, Eden had inherited the softer edges in the family. But soft edges could hide a stubborn nature, as he knew only too well. On the other hand, a steely facade meant little if the veneer cracked to reveal southern mush.

Not a breath of air stirred the moss. He caught another movement and this time saw the door swing inward. Actually, it was yanked, but because it wasn't slammed when Eden emerged onto the porch, he reasoned that, while she might not be happy, at least she wasn't in a temper.

He decided to watch her for a few minutes before revealing himself. Watch and fantasize about those long, lovely legs and a mouth more tempting than any wine he knew of.

If he was lucky, the fantasy might even win out over the guilt.

EDEN PACED AND SIMMERED. The witness, one Robert Weir, had been Maxwell's business partner for decades. According to Lucille, they'd been neither friends nor enemies. They'd simply worked together, with Maxwell assuming the role of the business lion and his partner that of barnyard rodent.

Their shares in the various companies had remained separate. Neither stood to inherit anything from the other in the event of death.

So much for motive, Eden reflected in annoyance.

Halting, she inhaled the thick, bayou air. She found it difficult to believe that Robert Weir had liked his situation. Endured it for a profit, however, now that was possible. Not having met the man, she couldn't say. She only knew she wasn't about to take Lucille's assessment of him at face value, not when her birth mother had so obviously despised Maxwell.

Taking one last deep breath, Eden focused her eyes. "He lied about seeing Lisa, though," she said to Dolores's climbing roses. "Lied or can't see beyond the end of his nose at night."

Lightning crackled through the clouds. Seconds later, the thunder rumbled overhead. The storm was on top of them, and still not a drop of rain had fallen. Not a single leaf or flower moved in the garden, and the water behind it sat dead calm.

Something stirred, however. As more lightning lit the sky, the bushes beside her rustled and a man stepped out. If he hadn't been ten feet away and stopped when she spotted him, she probably would have jumped through the wall of the house. Instead she dealt with a racing heart lodged somewhere near her throat and forced an even tone.

"Why?" she demanded simply and hoped the fingers she wrapped around the wooden railing didn't give her away.

Armand almost smiled. He wanted to. She saw the amusement in his eyes. Disarming in faded jeans and a long-sleeved white tee, he shrugged. "Would you believe me?"

Eden pressed a fist to her breastbone and concentrated on breathing. "You never know. I might. It's been a weird sort of night."

He leaned on a peeling column. "I came to talk to your mother. I called her club and found out she was here. I'll admit, it took me a while to discover exactly where here was, but I managed, with some help from a kid at the crossroad filling station."

Could she go for that? Eden wondered. She wanted to, but then she'd had faith in Santa Claus until she was ten—and her ex until there was no hope left.

Sighing, she pushed off from the rail. "Lucille's not my mother, Armand. My mother's name is Alice Anne. She teaches philosophy at Florida State University. As we speak, she's somewhere between Bridgetown and Crab Hill, visiting her cousin."

"Lucky woman. All I have is an estranged aunt in Vanuatu."

"The South Pacific's not lucky?"

He smiled. "You watch the Travel Channel."

"I watch lots of things." Including him at the moment. Eden didn't want him getting any closer. She was aware enough of this man without remembering what it felt like to kiss him.

Rubbing her suddenly tingling arms, she prowled the length of the porch. She caught a hint of wood smoke as more thunder rolled through. She pictured one of Dolores's neighbors firing up his still and wondered with amusement how Armand would respond if he stumbled across it when he left tonight.

"Have you been here long?" she asked over her shoulder.

She didn't realize how close he'd gotten until he answered almost in her ear. "Not very." A pause, then a teasing, "Does my being here upset you?"

She faced him with calm resolve. "Should it?"

"That's for you to say." Reaching out a finger, he brushed

the hair from her cheekbone. Then he ran his knuckle along the curve of her jaw. "You have beautiful features, Eden. Like your sisters and mother, but softer in so many important ways."

She narrowed her eyes at him. It was either challenge him or lean in, and they weren't going there tonight. "Did you buy a jug of moonshine from that kid at the filling station?"

He grinned. "They sell it by the jug?"

"Sometimes, although the kids probably wouldn't. This is a God-fearing town." The tang of wood smoke reached her again. Behind it came the loudest clap of thunder yet and a trio of lightning bolts that sizzled in the already charged air.

"Lucille is inside with my grandmother."

"Dolores Boyer."

"You'll want to talk to her as well, I suppose."

"If she knew the victim, yes."

"Oh, she knew him." Eden wrapped her arms around her waist and stared at Dolores's magnolia trees. "She also knows the man who accused Lisa of murdering Maxwell."

If Armand was surprised, he didn't show it. When Eden glanced back, he was staring up at the roof and frowning slightly.

A fat drop of rain landed on the railing. Another splatted on the top of Eden's head. "Is something wrong?" she asked.

His eyes traveled past the chimney to the tree line. "Do you smell smoke?"

"I did a minute ago." She followed his gaze, then pointed to a sycamore tree on the far side of the house. "Something just drifted through the branches."

Visions of an overheated car engine sprang to mind. It had happened to Mary once last summer. But a fire wouldn't take that long to start—unless it had been smoldering under the hood all this time.

"Mary," she said softly and started for the garden steps. "She's in my car with a bottle of wine. If the engine's burning…"

Armand caught her. "It's not electrical smoke, Eden. And

Mary's not in your car. At least I didn't see her when I went by there a few minutes ago.''

Large raindrops plopped down. A gust of wind, eerily silent, swept past in a thin stream.

It felt like ghosts passing over her skin, Eden thought with a shiver. Then she had another thought, and she swung to face the door. ''Dolores and Lucille are inside.''

But Armand stopped her again, this time by snagging her wrist. ''The smoke isn't coming from inside the house.''

''The windows...''

He shook his head and, keeping a firm hold, drew her with him up the garden steps and along the path to the driveway.

Behind her, Eden heard the bayou trees starting to creak. Water lapped against the low bank and rain splashed the surface.

It would be a deluge in a minute. She'd be hard-pressed to drive out of here even if she left right now. Still, water doused fires, so she really shouldn't mind. All they had to do now was find the fire.

Armand kept her glued to his side. In a dress and high-heeled sandals, walking on stones was difficult, and increasingly treacherous the wetter they became. Eden lost her footing more than once and would have fallen if Armand hadn't been there to steady her.

''It's the front porch,'' he said.

A blast of wind whipped up from the water. It carried his words away and at the same time seemed to unleash the full fury of the storm. The rain didn't so much fall as sweep in, driven by air currents so strong Eden felt as though she were being slapped.

The iron and glass baubles Dolores had strung from her eaves rattled and clanked. On the porch, a blurry wall of flames crept up the side of the voodoo cupboard. The cupboard stood exactly as it had when Eden arrived. Except...

''Someone's pulled it forward.'' She had to shout to be heard. Using her hands, she mimed the change. ''It's been moved away from the house.''

Away, but not out from under the overhang. The rain had no effect on the flames which were already engulfing the lower shelves as they now worked their way toward the top.

"I have to find Mary." Eden ran to her car while Armand headed for the burning cupboard. She couldn't see her sister inside and fumbled the key ring from her pocket.

"Mary," she called, swiping wet hair from her eyes. "Are you in there?"

She found her keys just as the driver's window rolled down. Mary's groggy face appeared. "What's going on? Is Lucille gone? What's hitting the roof?"

Relieved, Eden replied, "Nothing. Put the window up and go back to sleep."

She saw rather than heard the door to the house open.

"*Mon Dieu,* my collection!" Dolores rushed to the cupboard. Armand intercepted her. He said something in Cajun and she answered with an angry fling of her arm.

The hose, Eden recalled suddenly. Dolores hung it next to the house so she could water her planters.

She got there at the same time as Armand, almost colliding with him in the process. "Do you know where to turn it on?" he shouted above the wind.

Eden thought for a moment—she'd watered Dolores's plants many times—then nodded. Kicking off her sandals, she ran to the trellis, reached through the wisteria and gave the tap a firm twist.

The rain drenched her. The yard was a submerged watercolor, with green melting into red and then into brown. Her task complete, she located the vertical slats of the railing, set a foot on the facing and hoisted herself up.

Climbing was no problem. She'd done it often in her parents' yard as a child. In this case, her dress hindered her, but by hiking it up, she was able to swing her legs over the top and land on the dry deck boards.

Dolores supervised Armand with critical words and sharp gestures. Lucille said nothing, merely watched the proceedings from a safe distance.

Smoke swirled around them. It billowed up and out, until the wind finally seized it and sucked the whole choking mass into the yard.

Eden's eyes stung. Even Lucille gave a wave and a cough. "Something just went up in flames," she noted. "Probably an old cornhusk."

But Eden knew Dolores's taste, and cornhusk dolls had no place in it. She liked stones and bones and smooth, colored glass. The rest of her collection ranged from alligator teeth and rusted iron keys to five carved amulets, three of which she firmly believed had been used in voodoo rituals.

Once the flames were extinguished and only a haze of smoke remained, Eden moved forward. It surprised her when Lucille set a restraining hand on her upper arm.

"The fire might not be out yet."

"But you can see it is, Lucille."

"Don't believe everything you see." She offset the warning with a shrug. "Better to let your grandmother assess the damage. You know she'll see this as the worst kind of omen for you."

With a small hiss of pain, Eden pried Lucille's fingers from her arm. "You don't have to cut off my circulation to make your point. I understand how Dolores feels about her voodoo paraphernalia, and her curse."

Lucille's gaze traveled to the scorched cabinet. She looked pale in the strange light of the storm. Pale and distracted and— Mary was right—far too thin. Her fingers continued to dig into Eden's arm.

"Lucille." Eden endeavored once again to dislodge her.

"What? Oh, I'm sorry." She relaxed her grip. "I was thinking. That man with Dolores, is he the police detective Mary mentioned earlier?"

"Armand LaMorte." Eden rubbed the red marks left by Lucille's fingers. "He came here tonight to talk to you."

"Did he indeed. An intriguing development. Eden, no stay with—" Lucille sighed "—me."

Eden heard her but something had captured her attention, and she wanted a closer look at it.

There had been three boxes on the top shelf of the cupboard when she'd arrived. Now, another object had taken their place. It was perched right in the center, but it wasn't box-shaped. It was Dolores's green-eyed doll, and without words or movement, it called to her.

Voodoo child with Carib blood, and eyes of green. This is foreseen: The eldest born to eldest grown, my pain shall bear. Believe. Beware…

The words of the curse ran through Eden's head. She saw them superimposed over the doll's green glass eyes.

For a startled moment, she thought she saw a tear in those eyes, but of course it was only water. The doll was wet from the spray of the hose.

The storm's noise didn't block out Dolores's harsh intake of breath when she saw the doll as well. Eden sent her grandmother a grim look and fixed Armand with a mildly suspicious one. His features, however, remained completely unopen to interpretation.

"Did you do it?" she demanded.

He dropped the hose and swiped a sooty arm across his forehead. "I'm not an arsonist, Eden."

"I don't mean the fire." She knew she sounded testy, but she didn't care. "Someone moved that doll. It was on the third shelf when Mary and I got here. Now it's on the top, and the cabinet's been pulled forward, and everything in it, including the doll, has been scorched."

Dolores uttered a quick prayer.

Shifting her mistrustful gaze, Eden splayed the fingers of her right hand. "Don't say it, Dolores. Not one word about that damned curse. Dolls don't move by magic and neither do cupboards. Someone did this deliberately, and if the only name you can give me is Eva Dumont's, then I'm out of here."

Dolores reacted swiftly. Before Eden could turn, she caught her granddaughter's hand in a tight grasp and squeezed. "You've scoffed at this curse for every one of the ten years

I've known you, Eden. I don't expect you to believe overnight, but you see now that something is happening here. Maxwell's death—''

Eden's hand went cold, but she kept her voice steady. ''Alive or dead, Maxwell Burgoyne has nothing to do with Eva Dumont's curse.''

''Could be not directly, but I believe his death might have been a catalyst.''

Impatient, Eden frowned. ''What do you think about family curses, Armand? Do you believe in them?''

''I believe in many things, *chère,* some supernatural, most not. In curses handed down through blood, not so much.''

As answers went, it was ambiguous enough to quell the fear that had been rising inside her. Or if not quell it, at least shove it back far enough for her to rally.

With lightning flickering over the bayou, she looked first at Dolores, then at Armand. ''Maxwell's dead and a witness lied about how that happened. Lisa's involved and so am I. Someone with blue-tinted headlights has been following me, a planter fell from a balcony and now a doll's been moved inside a burning cabinet. That's not voodoo, Dolores. You're not doing your job, Detective, and I—'' she tugged free of Dolores's increasingly painful grasp ''—am going home.''

She glanced at Lucille behind her but avoided looking at Armand again. Seeing him confused her, and she was muddled enough already.

She was also hearing something, or imagined she was. As she turned, a voice seemed to whisper in her head.

''For deeds long past, *chère* child will reap, my vengeance curse, of death—or worse.''

Unable to resist, Eden shot one last glare at the green-eyed doll. And on a drying shelf saw twin drops of water trickle like tears down her cheek....

Chapter Nine

Armand considered going after her, but he knew better than to pursue an angry woman. She didn't trust him, and who could blame her? Not him of all people.

So he spent several soggy, smoke-filled minutes talking to Lucille, refused Dolores's offer of a shower and, with his cell phone activated, drove back to the city.

Grimy and out of sorts, he cruised the narrow streets of the French Quarter in his SUV, listening to Dixieland jazz and forcing himself not to go past her apartment. She wouldn't want to see him, certainly wouldn't want to talk to him right now.

His cell phone rang. He checked the screen and answered. Two minutes later and against his better judgment, he parked and made his way into a walk-up restaurant called La Bouche. He tried another call, but couldn't connect, and ignoring the speculative look he received from the owner's wife, seated himself at the only empty table in the room.

Still out of sorts and now wishing he'd taken Dolores up on her offer, he went over in his mind his reasons for doing this. They boiled down to two words: parental pressure.

"Hell." Annoyed with himself, he ordered the first thing he saw on the menu which was boudin, a spicy pork and rice dish. He was tempted to add a glass of whiskey but opted for beer instead, then rolled his shoulders and waited for Al to arrive.

Twenty minutes and a bottle of lager later, the older cop slapped a newspaper onto the table and took a seat in one of the hard-bottomed chairs.

"Coffee," he grunted at the server. "No chicory. Makes the coffee sit in my stomach all night."

"Have a beer," Armand suggested, taking a long swig of his second bottle.

"I'm on duty."

"So am I."

He handed over the bottle. Al hesitated for half a second before taking an even deeper swig.

"You finish that while I check out the news."

Al set the bottle on the paper and belched. "Not here, okay? Think pension, Mandy. Not yours, mine." He picked uneasily at the label. "That doc friend of yours was good, by the way. Gonna do an MRI next week."

"I'm glad to hear it." The food arrived then, its spicy scent mingling with the other smells around them—exotic perfume, crushed garlic and a full-bodied French wine that brought to mind any number of images, all of them involving Eden. He was in bad shape, Armand reflected, if something so basic could mess him up so completely.

Amused at himself, he sat back. "Word of advice, don't do favors for people. The consequences are hell to deal with."

Al snorted. "Now there's a philosophy. Does that mean I can take my newspaper and blow?" He sniffed the steaming pork dish. "You gonna eat that or just poke?"

Armand tossed his fork down and shoved the plate across the table. "Do you believe in voodoo?"

"Nah. My oldest does, but she's in college, going through a phase. It's all crap to me. I get a backache, it's because I moved a sleeper sofa on the weekend, not because Francine's old lady's sticking pins in my spine." He pulled a piece of fat from his mouth. "What happened? You run into a zombie or something?"

"Not yet, but who knows what arrangements Maxwell Burgoyne has made for his eternal soul."

"Huh. Well, he won't be too fresh by the time the voodoo resurrectors get hold of him. His body's still in the morgue." When Armand didn't respond, he ate a forkful of rice, then looked across the room. "What's so fascinating out there? You see someone you know?"

Armand kept the man who'd just entered in sight. "Yeah, a guy who shouldn't be here."

"Well hell, Mandy, you shouldn't be here." A slow smile spread over Al's homely features, and he craned his neck for a better view. "My, my, now there's a coincidence. Lisa Mayne's pretty sister. 'Course she lives around here, doesn't she, so maybe it's not such a coincidence after all. Make that coffee to go," he told the passing server. He polished off Armand's dinner and breathed in deep. "I'm gonna say it again, Mandy, you're walking a fine line on this one."

"You think?" Armand kept his eyes on Eden, who also wasn't supposed to be here. "If I drop off, I'm screwed. Don't worry, old friend, I don't clutch and grab when I tumble. Your pension's safe. Thanks for the paper."

Al left with a weary grunt. Armand didn't look because he didn't want to lose sight of Eden in the crush of laughing, flirting bodies.

She was searching for someone. Probably not for him, though. Their coming together here was a coincidence, or if not that, at least he hadn't expected her to choose tonight of all nights to dine out.

This was her favorite restaurant, close to her apartment and with a reputation for authentic Cajun dishes. She'd known the owners for years. And wasn't it just a fitting end to the day, he thought with a sigh, that they would wind up in the same place at the same time, with neither one of them likely to be in the best of moods.

She'd showered and changed in the two hours since he'd seen her. She wore a black halter top, a short, white skirt and black, high-heeled sandals that made her mile-long legs look even more incredible.

Armand watched her scan the crowd. As he drank his beer,

he wondered how many four-letter words would occur to her when she spotted him.

It took her a few minutes, but her gaze finally settled on his table, then on him. With a determined expression, she tucked her purse under her arm and made her way through the throng.

The restaurant was steaming at 10:00 p.m., partly from the rainstorm which had passed through the city earlier, but mostly from the heat of God knew how many bodies packed into a single tiny room. The food was the draw for the locals. For the tourists, it was the atmosphere. For Armand, it was all Eden.

He continued to sip his beer, offering no reaction to her arrival beyond the faintest arch of one brow.

When she didn't speak, he took another drink and said, "Aren't you going to accuse me of following you?"

Whatever reaction he'd expected, it definitely wasn't the humor that flickered across her face. "I do that a lot, don't I? With reason, I might add, but not in this case. Mary and I were across the street. She saw you come in here, so I followed."

"You want to know what I said to Lucille, right?" Because he couldn't think of any other reason.

Snugging a chair up next to his, she set a hand on his wrist. "Tell me the truth, are you drunk?"

He almost laughed but managed to keep it to a smile. "Do I look drunk?"

"No games, Armand." Her fingers bit in just enough to emphasize her point. "I need your help. I took Mary home earlier and went in to see Lisa. She wasn't there, so I drove to my apartment."

"And?"

"Mary phoned. She said a neighbor told her Lisa left ten minutes before we got there. She has an appointment tonight… with a voodoo priestess."

"The woman's known," Eden explained five minutes later at street level. "Not well-known because she doesn't do readings or present herself in a particularly appealing way. Her name's Madame Kafkha, and I guess you'd call her a seer. She lives in the Irish Channel, in a third floor walk-up that never gets burgled even though it's in a bad neighborhood." Eden wondered how detailed she should get, then continued. "Lisa's not an unbeliever where voodoo's concerned, but she's never gotten anyone to read the bones for her before, and even if she wanted to try it as an experiment, Madame Kafkha isn't the sort of person I'd expect her to pick." She paused again, then went for it. "Bottom line, Armand, I want to call a truce. I need you to help me find Lisa and figure out why she's not acting like Lisa."

Armand regarded her over the hood of his Explorer. "Lucille thinks she's taken the disappointment she feels about her biological father and twisted it into a sense of guilt now that he's dead."

"You mean if she hadn't left the restaurant, he wouldn't have gone to the auction preview early, and maybe he wouldn't have wound up dead? That's crazy."

"You don't think it's possible?"

"No, it's totally possible. I just—" She made an obscure gesture. "I can't see her turning to a voodoo priestess for absolution. Father Michael, yes, but not Madame Kafkha of all people."

Armand unlocked the SUV, climbed in and, from the driver's seat, gave the far door a kick. "It sticks," he said and held out a hand to her. "I agree to your truce, *chère*. We'll find your sister. And on the way, you can tell me how it is you know so much about a seer who lives in the Irish Channel and has the power to intimidate thieves."

For the first time since she'd approached him in La Bouche, Eden smiled. "That's an easy answer, Armand. I'm her dentist."

SHE'D KNOWN SHE WAS TAKING a risk enlisting his help. But Mary had been adamant. She wouldn't spy on Lisa, not for any reason. Eden recalled the conversation.

"You got her off the hook with the witness, Eden. That's all I asked you to do."

"You asked?"

"Okay, I was a little pushy, but we both know Lisa would no more bash someone's head in than she would set fire to her garden or poison all her precious greenhouse plants. In other words—not gonna happen."

Out of patience, Eden retorted, "So you think we should let her go to Madame Kafkha's even though she thought you were having a serious reaction to your allergy medication two years ago when you paid some harmless street corner psychic to do a two-dollar reading for you?"

They'd been standing outside one of Mary's regular night-club haunts off Bourbon Street and arguing steadily since meeting for the second time that night.

Mary pulled Eden out of the doorway and tapped an irritated foot. "Look, I agree this is an unusual thing for Lisa to do. I mean, who called whom in the first place tonight? But when I said we needed to talk, I didn't mean we should rush out after her. I figured we'd have a drink, and you'd come up with a plausible explanation for her behavior."

"Because I'm so into curses and voodoo?"

"Don't be sarcastic." The beat of her foot quickened. "Sometimes you see the big picture when I don't. And stop giving me that look. I told you on the way back to the city, I didn't see anyone sneaking around Dolores's house. I had some wine, dropped the seat back and fell asleep. Next thing I knew, rain was hitting the roof and you were shouting at me. As far as Lisa goes, I think she's just plain crushed to a pulp that Maxwell turned out to be a bastard. He makes up half our gene pool, don't forget, so maybe some of the creep in him is in us, too. Add that to Lucille's half and we're all three of us walking cesspools of screwed-up DNA."

Eden had almost snapped at her, then she'd remembered Mary's unhappy childhood and backed off. "Don't be an id-iot," she said without rancor. "The only cesspool personality was Maxwell Burgoyne's. Lucille cares, whether you believe that or not. You know Dolores is a good person, and I don't know about you, but I haven't committed any major crimes lately."

As soon as the words left her mouth, Eden regretted them. Because while visiting a voodoo priestess might be out of character for Lisa, it certainly wasn't a criminal act.

Before Mary could point that out, Eden raised her hands in surrender. "Okay, I get it. I should leave her alone. But she has a right to know about Robert Weir and Maxwell being partners."

"Absolutely." Her sister fussed with the neckline of her dress. "You tell her."

"You live with her, Mary."

Although she'd tried not to let them, Mary's shoulders jerked. "I know but—well, just because I don't think we should chase her to Madame Kafkha's, doesn't mean I haven't been finding her a little hard to deal with. She talks plants, Eden, and nothing else. Okay, she's crushed. Maxwell's a jerk etc. but until Lisa's Lisa again I'm avoiding mealtime chats. I mean, how many ways can there possibly be to cross-pollinate roses. On top of that, she keeps putting speckly flower arrangements on the mantel, and if I try to use any of her garden produce to cook, she freaks." Mary fluffed her hair in the club's smoked glass window. "Not that I cook much, but you get the idea. D'you think she's taking tranqs, or something…?"

The question echoed in Eden's head. No, she didn't think her sister was taking tranquilizers, but that belief was based on ten years of relatively peaceful history. With Maxwell dead and a murder charge barely averted, who knew?

Inside Armand's truck, with Louis Armstrong on the stereo and the city lights winking around them, Eden massaged the back of her neck. When she focused her eyes, she noticed a bluish beam behind them and twisted in her seat to look.

"It's a white Mercedes convertible, Eden," Armand told her. "I saw the headlights two blocks back."

"I guess I'm on blue alert these days." Eden studied the

car and its female driver for a moment then turned back. "Actually I haven't seen blue headlights since that night at Montesse."

Armand offered no comment. "Tell me about your second family," he said. "I can see that Mary dislikes Lucille, and she wasn't as fortunate as you and Lisa with regard to her adoptive parents, but I don't know much about you, past or present."

Eden shrugged. "I was born in New Orleans, but my parents came from San Francisco to adopt me. They were hippies through the seventies, which was fairly commonplace in California. My older brother Brian, also adopted, lives in Utah and works at a resort outside Salt Lake City. My father passed away five years ago and I already told you about my mother."

"When did you move to New Orleans?"

"When I was seven. That could be why I don't believe in voodoo. My uncle Joshua, who is my mother's brother, does special effects for a major studio in Los Angeles. Plus you only have to look around L.A. to see how easily what's artificial can be made to appear real."

Armand draped a hand over the steering wheel. Eden wondered why on earth a simple act like that should seem so sexy.

"New Orleans has its own brand of artifice," he said. "Or maybe a better word would be illusion."

"It sells."

"Yes, but not all of what you see is an illusion, is it? You want to believe voodoo's groundless, yet you can't quite dismiss your natural grandmother's beliefs."

It vexed Eden that he could read her with so little effort. She stared at the traffic ahead. "I'm not so closed-minded that I dismiss other people's beliefs out of hand, Armand. But I won't buy into a family curse, especially one that involves me."

It was hot and muggy in the Explorer. A large portion of that heat, Eden knew, was coming from inside her. If Armand was sexy at a distance, it was nothing compared to his effect on her in close quarters. This hadn't been one of her better ideas.

Louis Armstrong sang on, a gritty blues tune that fit the moment perfectly. Because she couldn't read his expression in profile and felt a somewhat desperate need to keep the conversation flowing, Eden eased her way back to his chat with Lucille.

"Did you learn anything useful?" she asked.

He sent her a sideways look that had her grinding her teeth and thinking about sitting on her hands. "Mostly that she disliked Maxwell."

"I could have told you that days ago."

"She also loves you and your sisters more than I expected."

"Lisa and I think she does, but you'll never convince Mary. Lucille's a gorgon to her. We were given up for adoption after—well, Lucille said it was after her husband died, but we know that was a lie."

"And the truth is…?"

"Probably the same one she gave us before we learned about Maxwell. She knew she wouldn't be able to raise us properly, and she wanted us to have the lives she felt we deserved. It worked out well for me and Lisa, not so much for Mary."

"Until Mary met Lisa."

Eden conceded the point. "I know you won't have seen this because you're not catching her at her best, but Lisa's one of the most generous people I've ever met. She inherited a fortune when her parents died, but I swear, if she only lives to be sixty-five, she'll die a pauper, and not through bad investments or selfish spending."

"Does she know about Robert Weir?"

"Not yet. I told you, she was gone when Mary and I got back from Dolores's tonight." She hesitated a moment, then asked, "Do you like her?"

"Lisa?"

"Hardly, Armand. Dolores."

She thought his frown deepened, but she couldn't be sure.

He surveyed the road ahead. Instead of answering, he nodded forward. "Is that your seer patient's building?"

It was a dingy concrete box, with sagging shutters, rusted iron railings and a fire escape ladder that appeared to be hanging by a single bolt. Candles glimmered in several of the windows behind cloth remnants that barely covered the glass.

Eden indicated the curb lane. "There's Lisa's car."

"I see it. Did you introduce Lisa to this woman?"

Eden pushed on the stuck door. "No, Dolores did. Do I have to kick my way out?"

"It's being temperamental tonight." Armand reached over, and she held her breath as his shoulder pressed into the V of her halter top. "A firm nudge is all it needs." His mouth was mere inches from hers. "Like some people I know."

Eden didn't understand the allusion, and to be truthful, she didn't want to. She'd requested a truce—a big mistake, she was discovering. This weird attraction she felt for him was simply a side effect she'd have to deal with. Breath held and feeling like a skittish teenager, she slid from the truck.

The air smelled of jasmine, cigar smoke and catfish. Madame Kafkha lived at the back of the building in a corner apartment that she shared with two boa constrictor snakes. On her first visit to Eden's office, she'd brought the smaller of the pair along in her oversize handbag. Phoebe had taken one look at the thing, shrieked and locked herself in the bathroom for the duration.

"She'll probably have five snakes by now," Eden anticipated with distaste. "What is it about weird magic that reptiles have to be involved?"

"Voodoo is considered a religion by some, not weird magic." Armand draped an arm over her shoulders. "At least that's what a friend who spent his childhood in New York tells me."

"And he knows how many voodoo queens?"

"None that I'm aware of, but he has a daughter in college."

Incense joined the array of smells. Eden let Armand's arm

remain where it was for two reasons. One, she liked it there, and two, she felt safe having a cop so close beside her.

The front door was made of iron and cracked glass, and it creaked like a coffin lid when Eden pushed it open. The stairs were worse. They groaned like the dead. She saw red X's scratched on the walls and trailed a finger over one of them as they climbed.

"I thought this ritual was specific to Marie Laveau's crypt. Draw an X, make a wish." Her finger came away smudged with lipstick. "I like wishing on a star and blowing out birthday candles better."

Armand checked the landings they passed. "Which floor did you say was hers?"

"Third. Rear apartment. No locks, no need. I made a house call last year when she broke both her foot and a bridge in the same fall. Her snakes watched me the whole time."

"How old is she?"

"She says eighty-three. I'd add ten years to that."

"And your grandmother believes in her?"

"Yes, but I made a deal with Madame Kafkha. She doesn't talk voodoo or curses, and I give her a thirty percent discount off her dental work."

"Good deal on her side. I've seen five rats already."

"I was trying to ignore that. Here." Eden indicated a door with a red squiggle where the apartment number should have been. "She won't answer if she's in a trance."

"What about Lisa?"

Smiling, Eden raised her hand and knocked.

The door opened instantly to reveal her white-faced sister. "Claudette? Oh, Eden, thank God!"

Whatever Eden had been anticipating, it wasn't this. Before she could respond, Lisa hauled her inside.

"Hello, Detective. I'm glad you came. I don't know what to do. I've been waiting for Claudette for hours." Lisa indicated a form which, from a distance, resembled Norman Bates's shriveled mother. It was lying prostrate on a cot. "Claudette is Madame Kafkha's niece. She phoned me tonight and asked if I knew of any poultices that would work on a bad infection. She said she called you as well, Eden, but you weren't home. I tried your cell, but you must have turned it off.''

Eden regarded the woman on the cot. She thought she saw her chest rise and fall.

"When I got here," Lisa continued, "I sent Claudette for a doctor, but you know Madame Kafkha. She doesn't trust many people, so I think Claudette's gone to the bayou.''

"To find a witch doctor?" Armand assumed.

His tone made Eden's lips twitch. "To fetch Dolores's doctor, I imagine. What's wrong with her, Lisa?''

"She cut her leg two weeks ago and tried to deal with it herself. As you can see, though—" she waved at the cluttered room "—this place isn't exactly sanitary.''

Eden's gaze swept the floor which was littered with feathers, leaves and broken, yellow objects that were probably bits of bone. "Where are her snakes?''

"Claudette locked them in the bathroom.''

It was something. Armand walked to the cot and crouched. Eden peered over his shoulder, then laid a hand on the old woman's forehead. "She has a fever, but she's breathing.''

"'Course I'm breathing.'' Madame Kafkha spoke in a harsh rasp. Her eyes remained closed. "Little nap is all. Fell down. Bone got stuck in my shin.''

"I made a poultice,'' Lisa said from behind. "It's that bulge under her skirt.''

Eden removed her hand. "You should be in the hospital, Dali.''

"No.'' The old woman's eyes cracked open, but Eden doubted if she saw much in the dim light.

Groping, she wrapped a clawlike hand around Eden's wrist. *"La morte,"* she said with a rough sound that was probably a cough. "I see it for you—have always seen it for you.''

Eden managed not to shake her hand off. "You're breaking your promise,'' she warned. "I'm not going to die from a curse.''

Again the old woman coughed. Her eyes sought out Armand's face and her brow furrowed. Then her eyes closed, and her breath rattled out. "I see it now... Worse maybe than before... Never the strong ones... Never."

From his crouch next to the cot, Armand glanced up at Eden. "Do you want me to carry her out?"

Lisa checked the poultice. "We have to do something, Eden, or *she'll* mort."

"You didn't feel her grip." Eden flexed her wrist and, perching on the cot, examined the discolored area. "It's a bad infection," she agreed, "but it appears to be localized. She could be fixed up with antibiotics."

Again, the old woman's eyes opened. "Eldest born to eldest grown," she whispered.

Her head turned on the lumpy pillow. The slow-motion effect sent a chill down Eden's spine. She envisioned a mummy returning to life, but just barely.

Madame Kafkha's index finger trembled as it pointed. "I foresee worse than death, *chère* child. A cut bleeds. Unattended, it throbs with the poison inside. The past bleeds, becomes the present. Anger festers. The curse continues..."

Eden smelled the poultice and heard Lisa sigh behind her. "She's delirious, Eden. She can't know what she's saying."

Yes, she did, but she also needed help. Eden set a hand on Madame Kafkha's shaking arm and pushed it gently back to her side. "Rest," she said. She looked at Armand. "Do you mind taking her out of here?"

He nodded, and with a cautionary word to the old woman, lifted her from the cot.

"This is blasphemy," Madame Kafkha accused in a thready voice. "The past festers..."

"So does the cut on your leg," Armand told her. "Lie still, and I'll get you downstairs."

"I was wrong," she mumbled to Eden, "to make a deal with you. Felt it all along. For deeds long past, and some not so long past, *chère* child will reap, a vengeance curse. Perhaps of death, but likely of far, far worse..."

Chapter Ten

Even the maledictions of an old witch weren't enough to make her believe. But much later—sometime after 2:00 a.m.—Eden agreed to let Armand walk her to her apartment.

He leaned against the jamb while she used her hip to open the stubborn door.

"There, you see?" he said with a smile. "We have something in common, after all."

"Warped doors? It's not much to build on, Armand." But the tweak of humor felt good after the evening she'd spent.

His smile widened, and he cocked his head. "I can think of a better thing."

She saw his expression and this time offered no resistance as he drew her toward him. He smelled of smoke and soap and man, and when his mouth covered hers, she added danger to the list.

No cops, she reminded herself, then shoved the thought aside. To hell with caution. *La morte*—death—was her fate, or so Dolores and Dali Kafkha insisted. That being the case, she might as well enjoy herself before she went.

It surprised her how gentle Armand's kiss was. His tongue dipped and tasted, but he didn't push, didn't really touch her beyond the kiss. Her head went into a delicious tailspin anyway.

It smoldered, she decided, like the fire tonight. There was warmth and comfort, yet an underlying sense of wickedness as well. Maybe she should deepen the kiss and see where it led.

Before she could do anything, however, Armand raised his head, and she saw his lips curve. "You're not fighting me, *chère*. Why is that?"

"I'm—" She thought for a second. "I guess I'm tired."

He ran his thumb over her lower lip. "That gives me an unfair advantage."

She felt herself sway and realized she'd been propping her eyelids open. "Maybe," she agreed. "Nothing's clear right now. But I do like kissing you, and I'm thinking I might have been wrong to doubt you."

She also thought she was crazy to be talking when his mouth was only a few tantalizing inches away. But as she ran her hands over his shoulders, she felt his muscles tighten.

He did kiss her, but it was a hard kiss that caused her eyes to widen in surprise.

Puzzled, she demanded, "And that was...?"

He trapped her chin. "Conscience, Eden, restraining desire. I want you awake and aware, not fighting fear and questioning how long you have to live."

"A curse of death," she repeated. Then she frowned. "Except Madame Kafkha said 'perhaps of death, perhaps of far worse.' This just keeps getting better and better, doesn't it?"

"Only if you believe."

"Which I don't—won't. Can't."

Amusement quirked the corners of his mouth, and he kissed her softly. "So there you see, your own convictions will keep you safe."

Eden started to respond, but before she could, a movement at street level sidetracked her. She dug her fingers into Armand's shoulders and hissed, "Someone's standing inside the gate."

"I see it." He set her behind him. "Go inside and turn the lock. Now."

His kick sent the door stuttering inward. Then he vanished,

and Eden was left alone and bemused on the threshold. She felt as though a tornado had just blown through.

She saw three cars on the street below. The closest one, a charcoal gray import with hideaway headlights, had a long tear under the passenger door. She envisioned a zombie with a chainsaw carving the low gash as he plodded toward the St. Louis cemetery. The image came from too much Madame Kafkha, she decided, not enough food.

The steel drums of a Caribbean band reached her from the club a block over. In the complex next door, a saxophone soloist played an old Miles Davis tune. But those were everyday sounds. No one cried out or fired a shot or even pounded along the sidewalk at a dead run.

She heard the phone in her apartment. It stopped after three rings, and when it did, she thought she noted a thud. In the courtyard, perhaps? It made sense that an intruder would try to escape that way, and knowing about it, Armand would undoubtedly have gone in the same direction.

Lulled by the music, Eden lingered on the balcony. Then she heard a crash of glass and whirled.

She started to call Armand's name, but something snaked around her throat from the neighboring balcony, cutting off not only her shout, but also her oxygen supply.

The shadows of the Quarter swam before her eyes. There was nothing she could ram her elbow into. Whoever held her had used the wall between the balconies as a barrier.

The cord dug into her throat. Her assailant breathed in grunts and exerted more pressure. Eden smelled mothballs, wine and some kind of chemical.

Using her fingernails, she clawed at the makeshift garrote. The wall helped as she used her whole body to fight. Maybe the cord slipped, or maybe her struggles simply worked, because the pressure on her windpipe lessened.

"Armand!" She got his name out once, then again as her attacker attempted to regain control.

Above the pounding of blood in her ears, she heard a grunt

and noticed the chemical smell again and finally felt the cord being torn away.

Coughing, she stumbled forward, away from the wall and the shadows. When she turned, she saw nothing except darkness and the outline of her neighbor's planters.

Black spots marred her vision. *Run,* was her first thought. But she had to find Armand. Where had he gone? Was he hurt? Had the same person who tried to strangle her caught him off guard and knocked him out?

Panting, she braced her hands on the railing—911 was the answer. She needed to call for help. For both of them.

ARMAND HAD THE MAN cornered. All he had to do was skirt the divider wall, and he'd have him. But then he heard Eden scream, and he came to a dead stop.

When she screamed a second time, he abandoned the chase and raced back to the street.

"Eden!" Taking the stairs three at a time, he arrived at the top with his gun drawn and his eyes combing the shadows.

She rushed through the apartment door, obviously relieved. She said something into the handset she held, then threw her arms around his neck and hugged him hard. "I thought he'd gotten you."

"Who'd gotten me?" Confused but gentle, Armand eased her back so he could see her face. His expression hardened when he spied the red mark on her throat. "What happened? Who did this to you?"

"I don't know. I thought it was whoever you were chasing, but maybe not. It might have been Kenny inside the gate."

"I didn't chase your neighbor's son," Armand told her.

"You saw a face?"

The mark on her throat agitated him almost to the point of fury. Collecting himself, he said, "No. This person was large and stocky. And he limped." He trailed a finger over her skin. He was angrier than he'd been in years. "I'll put some antiseptic on this." Then he tipped her head back so he could look into her eyes. "What happened here? Can you tell me?"

"I heard island music playing. It made me feel safe. Stupid, I know. I was worried about you, and I guess a little shell-shocked over everything that's happened lately." He felt the shiver that ran through her as she glanced into her apartment. "The phone rang, then it stopped. I heard a thump. I thought it came from the courtyard, but now I'm not sure. It might have been—whoever."

"Did you see whoever's face?"

"No. He came at me from the balcony next door and got a cord around my neck." She drew her brows together. "My neighbor goes to Baton Rouge every other week. She left this morning. But how would he have known that?"

Armand stroked her cheek. "Information is easily obtained, Eden. Don't trouble yourself over the how of it. Rather know that whoever he, or possibly even she, is, it's likely that person who followed us to Madame Kafkha's tonight."

"I didn't see blue headlights." She paused and looked down. "What just crunched?"

"When?"

"You moved your foot, and I heard a sound like glass breaking."

Armand went to his haunches. "It was glass," he said. He regarded the wall beside them and ran his fingers over a wet spot beneath the shattered fragments. The smell of the liquid struck a familiar note in his mind.

That's when he spied the needle.

IT HAD BEEN, Lucille admitted, a long and dreadful night. She rested briefly against the door of her office, her forehead pressed against the panels while she pictured Eden's face and Mary's. And, dear God, Lisa's.

She began to shake, but stopped. Such a reaction was not permitted. She would do what was necessary, as she had from the start. However grotesque the task, however loath she was to continue, she would see this nightmare through to its conclusion.

Muttering an oath in French, she pictured Eden again. Then

she shook it all off, summoned her strength and strode to the safe beside her desk. First things first.

Disengaging the lock, she reached inside for a box of fresh syringes.

ARMAND INSISTED ON SPENDING the night in Eden's apartment. On the sofa, he said, and it was a promise he intended to keep. He felt low enough these days without taking advantage of her in her current state of exhaustion.

So he did his Cajun mama proud. He tucked Eden into bed with a glass of brandy-laced milk and told her he would be in the next room until morning if she needed him.

Afterward, he poured a shot of bourbon from the bottle she kept under her kitchen sink. He allowed himself a fantasy about her wrapping her long legs around him while he set aside guilt and duty and made love to her through the night, then turned a hiss into a growl and got down to business.

The broken syringe angered him. He had no idea what had been inside. He would, though, once the contents were analyzed. As for prints, Armand doubted there would be any, not unless they were dealing with an idiot.

He recalled the chemical smell, but couldn't quite place it. It was toxic, he felt certain. Eden's assailant must have planned to stick the needle in her neck and kill her that way. So did that mean the strength necessary to strangle her had been an issue, or had an injection of poison simply been a more effective murder weapon than a cord?

Eden's neighbor's apartment had indeed been broken into. Armand had seen the signs of forced entry on the lock. The would-be killer had snipped the cord from a floor lamp and used it as his or her weapon, which seemed to suggest that injection had been the method of choice from the outset.

Because he couldn't make any determinations in that area tonight, he turned his attention to the file folder concealed inside the newspaper Al had given him at La Bouche. It was labeled L.C., which stood for Lucille Chaney, and had a large R in quotes below it. The R was for Roccolo, and Roccolo,

Armand acknowledged with a fatalistic sigh, was a name law enforcement officers across the United States knew all too well.

Admittedly Lucille's connection to the New York crime family was less than direct, but that it existed at all was not, in his opinion, a good sign.

On the other side, so far there'd been no link made between the Roccolos of New York and Maxwell Burgoyne, beyond the fact that Lucille and Maxwell had been married once upon a time.

Married, divorced and with no prenup, Armand noted. Maxwell had accepted that he'd been the father of Lucille's children. His name appeared on the registration of birth for Eden, Lisa and Mary. He'd acknowledged paternity, yet as far as Armand could determine, he'd never paid a cent in child support.

Nor, it appeared, had Lucille requested any. They'd gone their separate ways when Mary was six months old. Lucille had kept her daughters for another six months, then quietly put them up for adoption.

Maxwell had been a bastard in the basest sense of the word. Armand shook his head as he went through the printout a second time. Unless Al had missed something—and he doubted it—Burgoyne had washed his hands of his children from the point of divorce on.

Pushing on a throbbing temple, Armand scanned the first two pages again. He'd known for years that Burgoyne possessed no morals. This new information, while unpleasant, came as no real surprise. It was the Roccolo connection that niggled.

Lucille's grandfather had changed his name from Roccolo to Rockland near the end of his life. It was speculated that he'd been on the outs with his famous family. He'd purchased land along the river and run boats up and down the lower portion for several years. He'd called them tour boats, according to Al's information, which might have been the truth or a complete fabrication.

Whatever the case, time moved on. Two children were born, followed by three grandchildren. Two of the grandchildren were dead. Only Lucille remained alive.

She'd left home at age fifteen and worked in nightclubs from her sixteenth birthday onward. She'd gone from waitressing to hostessing to manager's assistant. She'd met Maxwell and invested the money she earned over the years very well. She'd purchased properties in and out of New Orleans then flipped them for a handsome profit. These days, she owned a sex boutique in the French Quarter, a pair of gambling houses, her nightclub, Nona, and a bakery on Decatur. The name Chaney had been her choice, legally changed from Burgoyne after the divorce.

All of which added up to what?

Armand sat back in broody silence. With the windows open, Eden's cat purring beside him and Ella Fitzgerald's voice filling the air, he didn't hear the bedroom door open. It wasn't until the shadows shifted that he saw her. She stood as he had earlier, with one shoulder resting against the door frame, watching him out of those amazing green eyes.

She wore a long red robe made of some kind of slinky satin fabric and the barest hint of a smile on her lips.

"I've never seen you look grumpy, Armand. It makes you seem human somehow."

He regarded her half-lidded and decided he could use another shot of bourbon. "You don't see cops as human?"

"My ex wasn't, not after a while anyway. Friends said he let the job in, and that's when it started going wrong. I think he wasn't cut out for law enforcement. He laughed a lot when we first met, not so much after a few years, not at all once he transferred to Vice." She indicated the file on the coffee table. "Do I want to know what you're reading?"

"It involves a mutilated body," he lied.

"That's a no." She made a restless circle of the room. "Would you like some coffee?"

"If you're making it, sure."

She smiled. "I'd rather have cake myself, but I'll settle for

French roast." She hesitated a moment before asking, "Why does someone want to kill me?"

She had to have rehearsed the question for it to come out so calmly. Standing, he crossed the room to her. He reached out but didn't quite touch the mark on her throat. "I think these attacks could be a warning to you."

"Provide an alibi for myself for the night of Maxwell's murder, or die? To what end?"

He shook his head. "All I can think of is that someone wants Lisa charged with that murder."

"A someone who can only be Robert Weir, right?"

"I'd agree," he said, "except he has no motive that anyone in the department can find. By all accounts, he'll inherit nothing from Maxwell."

There was, of course, another possibility but she would kick him out of her life if he so much as hinted at it. Besides, he had no proof at this point, and only a halfhearted desire to find any.

Eden considered his remark. "Maybe Maxwell was going to phase Robert out of the partnership, and Robert didn't want that to happen."

"It's being looked into," Armand told her. Up close, her eyes were a deep sea-green, and her mouth…

He slid his thumb over one soft corner, then across her cheek until his fingers tangled in her hair. "You're making my conscience work very hard tonight, Eden."

She didn't step back, or even move. Her eyes remained steady on his. "You can kiss me, Armand. I won't accuse you of taking unfair advantage of a situation I created."

"I know." Unable to resist, he lowered his head for one brief taste. "But I'll accuse myself, and that would be almost as bad. One cup of coffee, then we should both get some sleep. If you're interested, I had a phone call after you went to bed."

"And?" she prompted when her eye color sidetracked him again. "Has something happened?"

"The autopsy's as complete as it's going to get. The coroner is releasing Maxwell's body for burial. The will is set to be probated two days from now.''

ARMAND SPENT THE BULK of those two days immersed in the Burgoyne case.

He put his father's phone calls on hold and set his mind on his computer. He watched Eden from a distance and kicked himself again for his involvement in this. He sent the splintered syringe and substance samples for analysis, ran background checks on Lucille, Mary and Lisa and went after Robert Weir with a vengeance. He also checked out Maxwell Burgoyne from every conceivable angle, both on a personal and a professional level.

Finally, on the morning of the funeral, he gave in and drove to his father's home which was much deeper in the swamp than Eden's grandmother's place.

J. C. LaMorte had been a large, powerful man in his prime. He'd played football in high school and might have turned pro if he hadn't met Armand's mother and fallen in love. He'd gone to work instead of college and done better than most in his position. Unfortunately his wife had died, and work in the area had declined. His job had grown increasingly difficult, so much so that his shoulders, once broad and sturdy, had begun to sag.

Today, he sat in his chair on the porch, puffing on a cigar he wasn't supposed to smoke and poring over the photos in his favorite old album.

He knew Armand was there but didn't look up from his pictures.

"She was a beauty, sure enough," he said and ran a thick finger over his late wife's face. "French on her mama's side, Venezuelan on her pa's. She shouldn't have died so young. Shouldn't have died at all, come to that. We were gonna go to South America when we retired. Had it all planned. Just needed to work hard and put money away every year. But you and I both know those plans would've blown up on us even if she hadn't passed on.''

Armand hoisted himself onto the weathered porch rail. "I know you hold a grudge better than anyone I've ever met."

"Not a grudge. When it's about friends and family, it's loyalty. You need to learn the difference if you haven't already. You planning to be at the reading tonight?"

Armand's gaze strayed to the murky bayou water. "I told you I would."

"Wish I could go, too."

"Why? So you can drink a toast to his death?"

"Murder," his father corrected. "Be clear on that point, boy. Everything's riding on you keeping what needs doing in the forefront of your mind." He stabbed the air with his cigar. "Remember, as paybacks go, this is top of the heap." He puffed again and turned to the next page in his album. "What's eating at you, anyway? Lots of lies have been told in that police department over the years. What'll a few more hurt?"

"Maybe I'm still not comfortable with the idea of murder."

His father waved him off. "I told you before, no one's gonna shed tears over Maxwell Burgoyne's being gone. Unless…" He sent his son a shrewd look. "I hope you're not developing any untoward feelings here."

"Hope I'm keeping up my end of the bargain, and leave it at that."

Resignation was written all over his father's face. "You have too much of your mother in you to be a good cop, Armand. Or even a bad one."

"You got that right," Armand agreed. He watched strands of moss float lazily on the water. For the most part it was peaceful here. No cars, few people, little deceit. And then there was New Orleans, and a dead man, and Eden. And him.

His father released a rattly breath. "Why did I know deep down that this would screw up?"

Armand slid his gaze sideways. "Murder has a way of doing that. It's one of the few things in life you can count on."

His father stared up at a cloudless sky. "Well, go on then. Go inside and fetch us a cold beer. You can tell me, straight

and detailed, how it's all going down in the city. And how—"
he aimed a stern glare in his son's direction "—with more
attention to job and less adherence to conscience you're gonna
make it come around to the end we want."

Chapter Eleven

It was a perfect day for a funeral. The sun shone but menacing clouds had scudded up from the south and currently hung over the Mississippi.

Eden surveyed them while Lisa finished tending to her rows of bougainvillea. "I wouldn't bother watering anything, Lisa," she called out. "From the look of the sky, your whole garden could be washed into the river before we get back." Armand was examining one of Lisa's stone statues. Because her sister was long gone, Eden turned her attention to him. "What are you fiddling with down there?"

"Examining."

It was a statue of a young nude boy. The nose was chipped and part of the base had broken off. Armand regarded the cracked footing, then compared it to the photograph in his hand. "Do you know where your sister got this?"

"A junkyard, I imagine." Armand looked up, and she released a breath. "Okay, what's the deal? Do you think she stole it?"

He flipped the photo around. "This is the garden cemetery where Maxwell was murdered. Something heavy was removed between the time it rained, which was maybe fifteen minutes before he arrived, and the discovery of his body. The object had a broken base."

Eden stared at him. "And you think Lisa took it? Because if you do, then you must also believe she bludgeoned him."

"I don't believe she bludgeoned him. You told me once that Lisa collects statues. I'm curious to know where she collected this one from." He shrugged. "I could ask her, but I think she'll be more receptive to you."

Eden checked her watch. "I'm really glad I'm a dental surgeon." She raised her voice. "Lisa, we have to go. Now." Then she lowered it. "I'll talk to her, Armand, although I can't imagine such a detail will help your investigation."

He had his fingers curled around her neck and his lips on hers before she realized he'd moved. A smile touched his mouth, and he nuzzled her ear. "It's all in the details, *chère*. In death, in life—and in love."

HE DIDN'T LOVE HER, and she most certainly did not love him. But it was a heady prospect all the same, and it left Eden feeling breathless and a little unsure because she'd dreamed about him for three nights now.

They'd been sexual dreams, wild and abandoned. True, they'd been interspersed with zombies, voodoo queens and scorched dolls with lamp cords wrapped around their necks, but the sex had been incredible, and three nights of fantasy had melted into three mornings of delicious memories. Until her common sense had reasserted itself, and she'd banished them to the darkest corners of her mind.

Dark or not, however, the longer she stood at a dead man's grave site, the more she considered revisiting those dreams.

Maxwell hadn't chosen the most promising spot for his eternal resting place. The graveyard was small and dingy, set behind a ramshackle stone church fifteen miles north of New Orleans. Several of the surrounding large trees were dead and twisted, as if they'd been human once then transformed into trees as part of some horrible curse.

She sighed as she thought the word, but knew where it had come from. Clouds continued to roll in. Dolores had been hovering since she'd arrived and Maxwell's lawyer, the quintessential Hollywood undertaker right down to his bony fingers, sunken eyes and a prominent Adam's apple, seemed to have a worried scowl etched into his features. The whole scene felt cursed.

Armand prowled in the background. Eden was aware of him even if the others were not. Maybe too aware, she thought and looked away. Lucille stood stony-faced with only her hair moving in the breeze. Mary, who'd brought her muscle-bound friend, B.J., appeared utterly bored, and Lisa's skin had been the color of chalk all day.

Eden knew Lisa hated funerals, but then who except a ghoul would enjoy them? She let her sister clutch her arm and tried to concentrate on the reverend's words. Unfortunately the man was dull beyond belief, and her attention wandered.

Robert Weir stood to one side. He looked British in every sense of the word, dignified and proper, with a receding hairline, nondescript spectacles and features that fell somewhere between attractive and bland.

He wore a tweed jacket even though the temperature had climbed to the mid-eighties, and seemed neither pleased nor upset that his business partner was dead.

Armand passed behind him, and something in his expression brought a smile to Eden's lips. He didn't trust the man, either. Good.

Beside her, Mary drummed her fingers on her crossed arms. "Come on, chop the speech already. You didn't know the guy, so say *au revoir,* and let's get to the meat."

"Maxwell didn't leave us anything," Lisa said from Eden's other side.

"Didn't leave us anything, didn't leave his partner anything and only a handful of mourners showed up to send him off to wherever. Aren't either of you curious as to why there aren't more vultures in the vicinity? Count them guys. Besides the people we know and his Milquetoast partner, all I see are a pair of middle-aged women, a moon-faced man who keeps licking his lips and a lawyer who looks like a character from a Disney cartoon."

The last was so true that Eden almost laughed. She shouldn't have though, because Robert Weir chose that moment to raise his head. His own smile was tentative and, for a moment, Eden sensed, somewhat speculative.

Mary must have thought the same thing because she snorted and said in an undertone, "Oh, yeah, pal, Eden's got the hots for you all right. There's only a gorgeous cop ten feet away who has the hots for her, so why wouldn't she go for you? Unless everyone's wrong and you do stand to inherit Maxwell's business holdings. Then even I might find tweed and pop-bottle glasses attractive."

Eden had noticed the glasses but not the thickness of the lenses. She wondered if, as nearsighted as he must be, Robert Weir had simply mistaken someone else for Lisa. Of course that idea held absolutely no comfort since the only two people who looked enough like Lisa to be mistaken for her at thirty feet were herself and Lucille. Well, unless you included Mary in a punk rock wig and contacts, which was an absurd and unworthy thought and one Eden immediately shoved aside.

"He's not improving," Mary stated as Robert Weir pulled out a wrinkled cloth handkerchief and blew his nose. She caught Eden's glance and frowned. "What? I haven't asked you for a cent in weeks. Why the disapproving look?"

Eden gave her mind a shake. "I was thinking about you in *Cat on a Hot Tin Roof.*"

"My eyes are blue," Mary reminded in an emphatic tone. She blinked widely so Eden could see. "Not a hint of green, and I'm the youngest anyway. The curse'll get Lisa before it gets me, and it has to go through you to get her. So of the three of us, I'm the safest—and why do you keep staring at me as if I'd just turned into freaky old Madame Kafkha?"

"I'm not." Eden squinted past her at the road. "That gray car down there, the one with the gash under the passenger door. Do you know who owns it?"

"Maybe it's Smiley's." Mary wiggled her fingers and received a hopeful look from the moon-faced stranger.

Lisa swiped a strand of hair from her cheek. "You're so irreverent, Mary. And completely wrong in this case. The man you're waving at is, or rather was, Maxwell's chauffeur. He has two sons, both in jail. And I'm pretty sure he drinks.''

''No inheritance?''

''I doubt it.'' She indicated a gnarly oak tree across the road. ''The man who came in the dark car is over there, Eden. He arrived after we did, but I guess he didn't want to be part of the service because he went and stood over by the tree.'' She fussed with a bouquet of spotted white flowers she'd brought along. ''Is it me, or does this day feel really bizarre?''

''It's not you.'' Eden glanced at Armand, but he was watching Mary's friend who'd wandered off to a nearby crypt.

She returned her gaze to the stranger, half hidden behind the oak's massive trunk. He seemed to have realized he'd been spotted. He was hastening back to his car.

And limping.

''HE WAS BIG and heavyset, and he limped,'' Eden said to Armand. ''You told me the man you chased last night had a limp. And there was a gray car with a gash parked outside my apartment.''

''I believe you, *chère*.'' Armand pushed the button for the old-fashioned elevator and regarded the floor indicator above. ''But, one, the man you saw today took off before I could get a license plate number, and two, there's no sign of either him or his car anywhere near this building. I've checked the streets and the parking lot twice.''

And gotten soaked in the process, because it was raining.

Eden shook her umbrella. ''I appreciate the effort, Armand. I'm just feeling frustrated right now.'' She secured the automatic handle. ''Have you noticed how thick the lenses on Robert Weir's glasses are?''

''I noticed he was staring at you in the cemetery.''

Eden's eyes sparkled. ''Maybe he thought I was Lisa, and it suddenly hit him that there are other ways to get hold of an inheritance.''

''Lisa was standing beside you, Eden. He couldn't have

missed her. Besides, he wouldn't accuse a woman of murder in one breath, then come on to her in the next."

"He wasn't coming on to me, Armand."

"But you did smile at him."

"I smiled, yes, but not at him. Mary made a comparison that I found amusing. He looked over, and—" She stopped. "Why are we discussing this?"

"Because the elevator's slow, and I'm feeling as frustrated as you are, about many things. Robert Weir is one of them."

"Robert Weir is nothing for anyone to worry about." Lucille spoke from behind Eden. "Consider him the garter to Maxwell's cottonmouth snake. Are the others up in Franklin's office?"

"Franklin?" Eden repeated in surprise. "You know Maxwell's lawyer?"

"Of course. He's my lawyer, too, has been since before you were born. He handles my business affairs. He might look like a ghoul, but I assure you, he's a master when it comes to dealing with legal ruts and potholes."

Eden didn't know why that piece of information bothered her, unless it had to do with Lucille having still been connected to Maxwell while her daughters remained oblivious to his existence.

Reading her expression, Lucille shrugged. "Don't analyze it, Eden. Where Maxwell was concerned, my goal has always been to protect you and your sisters." She bestowed a smile on Armand. "You look well, Detective, albeit wet. I saw you on the street a moment ago. Searching for something, were you?"

"Someone. Your daughter's picked up a shadow."

Lucille's eyes came up. "What kind of shadow, Eden?"

"A man. I don't know what he wants yet."

"But you can guess."

"I can. Right now, I have other concerns. Robert Weir, Dolores, the curse."

"I'll deal with Robert," Lucille promised. "As for Dolores—" she spread her fingers *"—c'est une problème."*

A nagging problem, Eden concurred as the elevator finally put in a clanking appearance. But no more so than the questionable wiring in a building that had to date back to the thirties, or the fact there was no air-conditioning anywhere.

It got worse. Because he hated thunderstorms, Maxwell's lawyer kept his windows tightly closed and used only fans for ventilation. His office smelled like dust and incense, and he had a pair of dirty human skulls shoved into the corner of his bookshelf.

His name was Franklin Boule, and he seated everyone in hard chairs around his desk. He offered tea that no one wanted but took anyway, then set the used cups in a straight line on his sideboard.

Eden didn't want to think about him or any of it. Mostly, though, she didn't want to think about Armand, whose presence was by far the most distracting element in the room.

It really had been too long since she'd been involved with a man, she thought with a sigh.

Claustrophobic from the heat and no fresh air, Eden sat between Lisa and Lucille and listened to the lawyer drone on. Snippets of information registered, minor bequests made to Maxwell's housekeeper, his chauffeur and a recently hired nurse.

Then it got interesting.

"To Lucille Abigail Chaney," the lawyer read, "I bequeath my condominium in the Warehouse District and my house in the Garden District, together with the personal effects contained therein. To my associate, Robert Weir, I leave my burgundy leather office sofa."

Robert's smile was rueful. "As I expected. Congratulations, Lucille. You appear to be the big winner."

The lawyer fixed the restless gathering with a stern look while rain pelted the windows. "There remains the matter of Mr. Burgoyne's business holdings."

A hush fell, and Franklin Boule began listing companies by name. MamaDees Molasses and Sugar Mills, LoBo Records, a radio station and a line of tools. There was also a window screen manufacturer, pulp and textile mills up the coast and a small charter fishing company that operated out of southern Florida.

Although she listened, Eden was increasingly diverted by Armand in the background. Boule had objected to his presence at first; however, after a hushed but heated exchange, Armand had prevailed. He had positioned himself now behind the lawyer's desk. As he scanned the printout of company names, a crease formed between his eyes.

"Are those the percentages of Maxwell's shares?"

Annoyed, the lawyer twitched his fingers on the blotter. "I have my instructions, Detective, and divulging percentages is not among them. Now, if you don't mind."

Armand nodded, but didn't, Eden noticed in amusement, make any attempt to move. He read over the lawyer's shoulder until the man began to huff. Finally, when he reached the last page, Boule swiveled his chair away.

"Disposition of my shares in the aforementioned companies," he continued on Maxwell's behalf, "shall pass to one person, to sell, trade or retain as she sees fit. Whether she is present at these proceedings or not, I wish to convey this brief message—I'll keep a place reserved behind me, Mama dear. In hell."

ARMAND HAD NO INTENTION of letting Eden sleep alone, not that night or any other in the foreseeable future. But whether his decision was generated by concern or something far more complex wasn't a point he planned to explore. So he made himself at home on her sofa, with his laptop, a beer and his cell phone and told himself she would be perfectly safe visiting a hospitalized voodoo queen in the company of her mother, grandmother and sisters.

She'd been shocked at the reading to learn that Maxwell's mother, her natural paternal grandmother, was alive and apparently in line to receive all of her son's corporate goodies. Almost everyone in the room had been stunned by the disclosure. Only Lucille hadn't reacted.

"You're joking," Mary had exploded after Boule dropped his bombshell. "A father we never knew about has a mother we still don't know about? We've got blood relatives coming out of the woodwork, Eden." She'd tapped Lisa's shoulder. "Your PIs are grossly overpaid." Then she'd looked around. "Does anyone know this woman?"

A disgruntled mutter had been her answer, that and Dolores's sharp, "I knew he would leave nothing to his children. Dali warned me, and she was right." She'd reached for Eden's hand. "I have to visit Dali Kafkha today, before she sneaks out of the hospital. Come with me, and we'll talk on the way."

Armand had watched Eden from the outset. When he'd asked her what she was thinking, she'd merely frowned and replied, "About snakes mostly. I'm wondering why so many of us compare them to people like Maxwell while others like Madame Kafkha keep them as pets."

"Cherished pets," Lisa put in. "We all have our bents, Eden. Mine is plants, Madame Kafkha's is snakes, yours is teeth."

"And Mary's is money," Lucille inserted. "I'll go to the hospital with Dolores, Eden. You three go on home."

"Good," Mary said.

"Good is all you have to say?" Dolores had demanded in exasperation. "You offer no defense about what matters most in your life? That's sad, Mary, very sad."

Outside the circle, Armand had glanced at Eden. "Is money Mary's only concern, *chère?*"

Eden had shrugged. "You have to understand her background, Armand. Growing up, she ate black bean mush for dinner every night. As a teenager, she waited tables to bring in money. She developed an attitude, but at least she didn't wind up on the streets like other girls her age. Money will always matter to her...."

Money, yes, Armand thought now, booting up his computer, but apparently not discretion or loyalty.

In the end, Mary had gone to visit Madame Kafkha, not because Dolores had wanted it or even because Lisa had entreated her to join them but because Eden had pointed out that she would be able to snipe at Lucille while they drove. And Mary was, Armand reflected, in the perfect mood to snipe.

Having no siblings of his own, he often marveled at the differences within families. The fact that these three woman hadn't grown up together undoubtedly made those differences more pronounced, but he suspected they would have been unalike even if they'd been raised as one.

Of the three, Eden was by far the most intriguing. She was also the only one he really cared about—which brought him full circle to his earlier thoughts.

He knew he was crossing a dangerous line when his gaze strayed to the bedroom door and he began picturing what he would do if he ever got her in there.

His body reacted to the possibilities even as his thoughts darkened. He would not make love to her in deception. Which meant he would likely not make love to her at all.

The realization did nothing to improve his own mood.

Turning his attention to his laptop and using half-remembered access codes, he went for Maxwell's business holdings, his links and affiliates. There was a partner who'd inherited an old office sofa, an ex who'd copped two pricey New Orleans properties and, most significant, a maternal heir no one had appeared to know about, not even—and this had surprised him—Robert Weir. There were several figures he should go over as well.

And yet, he hesitated.

Unethical aspects aside, this was going to be a tricky search. One fumbled element, and more than his career might end. Friends would pay for favors he'd called in. Friends, family and possibly even Eden.

He noticed the envelope icon as Amorin settled on his lap. Reaching around her, he hit the e-mail button and waited.

The message was from Al. Only three words long, it sent his emotions into a tailspin. The words spoke of death more surely than any voodoo curse and read simply:

Syringe Contained Strychnine.

Chapter Twelve

Eden's head pounded. She called Armand's name as she came through the door. When he didn't answer, she dropped her purse, stripped off her jacket and headed for the kitchen.

Madame Kafkha had been in top form tonight. The hospital doctor had introduced a sedative painkiller into her IV, so she'd been drifting. She'd mumbled about emotional suffering being worse than death. She'd babbled about treachery, tricks and lies. She'd mentioned rats, poison and hidden truths. Then she'd looked from Eden to Lisa and back and whispered, "Such an ironic situation you have created. Lies compound. Murder forces murder." She'd blinked filmy eyes at Dolores. "This will not end well."

"It never does when you expect the worst," Mary said. She'd prodded Eden. "What was that you were asking Lisa earlier about a naked boy with a broken foot...?"

The conversation faded to memory. Eden wanted a glass of wine, a long bath and a dreamless sleep. Then she saw Armand rooting through her fridge while he talked on his cell phone, and she revised the thought.

What she wanted was him. In bed, in the heat, with jazz music floating through the open window while he made love to her, and she acted out every fantasy she could conjure up.

Like that was gonna happen, she thought. For one thing, who said he was into fantasies, and for another—well, he was a cop on a case.

"You sure?" Armand was asking into his cell. "Statue, syringe, debt?" He held out a bottle of Chardonnay and indicated she should find two glasses. Then into the phone, he said, "She's back… No, not yet… I don't know, maybe all of it." He glanced at Eden who was massaging her neck muscles en route to the cupboard. "Maybe none."

It was still early, and while Eden didn't like to believe she was in denial, she really didn't want to hear anything bad right now. Time spent with Dali Kafkha tended to sap her energy, and tonight had been no exception.

She didn't realize Armand had finished his call until she felt him behind her—directly behind her.

She really wanted to lean into him, to press her body against his and know one way or another if he wanted her.

His hands slid along her shoulders to the knotted muscles of her neck. "Bad night?"

Eden nodded. "Any voodoo talk is too much for me at this point. I like to think Dali was out of it, but I can't convince myself that's true. She unnerves me even when she's tranquilized, gassed and frozen in my dentist's chair?"

His thumbs made heavenly circles on her skin. "You do all that for a woman who boasts strong mental powers?"

"I've had boxers fall to pieces on me, Armand."

"An interesting remark. Maybe you're a witch, too. Is that better?"

"Mmm. Why?"

"Because I hate to see you in pain."

"No, I mean why am I a witch?"

He brushed his lips over her cheekbone. She heard the amusement in his tone, but sensed he was serious when he said, "Try the wine first. Then I'll tell you a story—about statues and rats and men who make stupid wagers."

"OKAY, LET ME GET THIS straight." Eden sat cross-legged while Armand poured more wine into her glass. "There was rat poison—strychnine—in the syringe. No prints, that's a given. A computer matched the picture of Lisa's broken statue

base to an imprint left at the site where Maxwell was murdered, and Robert Weir has outstanding gambling debts."

"*Had* outstanding debts," Armand corrected. "The estab-
lishments in question have all been repaid."

Eden's head swam, and she didn't think it was entirely due
to the wine. She and Armand were seated on the roof of her
apartment—in the moonlight, under the stars, with lovely shadows all around them.

Sipping carefully, she recaptured her train of thought. Something about gambling and rat poison. She went with the
money.

"Did Robert pay these debts before or after Maxwell died?"

"Before."

"How long?"

"Five, six months. Information's sketchy, but my guess is
he borrowed heavily from a loan shark."

"So now he owes the loan shark."

"Possibly. We'll see where that goes. The shark I'm thinking of has his fingers in more than one pie."

"Meaning?"

"He sponsors local boxers."

"Ah." She remembered and laughed. "That's the witch
thing you mentioned. Boxers faint at the sound of my drill."
She swirled her wine. "Loan shark or gambling house, Armand, Robert Weir still only got a sofa in Maxwell's will. It
can't be worth much no matter how good it is." She rested
her head against the low brick wall. "I guess we have a co-
nundrum, huh?"

Because there was no answer to it, she drew a line through
the stars overhead. "That's Orion's belt, up there. I never see
Orion, but I always recognize his belt. The Dippers are easy,
and I could pick out Centaurus when I went to Australia. But,
you know, I never got into stars much. It's all about astrology
on the West Coast—signs and houses and whatever's rising.
Here it's voodoo, creepy magic and curses." She regarded the
moon through splayed fingers. "I think Madam Kafkha fore-
sees a zombielike state for me when the curse is finished. She

keeps talking about a fate worse than death. Lisa says we should avoid her."

"Most people would, *chère*. How long has your grandmother known her?"

"No idea. Maybe forever. Madame Kafkha was born in the bayou, too. Can we go back to the rat poison and Lisa's statue?"

Rising to a crouch, he caught her hand. "I have a better idea. Let's forget danger, stop wasting a beautiful night and dance."

Tipsy, but still well within herself, Eden allowed him to pull her up and into his arms. "You're total danger, Armand. Strychnine's got nothing on you."

Dixieland gave way to Muddy Waters's blues. The music flowed up and over the wall. Eden knew she should back away, fight fantasy. You couldn't lose your heart to poison. Only your life. With Armand she stood to lose both.

"Tell me how you see your family, Eden." He held her against him with one hand in the small of her back and the other linked with hers. He kissed her fingers, then smiled at her uncertain expression. "Okay, your choice. What did Lisa say to you?"

Eden let him coax her head onto his shoulder. "She found the statue in the alley behind her house. She said it was lying near her trash cans looking forlorn, so she rescued it."

"Convenient."

"You sound like you half expected me to tell you that." She lifted her head. "Why?"

She couldn't read him by moonlight. "Because," he said and returned her cheek to his shoulder.

"She didn't bludgeon him, Armand. I mean, can you really see Lisa striking someone with an iron pipe, ignoring the blood and the deed, then working a stone statue free of the surrounding mud and dragging it out to her car? And if you want to talk rat…" She swallowed the rest as a picture of Lisa's exotic greenhouse sprang to mind. Had there been rat poison in a box on one of the shelves? "No," she said firmly. "Not Lisa. Anyone but her."

Armand's breath stirred her hair. He eased her closer, and she shivered. It was an unfair tactic. How could she think when she wanted him, and he obviously wanted her, when in her mind, she'd already begun to remove his clothes?

Aaron Neville sang now across the courtyard. She loved his voice. The heat from Armand's body brought a flush to her skin. His hair brushed her neck, and he smelled wonderful, like soap and wine and man. If he kissed her now, she might say yes to anything, especially with moonlight filtering down, and Aaron crooning about love and the Louisiana bayou.

Eden forced herself to breathe. She needed to steady her mind. She had to talk.

Going with his earlier question, she said, "I don't think of Lucille as anyone's mother. Mary and Lisa are my sisters, except that sometimes I'm not sure how well I know them."

Armand smiled. "Lisa loves her garden, and Mary loves money, you know that much." He kissed the spot behind her earlobe and the shiver it spawned spread right into her stomach.

"I guess." She struggled to keep her voice level. "Their pasts are sketchy, though. None of us talk much about our childhoods."

"Where does Dolores fit in?"

"She's a third grandmother. Actually, a second one in my case. My father's mother died before I was adopted. He called her a liberal ghoulie. She worked in a lab that processed diseased and abnormal organs which were later used to teach medical students. That was in the early twentieth century."

"And you think Dolores is strange for believing in a family curse?"

"No, I support her right to believe. I just don't want to be at the heart of it."

He trailed his knuckles along her spine. "You're still tense. You need to relax and not think about anything." His eyes glinted down at her. "Except me."

She saw it coming, but didn't pull away. His mouth covered hers in a kiss that undoubtedly accomplished the exact goal he'd intended. To empty her mind, then drive her out of it.

The same old tired objections remained, yet for the life of her, Eden had no desire to pursue them. She wanted Armand to go on kissing her forever. She wanted to feel him moving inside her. She wanted sex, the hot, steamy kind that a well-bred woman wasn't supposed to want, but really craved deep down if she was any kind of woman at all.

Sensations Eden had never experienced swept through her. Armand used his body to draw her to the edge and beyond. The air was hot, and so was she. His hands were doing amazing things to her breasts, and she responded by tugging his shirt free of his waistband and beginning an eager exploration of her own.

She felt satin-smooth skin stretched over muscle and bone. Not fair, she thought as she savored the taste of him.

She broke away just far enough to whisper, "You're making me crazy, Armand. This can't be right."

He stared down at her, breathing hard. "You don't know the half of it, *chère*."

Whatever that meant. Personal conscience, professional ethics—right then, Eden didn't care. She could feed on him all night and still not be satisfied. So did that make her a nymphomaniac, she wondered, or some kind of new millennium vampire?

Armand was touching his lips to hers when she felt a sting on her arm. She gave a quick hiss and a jerk of reaction.

"What?"

"Nothing." She didn't want the lovely haze of desire to fade. She ran the fingers of both hands through his long hair. "A wasp maybe. Don't worry, I'm not allergic."

But something wasn't right, because she felt a wet trickle slide along her bare upper arm.

Armand recognized it before she did. "Blood," he said and swore in French.

Eden drew back, astonished by—she couldn't imagine what.

Not a sting. That wouldn't bleed. A scratch? Maybe, but here were no rough edges nearby, and Armand wasn't wearing a watch.

''Get down,'' he ordered while her stunned mind worked. He unsnapped the leather holster at the back of his jeans and at the same time, made a quick inspection of her arm.

The truth blindsided her. She hadn't been bitten or stung, she'd been shot. She'd been dancing on the roof of her apartment building, kissing Armand and thinking about sex, and someone below had fired a bullet at her.

''My God,'' was all she could whisper. She stared at the blood, horrified, yet oddly fascinated. The wound felt numb. Shouldn't it hurt a little?

The night and whatever Armand was saying to her swirled away. She heard herself breathing, but couldn't seem to think.

Poison, cords, bullets, she saw all of those things superimposed over a pair of green glass eyes. She heard Dolores warning her about the curse, then saw Madame Kafkha shaking a skinny finger—''Such an ironic situation you have created. It cannot end well…''

''Oh, damn.'' Eden spoke softly and with a fatalistic sigh.

Armand had his gun out and an arm around her for support. ''What is it, *chère?*''

She knew he was scanning the grounds below. Knew it even as her mind drifted off.

Blackness rushed in. She couldn't stop it. ''I think I'm going to…''

It was as if she'd fallen into the bayou. She felt heavy all over. Then the murky water bubbled up, and she felt nothing at all.

SHE HEARD VOICES before she surfaced. Dolores's, Lisa's, Lucille's, and no one could mistake Mary's.

''The bullet only grazed you. No need to worry.''

Lucille's soothing tone gave way to Dolores's harsher, ''It could have killed her.''

"Or Armand," Lisa pointed out. "Please don't talk about the curse when she wakes up."

"Dali said…" Dolores began, but Mary cut her off with a snort.

"If your Madame K's so good, she should have foreseen her own cut getting infected. Eden's fine and Armand'll keep her that way."

Eden forced her eyes open. She was surprised to find herself staring into a pair of unfamiliar gray ones.

"Who are you?" Her voice was a dry croak, but at least she was in her own bed.

"Dr. Plante." He looked and sounded like Clark Gable. She thought she should recognize him, but couldn't remember why.

"Do I know you?"

"You'll have met my nephew Kenny. I'm visiting my sister for a week. I was out on her patio and—well, your young gentleman spotted me and told me to call 911. We took it from there to here."

She had no idea what he was talking about. "Where's Armand?" she asked as Lucille brought a glass of water to her lips.

"Out searching," Dolores said from her other side. She bent to kiss Eden's forehead. "He was frantic about you, pretty girl. We all were." Her voice trembled. Her hand on Eden's good arm tightened. "I spent too many years not knowing my grandchildren. I won't let this curse take you away."

Eden tested her shoulder. It felt more bruised than shot. Until she tried to sit up. Then it hurt like hell.

The doctor made a clucking sound. "As a DDS, Eden, you should know how pain works. Lie still until morning, and you'll feel much better. A painkiller would be a good idea."

"No pills," Eden said, although she did stop moving. "I want my mind clear." Which it wasn't by any means at the moment. Her eyes felt gritty. "No more statues, Lisa." Her thoughts crisscrossed. Faces popped in and out. "I still don't trust him," she murmured.

"Oh, but you should," Lisa insisted. Her sister's hand gripped hers tightly. "He flew out of here in a fury."

"You might even call it romantic in a weird sort of way." It surprised Eden when Mary set her hand over Lisa's and made a triad. "You're not going to die, Eden. It's not part of the deal."

"What deal?" Dolores demanded. "A curse offers no deal."

The voices became an irritating buzz. Eden felt oddly drugged, but she really shouldn't have fainted.

She wished Armand was here, but it helped to know he'd rushed out after the shooter. Cop or not, she believed he cared.

A man who dealt with loan sharks, however, now his agenda had to be questioned. Except that Robert Weir had only inherited a sofa. And sofas didn't satisfy sharks.

Unless, a voice far down in her head whispered, there was something of value hidden inside it.

ARMAND DIDN'T HAVE an explosive temper. But when he got angry, he got very angry. He'd surpassed that point when Eden had been shot. Now, on the hunt, he wanted blood of his own.

She would be all right, no damage done, the doctor had reassured. Dolores, Lucille, Lisa and Mary had all arrived within half an hour.

"Thank God I stayed in the city," Dolores had said, crossing herself. "Why won't this monstrous curse leave us alone?"

Eden would be safe in their company. No thanks to him, but for tonight at least, she'd be surrounded by people who loved her, who wouldn't harm her.

He hoped.

He didn't run to the alley that zigzagged off Dumaine. He walked and watched and breathed, all the while telling himself he would not use his gun when he reached his destination.

He smelled fried oysters, gumbo and andouille from a row of Cajun restaurants. Smoke, flowers and music spilled over balconies and through open doorways to sidewalks neon lit and teeming with life. People ate late in New Orleans. Actually, people here ate all the time. They also played music, danced and made love. He wanted to do all of those things and more with Eden. With no lies, no doubts and no evasions between them.

But a promise to his father was a promise he would keep. No one could dish out guilt better than J. C. LaMorte.

"Damn you," Armand swore under his breath.

He entered the alley and spied a man in the shadows. The man didn't wait until Armand was within range. He held up both hands and took several hobbling steps backward.

"I did what I was told, Armand. I went where I was told to go, and I waited. Then I..."

Before the man could retreat farther, Armand pressed an arm to his windpipe, shoved him into the wall and set his hand on his gun.

"No, wait I'm..."

"What?" It was a calmly put question, offered without a trace of hostility. Armand even managed a smile. "Are you sorry, is that it? You messed up again, and now you want to apologize?"

"I am sorry," the man got out. He seemed more startled then fearful, until Armand increased the pressure, then he choked.

"Get it straight." Armand's dark eyes bored into his. "You missed. You're not being paid to miss."

"I AM FINE, ARMAND." Eden removed the bandage Dr. Plante had applied and showed him. "It's only a scratch. It hardly even hurts."

It was morning, sultry and hot, but feeling better or not, the last thing she felt like doing was trotting around after him in her apartment.

"What are you searching for? There's no one lurking in my closets, if that's what you're thinking."

He sent her an unpromising look and opened her pantry door. "Why did you faint if it's only a scratch?"

"Too much excitement. Overwork. Over worry."

"A drug on the bullet."

She drew back in astonishment. "You can't be serious." She certainly hoped he wasn't. She inspected her arm from this new perspective. "Did you find the bullet?"

"No."

"Then you're only guessing." He left the pantry and went into the back hall. Eden replaced the bandage and followed. "Armand, what are you looking for?"

"Your suitcase."

That stopped her. "Am I going somewhere?"

He hunted through the containers in her storage closet. "You can't stay here, Eden. I want to know you'll be safe."

Lisa had an alarm system, she recalled. Lucille had a better one. Lucille also owned two new and highly secure properties.

"I'll have an alarm installed," she said and caught his arm before he could destroy the order she'd worked so hard to create. "My suitcases aren't here. They're in the attic."

"Where's the access door?"

"Outside my bedroom. Armand, if I go to Lisa's or Lucille's, I'll only be endangering their lives."

For the first time that day, he smiled. Cupping her chin, he gave her a disturbingly thorough kiss. "Staying with your family wasn't what I had in mind."

Eden shook her head to restore clear thought. "Where then? A hotel?"

"Better still." The amusement spread to his eyes. "Safer."

"Jail?" she guessed.

He pressed a thumb to the corner of her mouth, then replaced it with his lips as he murmured, "Church, *chère*. The safest place for you right now is in church."

Chapter Thirteen

"He lives in an old church, Lucille—with an altar and stained glass and crosses and all the other things churches have, including a disused graveyard in the back."

"Bats and cobwebs, too, I'm sure." Lucille weaved a cautious path through the many pots and planters that made up her nightclub garden. "I must have left it here. Look for a black portfolio case, Eden. I had it with me when I came through earlier."

Eden lifted the head of a drooping white lily. "Lisa should come over more often. She could keep your plants alive."

"She was here this morning." Lucille peered behind a wrought-iron bench. "She watered everything, then dug up four of my begonias and put in four different flowers. Snapdragons, I think."

Eden stood back and observed. The pink blooms were pretty. The weedy leaves weren't. "I've never seen snapdragons with red spots. Must be hybrids."

"Like you and your sisters."

"We're what we were raised to be."

"Mercenary, lost and stubborn. Ah, here it is." Lucille plucked the case from between two small lemon trees. "Mary needs to care more about family and Lisa less. And you—" she aimed a leather corner at Eden "—need to make more of an effort to know both of them."

The criticism stung. Eden recognized the truth behind it, but the pricks of conscience didn't sit well. "Bringing family members together is Lisa's forte."

"It's what she wants, and it's true, she tracked us all down. But intimacy is a difficult thing for Lisa. She's not touchy."

"And I am?"

"Physically touchy, Eden. You don't draw back from a hand on your arm the way Lisa does, or bat it away like Mary. My question is, do you know why the two of them react the way they do?"

Eden thought back. "Lisa had a creep for a boyfriend in high school. We were club hopping one night after we met and she mentioned him. She said he was a groper. Mary said if a man groped her, she'd blacken his eyes—ah."

"Exactly. One flinches, the other bites. Money isn't everything, is it? In many ways, and excluding Dolores's curse, I'd say you came away far better off than your sisters."

"As upbringings go, yes. But since they don't have people shooting at them or trying to poison them, I'm guessing they'd rather not trade places with me right now."

Lucille closed her eyes. "Needles." She sighed. "And lamp cords."

"On the other hand," Eden continued, "Lisa's got cops buzzing around her every day, and she almost wound up facing a murder charge. Maybe the family curse wants two victims this time instead of one."

"My hope is that it gets none."

Lucille wore a large black hat today. She'd angled the elegant brim over her face. She had lovely cheekbones, but Eden wondered if they might not be a little more clearly defined than they had been last year.

"Lucille, are you..." she began, but Lucille interrupted her with a shake of her head.

"No more talk of unpleasant matters, Eden. They unsettle me."

"I wasn't going to...

"Good, then you can walk me to my car—and go back to your tale of churches and a certain police detective who wants you to come and stay in one with him."

Eden didn't miss the gleam in her visible eye, and she released a gusty breath. "He's protecting me, Lucille. We're not involved."

"Yes, I noticed that last night when he took off after the shooter. No involvement there at all."

"I'm glad you agree." Eden changed the subject. "So where are you going?"

"To Franklin Boule's office. Afterward—I don't know. I thought perhaps a late lunch and a walk through the Quarter. If you'd like to come along, I'll buy you something tacky for your mantel. A papier-mâché doll maybe."

Eden pictured Dolores's collection of voodoo artifacts and gave a quick shudder. "As long as it doesn't have green eyes."

Percentages...

It wasn't until Eden pushed the button for the elevator in the lawyer's office building that she remembered Armand using the word. He'd been referring to Maxwell's shares in the companies Mr. Boule had rattled off, but she hadn't gotten around to asking him what he meant. She put the question to Lucille in the lobby and received a smirk in response.

"You didn't hear this from me, but apparently Maxwell's business holdings weren't as vast or as lucrative as his associates were led to believe. He owned shares in the companies on whose boards he sat. However, his was more of a figurehead position than one of financial control."

The elevator clanked to a halt, and they boarded. "So who…" Eden began, but stopped midsentence. "The phantom mother?"

"Apparently."

Although her expression remained serene, Lucille had the look of a cat who'd just been given a befuddled bird to play with.

Eden pulled the cage door closed. "You know who she is, don't you?"

"I have an inkling, but I'm not about to share it."

"Why not?"

"Because if she wanted you to know she'd tell you herself."

"Have I met her?"

Lucille smiled. "I've said all I'm going to. And don't badger Dolores about this when you see her."

Eden rolled her eyes. "What do you two do, get together once a month and go over your secrets so you can keep them straight?"

"I didn't say she knew anything, Eden. At the moment, she's so consumed by the curse and your part in it, I can't see Maxwell's disclosure mattering to her."

Leaning against the wall, Eden ran the names of several women she'd met over the past ten years. She could think of a dozen or more old enough to fit the part, but only a few savvy enough to pull off such a complex behind-the-scenes production.

And it must have been quite a production, with Maxwell in the role of lead puppet and his mother the master, controlling him on invisible strings.

When the elevator reached the seventh floor, Lucille shooed her forward. "You're over thinking this, Eden. I said I had an inkling as to the woman's identity. That doesn't translate to certain knowledge. Thus my reluctance to venture names."

Eden gave up. You could push Lucille Chaney only so far. She'd have to find another way.

She stepped through the frosted glass door marked Boule and Associates and into the empty outer office. "No paralegal or receptionist. No associates, either, it seems."

"His receptionist will be at lunch by now. Franklin has no associates, and his paralegal only works three days a week."

"Sounds like a crack firm."

"He has a small but lucrative practice. Franklin?" Lucille knocked on the inner door with a gloved hand. "Are you busy?"

"Seems unlikely." Eden ran a finger over the receptionist's desk, noting the dust trail left behind. The computer was shut down and a thin stack of mail sat unopened. "Are you sure he's working today?"

"Of course he is." Lucille twisted the knob. "We have an appointment."

She halted so abruptly that Eden bumped into her. "What is it?"

Lucille didn't remove her hand from the dull brass knob. "Franklin?"

Although she couldn't see past Lucille's hat, a lump of dread formed in Eden's stomach. When Lucille continued to stare, she closed her eyes briefly, then eased past.

She wasn't sure what she expected to see—possibly a man slumped over his desk, dead from a massive heart attack. Or heat prostration. The office was stifling, the shades drawn so that ghastly shadows fell across the carpet from the doorway.

Yet even surrounded by shadows, the blood revealed itself to her. It puddled dark and viscous on the blotter.

Franklin Boule sat in his chair facedown while blood flowed like lava from the gash on his head. His arms hung limply at his sides. On the floor next to his right foot sat what had to be the murder weapon.

Eden stared in shocked silence at the dirty face of the skull that had once sat high atop Franklin Boule's bookshelves.

The skull that had been used to murder him.

THE AFTERNOON PASSED in a blur of police officers, questions, more officers and more questions.

They talked to Lucille, then to Eden, then returned to Lucille. A detective named Al Janze finally drew Eden aside and told her he would need a statement. It wouldn't take long, he promised, and she'd be free to go.

"It's all routine, Dr. Bennett."

She rubbed the spot between her eyes, willing away the image of the leering skull. "Do you know if anyone's spoken to Lisa yet?"

The man put enough money for two coffees into a nearby vending machine. He handed her one before nodding. "She's been contacted and questioned."

Eden took a sip. "What reason could my sister possibly have for killing Maxwell's lawyer? Because she didn't like the terms of the will?"

"Chicory," the detective grumbled. He sent her a keen look. "You want a straight answer, or sugarcoated?"

"Straight."

"Your sister's a suspect in the murder of Maxwell Burgoyne. You did what you did, Dr. Bennett, and it worked. The witness's testimony was invalidated. But the investigation's ongoing, and Lisa Mayne is still plenty viable in the eyes of the law. We're not stupid," he added in a dry tone, "but we're also not looking for any old jack to pin Burgoyne's murder on."

Eden wanted to resent him for his lack of emotion, but she couldn't. There was sadness in his eyes if no hint of it in his voice.

She studied him over the rim of her cup. "Do you know Armand LaMorte, Detective?"

Al snorted. "We were partners once, but that was some time ago. I'm mostly partnered with a desk these days."

"Is he with Lisa now?"

Al grimaced and shook his head. "We sent a female officer to speak with her. Mandy marches to his own drum when he bothers to march at all. He'll show up, though, don't you doubt it."

"I don't doubt it." Eden gnawed on her lip. "I'm worried about my sister, Detective."

"Al. And you can see her just as soon as you give us your sworn statement." He studied her troubled face. "Are you okay with this—seeing a dead man and all? There are people you can talk to if you need help coping."

Eden glanced out the window. She started to answer but broke off when she spied a dark gray car with a tear along the underside. It cruised past, turned the corner and vanished.

"Who are you?" she murmured, frowning.

"Beg pardon?"

Eden banked her fear. "Nothing. I want an end to this nightmare, that's all."

"It's what everyone wants." Al finished his coffee, then glanced down and flexed his right knee. "I only hope the end we find will justify the means used to get there."

"I DON'T KNOW WHAT HE MEANT, Eden." Armand checked his rearview mirror on the winding back road. "Al can be as cryptic as the next person when he's in the mood. Now sit back, relax and be grateful everyone you love is well, and none of them stand accused of Franklin Boule's murder."

"Right, grateful." She tapped an agitated fist on her knee. "Lucille has no alibi for the approximate time of death, Armand. Neither does Lisa. No one's seen Mary since she left my place early this morning and, actually, come to think of it, I don't have an alibi myself."

Armand smiled. "We were getting hot and dusty in your attic."

"Says you. I'll deny it."

"You know for someone who proclaims her sister's innocence so vehemently, you seem awfully worried she'll wind up charged or at least suspected of this second murder."

The heat and humidity were unbearable. Eden lifted the hair from her neck and drew her brows together. "Wouldn't you be worried in my place?"

"You think someone's trying to frame her?"

"I think it's possible given the weirdness of this whole mess." Her eyes clouded. "At least Robert Weir hasn't made any noises about seeing her."

"If it's any consolation, Robert Weir has no alibi either."

"And his motive for murdering Boule would be...?"

"A question mark. Now stop thinking so hard and listen to Shirley Bassey."

"Uh-huh." Frustrated, Eden laid her head against the padded rest. "So where are we going, and why?" It struck her before he could answer, and she sat up with a start. "Wait a minute, this is the road to Montesse House!"

"You know the bayou better than I thought."

"I know this road well enough. Why here?"

"To visit a ghost."

She glanced at him, but as usual, his expression told her nothing. "To visit one, or to become one, Armand?"

Humor registered briefly. "Are you ever going to trust me, Eden?"

In truth, she did. Almost. "Whose ghost?" she asked. "Is this related to Dolores's curse?"

Bringing her fingers to his lips, he kissed them. "That," he said with a smile, "is for you to decide."

EDEN WAS UNDONE—and a little wary. Armand had put together a picnic dinner, complete with a blanket, cold beer, battery lanterns and a CD player. He carried the cooler to the rear of the plantation house and set it near the headstone Eden had discovered on her last trip there.

The remains of the planter sat untouched at the base of the porch. If this was his idea of visiting a ghost, Eden didn't really see the point, but maybe his sense of humor simply eluded her.

"What now?" she asked when he handed her an icy lager. "Do we drink a toast to the planter that missed me?"

"Wrong direction." He motioned behind them. "It's the headstone you need to see."

"Is it Eva Dumont's?" The idea intrigued her. "It looks old enough."

He opened the cooler. "Dinner first. Then we'll read the inscription."

Because she'd missed lunch, Eden was too hungry to argue. The chicken with Cajun sauce smelled delicious. So did the red beans and rice and the container of jambalaya that couldn't possibly have come from a restaurant. It burned her mouth and made her cough when she swallowed.

"Did you make this?" she asked after a much-needed gulp of beer.

"It's an old family recipe." He grinned. "My father likes his food spicy."

Eden picked through the chicken parts until she found a drumstick. "Is your father retired?"

Armand glanced at the bayou trees. "Last year. He should have stopped sooner, but you couldn't tell him that."

"Where did he work?"

"North of here, in a sugar mill. He was the foreman there, and in his element."

She smiled. "Likes control, huh?"

Armand shrugged. "He lives by his own rules."

"I've heard that before." Louder, she said, "What's his name?"

"Jonathan Calvert LaMorte."

It was a mouthful, like the chicken she stripped off the bone. "Do you get along well?"

A strange light flickered in his eyes. Or did it? Dusk had settled, and shadows from the surrounding bushes obscured his face from view. His beautifully boned face, she amended, although she'd do well not to think along those lines right now.

Last night's romantic interlude with Armand had ended with her being grazed by a bullet. Given her history at Montesse, who knew what might happen here?

No, for tonight she would eat, drink sparingly, talk and listen. And maybe fantasize just a bit. But she would not let her mind be clouded by thoughts of sex with Armand LaMorte.

"We have our moments." He answered her earlier question. "It was easier when he worked." He tore a chunk of bread from a fresh loaf and handed it to her. "I hear you met Al today."

Eden liked his hands. They were long and lean as he was,

but she sensed strength in them—as she did in him. "He says he doesn't do much field work anymore."

"Not much, no."

"He also said you were partners once."

Armand's smile was vague. "In Vice, years ago. We hated it."

"So you transferred to Homicide."

"It's less messy."

Eden recalled the blood puddled under the lawyer's head and set her drumstick down. "Depends on your point of view, I suppose." She picked up the beer. "So what's the news on Robert Weir? Have you found any money or drugs stuffed inside his newly acquired sofa?"

"No such luck, *chère,* but he has an ex who lives in Metairie."

"He was married?" Why that surprised her, Eden couldn't say. "Doesn't really seem the type to me."

"He also has a thirteen-year-old daughter."

She considered that. "Does he pay child support?"

"Yes."

"Any late payments?"

"None that have been reported."

"Of course, you've spoken to his ex."

"On the phone this afternoon. She says he keeps up. No more, no less. She insists he loves his daughter."

Eden tore off more bread. "He paid his gambling debts, and he supports his child. He inherited next to nothing from Maxwell, yet he's still a partner in the corporation."

"He's a minor player, Eden."

"Like Maxwell?" she challenged softly. "Lucille told me about his figurehead position, Armand. You might have mentioned it yourself."

Leaning forward, he ran a finger over her bandaged arm. "When might I have done that? Before I kissed you on your roof, or after someone took a shot at you."

She refused to be rattled, and countered with a sweet, "Maybe the shooter was aiming at you. I'm still not sure why anyone would want to kill me." Although some of the attempts had been very specific. She plucked a rose from one of the creepers on the path. "Tell me, Armand, does any of what's happening here make sense to you?"

"Not yet, no, but I can tell you this much. Preliminary reports indicate that Franklin Boule, like Maxwell, was struck from behind by a right-handed person."

"Meaning the same killer could have murdered both men..."

"Yes."

"Or not."

"Solving murders is a tedious business, Eden. Do you want another beer?"

She glanced at the broken marble slab some ten feet away on the garden path. "Maybe." Another thought occurred to her. "Have you located Maxwell's mother yet?"

Standing, Armand held out a hand to her. "Al's supposed to be on that, but he's backlogged to the max. It could take time."

"How's it possible for a person in a position of such control to be anonymous?"

"That's a fair question. Boule could have told us, and his records have in fact been confiscated, but so far there's no name."

She let him pull her to her feet. "I think Lucille knows."

His smile contained a note of mystery. "You may be right. Which brings us to the point of our trip here tonight. Tell me what you make of this?"

Eden wanted to resist, but ignoring unpleasantries wouldn't make them go away.

The scent of oleanders hung heavy in the air. Her sense of claustrophobia increased as the foliage enveloped her. Like a bug in a Venus flytrap, she thought and felt a prickle of unease crawl across her skin.

She'd never cared for overgrown gardens. Nature was one thing, excessive human cultivation an entirely different matter.

Armand led her to the edge of the slab, pulling her with him as he crouched. "Can you read the inscription?"

It was difficult, but she could just make out the words.

A most cursed life
A most cursed death
Rest as you will
Eva Chaney Dumont

Chapter Fourteen

Eden didn't know how many generations existed between Eva Dumont's father and her, and she really didn't care. But she was curious as to why the name Chaney appeared on both Eva's headstone and Lucille's driver's license.

It was after ten o'clock when she and Armand returned to New Orleans. As always, the city pulsated with life. A whiskey-voiced singer performed onstage at Lucille's club. The lounge was packed, and Eden had no doubt the other rooms were equally occupied. But there was no sign of Lucille.

"She was looking for you earlier, sugar," her assistant Ty said from the lounge entrance. "Mentioned something about an old church, then she gave up and called your sister."

Not Mary, Eden deduced and dialed Lisa's number on her cell.

"Is Lucille there?" she asked.

"Not yet, but she's coming." Lisa sounded tired, and Eden wished she could help. "She stopped to visit Dali Kafkha first."

As briefly as possible and aware of Armand's eyes on her, Eden outlined what they'd discovered at Montesse. She finished with a careful, "Do you know why Lucille took the name Chaney?"

But Lisa didn't know, and in the end, Eden and Armand made the drive to her Garden District home.

"I'll sweep the area," he offered. "Just in case."

"If he finds anything, it'll only be a police officer watching the house." Lisa examined the bandage on Eden's arm. "Has that been changed?"

"Yes. I'm fine. Lisa…" Eden caught her sister's wrist. "Just stop, okay?"

Easing away, Lisa balled her hands and folded her arms. "Let's go into the garden. This room's a mausoleum."

"That's because you have cremation urns on your mantel. How long do your parents' ashes need to be on display?"

"It was their house," Lisa defended. "They have a right to be here."

Eden studied a framed photo of the couple taken five years before they died. "Your father looks like Albert Einstein with his white hair and shaggy mustache."

Lisa's eyes misted. "He was a wonderful man, sweet. My mother—wasn't as sweet. She said women were put on earth to endure terrible trials, but that *as* women, it was our duty to rise above them."

The square-faced female did indeed look tougher than her husband. "She broke the jaw of a boy who tried to kiss her in college, didn't she?" Eden recalled.

"He wanted more than a kiss, and yes, she did. Very calmly apparently. His mouth was wired shut for six weeks."

"Don't get mad, get even." Eden fingered the petals of a spotted columnar flower with rough leaves. "Whatever this plant is, it's dying."

"Wilting," Lisa corrected. "It's out of climate here, but my mother would have appreciated it. That's why I put the pot next to her urn. I planted some for Lucille as well. Come outside. We'll have tea on the terrace."

Under attack from every flying insect in the state, Eden reflected, but followed her sister through the creaky old house to the kitchen.

It surprised her to find Mary rooting through the fridge.

"Hey, Eden. How's your arm?"

"It's—"

"Do we have any cookies?"

"Not in the vegetable crisper." Lisa shoved the drawer closed. "I'll check the pantry. Eden can tell you about Lucille."

Eden did so while, on the porch, Lisa's bug zapper annihilated a string of moths, mosquitoes and flies.

Mary opened the bag of Oreos Lisa gave her and began to munch. "So you're saying Lucille's last name and Eva Dumont's middle name are one and the same?" She paused mid-bite. "But Eva's the one who placed the curse on her father and his mistress, and we descend through them, right? So what's the deal? We know Lucille divorced Burgoyne, and she was born a Boyer, so she must have chosen to use the name Chaney after her breakup with Maxwell."

Which for anyone else might have seemed odd; however, the more Eden thought about it, the more she could envision Lucille making just such a choice. She had a wicked sense of irony and, at best, a dubious belief in the family curse.

"She probably did it to be perverse."

"The cursee flying in the face of the curser." Mary popped one last cookie in her mouth and brushed the crumbs from her fingers. "Except it's not Lucille who's cursed, is it? Unless she killed that funeral lawyer today, then she won't be feeling too good. Do you know, Eden, the cops actually tracked me to a club off Bourbon Street this afternoon? There I was, naked as a newborn, and they blow in and—" She stopped. "What?"

"What do you mean what? Eden stared though, God help her, she was tempted to laugh. "You were clubbing in the afternoon?"

"I was taking photos."

"In a bar? Naked?"

"Above the bar. For a massage therapist friend of mine. For a flyer. Stop looking at me like I've sprouted horns and look around the kitchen instead. Who's suddenly gone missing from our little family portrait?"

Eden made a quick sweep and realized that Lisa had vanished. "Where did she go?"

"Where she's been living lately. Out with her sacks of fer-

tilizer and her ugly tropical plants. Stupid greenhouses. Do you
know she's got henbane growing out there, and foxglove and
another flower that looks like someone wearing a robe.''

''Monkshood?''

''Yeah, and who do you think gave her the seeds and told
her that if she made a sachet from the petals and roots, it could
be used as a talisman against curses?''

Eden dropped her head back, laughing without humor as the
bug zapper wiped out another insect life. ''Let me guess—
Madame Kafkha.''

''The queen of voodoo curses herself.''

An idea, vague and unfounded, floated through Eden's
mind. The queen of curses, yes. But of what else might the
old woman also be queen?

LUCILLE HAD PRACTICED the art of deceit for much of her life.
She was a consummate actress, better than Mary, better than
any of her daughters. She walked a fine line these days, but
she was accustomed to that. She hadn't built her wealth
through luck, she'd done it with shrewdness and calculation.

Mary possessed those same qualities. Unfortunately, her
youngest daughter had never mastered them. If she ever did…
Lucille pivoted sharply from that thought.

The Mississippi flowed like a serpent before her. She could
watch it all night, though not this particular night. She'd visited
Dali Kafkha, now she needed to see Lisa. As for Eden—she
let that thought slide away as well.

While Lucille claimed no extraordinary mental powers, she
sensed something approaching, some kind of explosive situation.
Of course when you trod in a minefield, you had to expect that
one of them might go off. The smallest thing could do it. A rat
grown a little too fat, a snake that coiled up in the wrong spot….

Her thoughts were dancing away, she realized. That needed
to stop. So did the pangs of guilt. Sometimes death was the
only solution to a cursed problem.

Shoring up her defenses, she thought of Eden, closed her
eyes and plotted.

THE LOAN SHARK Robert Weir had dealt with went by the name of Steven Cruz. He sponsored three local boxers and could frequently be found watching them train.

Armand was typing the boxers' names into his computer when he felt Eden behind him. Whether she was looking at the screen or still marveling over his partly revamped church home he couldn't be sure, but he tuned in to her presence instantly.

"Do you like your room?" He kept his eyes on the monitor.

"It has its good points. Are you sure this was a church and not a monastery?" As she leaned over his shoulder, he caught the scent of Opium. "Lindell Jackson. I recognize that name. He's a light middleweight boxer from Alabama."

Scrolling to a photo, Armand sat back into her. "He's an up-and-comer according to this Web site."

Eden flipped her hair over one shoulder so she could see better. "Only his molars are real, and I see a lot of silver back there. He's got a knockout punch, though. If he connects early in a bout, he can win."

Armand hid a smile. "Are you a closet gambler?"

"Armand, at my most desperate, I wouldn't bet on this guy."

Part of Armand wished she would move away; a much larger part wanted to catch hold of her dark hair and tug her forward until she tumbled onto his lap.

She pointed at the monitor. "He trains near the St. Louis Cemetery, at a gym off Basin Street."

Armand gave in and pulled on a strand of her hair. "They all do."

"Who all?"

"Cruz's boxers."

"And Cruz is?"

"The shark who's rumored to have loaned Robert Weir his bail-out money."

"Ah." She smiled, and he couldn't resist brushing his lips over her cheek. "So what now?"

"Such a leading question. I wish my answer wasn't so mundane."

"To the gym?" she guessed.

"I'm afraid so."

Moving, she set a hip on his desk, arched a brow—then surprised him totally by leaning forward and giving him a thorough, openmouthed kiss. He felt her lips move against his as she murmured, "In that case, aren't you glad I brought my bag mitts along, Detective?"

HE MADE HER DO CRAZY THINGS, give in to erratic impulses. Kissing cops was bad. Initiating those kisses was just plain foolish. Until now, Eden had never considered herself a fool.

Upstairs, she stripped off her clothes in a bedroom the size of a monk's cell. "Married a cop, divorced him—lesson there, Eden, remember? You've got questions on questions, and all you can think about is how good this particular cop would be in bed. Hell."

With the lights out and wearing nothing except a black slip, she wandered to the window and gazed out at the graveyard. Shadows from the trees threw the tombs into freakish relief against the moonlit sky. She thought of Montesse House and the fallen headstone belonging to Eva Chaney Dumont.

Why had Lucille taken that name as her own? Why had she gone to see Madame Kafkha tonight? Was there more of a connection between them than anyone knew?

Dolores would know, of course she would. But would she tell? Unlikely. Still, Eden didn't suppose it would hurt to ask.

As for Maxwell's mother, evidently Armand's counterpart had too much on his plate to delve into that mystery. So maybe, Eden reflected, she should do it herself. A side benefit to her dental work was that her patients came from all walks of life.

Despite the heat, a chill swept through her. She kept seeing Eva's headstone. When she wasn't seeing that, her mind flashed tempting pictures of Armand. In his room. In the dark. Wearing...

"Don't," she warned herself. She didn't need to imagine him naked for the chill to be replaced with a surge of heat.

Her eyes combed the graveyard again. Leaves skittered across the raised tombs. The stones were scarred and weather-beaten. Graffiti adorned several of them. Kids, she assumed, partyers, midnight daredevils.

She was staring at a crumbling crypt when one of the shadows next to it shifted. She kept her eyes on the spot, not moving, not even breathing—until she began to feel light-headed, then she slowly exhaled.

Her fingers clenched on the stone sash. There it was again, that faint shifting of shadow. Someone was out there, hidden but there, watching her, or at least watching the church.

Eden eased away from the window. Halfway across the room, she whirled and ran for the door.

"Armand!" He was across from her, he'd said, directly across.

She had her hand up ready to pound when the door opened and there he stood, in a pair of unfastened jeans and nothing else.

Words clogged in her throat, and her lungs felt seared.

"What is it?"

She realized her hand was still poised to knock and she snatched it down. "Someone's in the graveyard. A man, I think."

Armand shoved her across the threshold into his room. "Stay here," he said. "I mean right here, Eden, and close the door. Do not follow me."

He was gone before she could point out that she hadn't followed him last time, and she'd almost wound up strangled.

Stepping back into the hall, she closed the door behind her—at least he couldn't accuse her of not listening at all—and promptly stifled a shriek as something slunk between her bare ankles.

A soft purr gave Amorin away. Pressing a hand to her heart, Eden listened but heard nothing. When her pulse rate slowed, she gave the cat's ears a quick scratch and headed for the stairwell.

Like much of the church, the stairs were constructed of stone. Since there was no wood to creak, she descended in silence with only the ticking of an antique clock to accompany her.

Careful not to bump into the furniture, Eden made her way through the living area, past what had once been a pulpit and over to a tall side window.

There was stained glass in the high casement, but at ground level, it was clear and open a crack. When she looked, she saw the crypt and more shadows. Then she saw Armand.

He was barefoot and searching. She noticed the gun in his right hand. He circled the stones like a predator, silent and wary.

Without warning, a shadow reared up behind him, like a ghost rising out of the mist.

"Armand!" She screamed his name, and he spun. Avoiding the blow to his head, he vanished with the shadow around the side of the crypt.

Not stopping to think, Eden grabbed a brass candlestick and ran for the door. She made it to the vegetable garden before she was blindsided.

Her feet left the ground and the air was torn from her lungs. She was flying, but she knew the landing would be rough, and likely not solo.

She hit the ground hard, so hard in fact that for a moment she saw black. It could have been worse, however. Blackness aside, whoever had tackled her had done so into a bed of hostas.

She fought to regain her breath, gathered what scattered wits she could and rolled. She had the candlestick and every intention of using it on the first thing that moved.

Except that nothing did. It was as if she'd run into an invisible wall and been flung to the ground by her own momentum.

Which was, she knew, impossible. What on earth was happening here?

She heard the ground cover rustle and, scrambling to her feet, swung around, candlestick raised. A slower person would have been knocked senseless. Fortunately this particular man was quick enough to intercept the base before it slammed into the side of his head.

Armand's dark eyes glinted. "This isn't my bedroom, Eden, and it's definitely not where I told you to stay."

Her breath rushed out. "Save it, Armand. You disappeared behind the crypt. I thought you'd been hurt."

"A thing you couldn't possibly have seen from my bedroom window."

"I'm not one of your underlings, Detective, and I don't like sarcasm. Who were you fighting?"

"I don't know. He was wearing a balaclava. We were exchanging punches when you screamed."

"I screamed?" She frowned. "I don't remember that."

"Well you did, and I had a choice. Keep fighting or find you."

She regarded his shadowed face. Was that concern in his eyes, or anger? She rested her spine against a live oak and relented. "Someone tackled me. I didn't see him coming and, afterward, he was gone. If I wasn't covered with dirt and leaves, I'd think I imagined the whole thing."

He brushed the hair from her face. "That's not good. It means there were two people here again tonight. Did you hurt your arm?"

"No, he came at me from the other side."

Armand checked to make sure the bandage was secure. "It was a man, not a woman?"

A hundred impressions danced in her head. "I don't know," she admitted.

Her resolve threatened to melt when he ran his thumb over her lower lip. He kissed her gently and said, "It's not fair, is it? Curses, poison, bullets, midnight attacks, and all because you want to help your sister."

Eden stiffened, but only a little. "Lisa didn't bludgeon Maxwell Burgoyne."

"She keeps rat poison in her greenhouse."

"To poison rats, Armand, not people."

"It's easily obtained," he agreed.

He sounded distracted, as if his mind wasn't on what he was saying. He had a hand wrapped around her nape, but his gaze was traveling through the graveyard and garden.

Always the cop. She supposed she should be grateful for that. Still…

Reaching out, she ran her fingers through the ends of his hair. It got his attention. His eyes returned to her face, and a slow smile curved his lips.

"You don't want to look at me like that, Eden."

No, she didn't. But she couldn't help it. The attraction between them had grown too strong for even her to ignore. And she'd given up denying it days ago.

"Why is life never simple?" she wondered out loud.

"Because it is life, *chère*." He hesitated for a moment, then, unable to resist, lowered his head and set his mouth on hers.

It was only a kiss, and yet it was so much more. Sensations Eden couldn't begin to describe darted through her mind. She felt hot and dizzy, hungry and needful. He tasted like sex, the fiery New Orleans kind she'd craved but never experienced. With her ex it had been white bread all the way.

The comparison amused her even as she ran her hands over Armand's ribs. He drew back just far enough to ask, "Something's funny?"

She gave his lower lip a playful nip. "I think I must be a New Orleans woman at heart. Maybe there's something to genetics after all.

"Ah." He ran his mouth along the curve of her neck, and she arched her body in response. She didn't know where or how far it would have gone if she hadn't heard the phone inside.

A groan escaped her as the ringing persisted. "Saved by the bell, I guess." She glanced at the welter of surrounding shadows. "I don't suppose this is the best place for us to be right now anyway."

Or the smartest thing for her to be doing given that nothing in her world these days made the slightest bit of sense.

The phone refused to stop, and Armand made an irritable sound.

"No machine, huh?"

"Broken," he said and glanced at the moon. "It must be important for someone to be so determined to reach me after midnight. Come on, *chère*. We'll go inside where it's safe. Tomorrow, when we're fresh, we'll try and figure out who was here tonight, and whether they came for a single purpose or two separate ones."

A BLOODY NOSE, bruised kidneys and three loose teeth had not been the plan. Curse or not, Eden was too lucky by half. Matters were not unfolding as quickly or as smoothly as they should. Thankfully, there was one element which had caused no problems so far, but then outmaneuvering a sloth was nothing to crow about, especially when you kept smashing into a wall afterward.

It was time to go for broke. It would work, or there would be more death. Eden's death. The family curse said so, and you couldn't argue with voodoo.

The lovely part was, you didn't have to explain it, either.

Chapter Fifteen

Eden met her friend Justine for lunch at an outdoor restaurant. It was hot and noisy, with traffic crawling past, people enjoying their food and a group of men singing Gospel on the corner.

Justine set her Merlot down with a click. "You were shot? That's what the bandage and all the cancelled appointments this week are about?"

"It was suggested that I should suspend my practice for a few days," Eden explained. "And I was grazed, not shot."

"Like there's a difference?" Justine fanned her face. "Okay, what's this favor you need that's going to net me a root canal and two new caps. You want a celebrity phone number or something?"

Eden handed her a card with Maxwell Burgoyne's name on it. "I need a list of all the phone calls this man made in the month before his death."

"Ghost file, huh?" Justine's brows came together. "You wanna tell me why I'm risking my squeaky clean work rep to do this?"

"I'm hoping the information will keep me from actually being shot."

Her friend winced. "Well, ouch."

"Can you do it?"

"It's in the system, Eden. Computers keep records of everything. I'll have to slip it by my supervisor, and it isn't legal or ethical, but for the sake of your life, I'm in." She ran her tongue over her left incisor. "You couldn't make that three caps, could you?"

Eden smiled. "If it'll end this nightmare, I'll even replace your old fillings. How long?"

"A day, maybe two."

"I'll put you on the shortlist. And Justine?" Eden caught her friend's hand. "Thanks."

ARMAND'S MOOD WAS NOT GOOD when he visited his father that afternoon. It declined further when he realized the old man had a visitor.

"You look snarly as a gator," J.C. noted from his chair on the back porch. "Aside from the fact that you're working parallel to an idiot, things are holding steady enough. Or so you said last night."

Armand glanced at his father's guest who was studying him with a keen eye from the porch swing. "He's not an idiot, he's just over his head. He's not used to shooting people, and his night vision's questionable."

J.C. glanced sideways. "You wanna maybe reconsider using a man like that, don't you think? My Armand—"

"Will make up for any and all inadequacies." The swing creaked as J.C.'s guest shifted position. "You'll do that, won't you, Armand?"

"I'll keep my word," was all he said.

"You like her, don't you?"

"I do."

"I'm not surprised." The swing creaked. "She's beautiful, looks like her natural mother."

"Lucille." Armand stared through his lashes. "Interesting choice of surname. Why Chaney, I wonder?"

"Maybe one day you'll find out, but it won't be me who does the explaining. Right now, all I want is for you to keep your word to your father, and through him to me."

"What about my word to Eden?"

His father fixed him with a glare. "It's my blood in your

veins. Mine and your late mama's. You do this for us, then you deal with the rest. How this started is how it goes on. It's too late now to change things up.''

Armand returned the glare. ''Eden deserves the truth. She's deserved it from the start. I should never have agreed to do this your way.''

''But you did agree,'' J.C.'s visitor reminded, ''and it's gone too far now for any of us to pull out.''

''It's payback time,'' his father said. ''A life for a life. My life for Eden Bennett's.''

THE ST. LOUIS CEMETERY after sunset held a certain lurid fascination for Eden. She'd accompanied Dolores there many times to visit Marie Laveau's tomb.

''Draw an X, pretty girl, make a wish.'' On every trip, Dolores would add her X to the wall, close her eyes and murmur something in French.

Eden hadn't asked why. She hadn't needed to. She'd known what her grandmother wanted.

It wasn't working. Dolores had called her three times today before dinner. Finally, with love and exasperation driving her, Eden had countered, ''Why the desperation now, Dolores, and not two months ago?''

''I told you, Maxwell's death was a catalyst. Your natural father dies, and there you go, Death's foot's wedged in your door.''

''But I didn't know about Maxwell until after he was murdered. How can his death affect me?''

''Not having known him doesn't make the fallout from his passing any less real, pretty girl. The curse is in motion.''

''In the voodoo world maybe, but I prefer science to magic—and, I know, you're going to say voodoo's religion, right?''

''It is.''

''But not my religion.''

''Beside the point. You listen up. You go into the cemetery

tonight, you keep that police detective of yours in sight. And make a good hard wish for me.''

Because she loved her grandmother, Eden agreed. "All right, I will, a good, hard one…''

"A good, hard what?''

Armand's question zapped Eden out of memory and back to the real world. He'd parked his SUV on Basin Street. She could see both the boxers' gym and the walls of the St. Louis Cemetery a block ahead.

"Not what you think,'' she said with a quick sideways look.

He curled his fingers around hers, squeezed lightly. "We'll let it go, for now.'' He nodded forward. "That's Cruz's Mercedes.''

"Isn't a red convertible a bit flamboyant for a loan shark?''

"This is New Orleans. Flamboyant's the standard here.''

She regarded the other parked vehicles. None of the darker models had gashed undersides, but then would a killer who was watching her and knew she'd spotted his vehicle at least once park it in plain sight?

Because she didn't want to think about that, Eden tied her hair into a ponytail, stuck a Saints ball cap on her head and squared up. "Let's get it done then. Is this guy big, small, guarded, armed?''

"I'd guess three out of four.''

"Is he a killer?''

"Not that I know of. Relax, Eden, he has no reason to harm either of us. The most he'll be when we leave tonight is irritated.''

"An irritated loan shark doesn't inspire much confidence, Armand. And since he'll probably lie to you anyway, what's the point of questioning him?''

"Because I'll know if he's lying, and if he is, it'll be more incentive for me to dig.''

"You think he had dealings with Maxwell?''

"Possibly.''

Eden nodded. She knew this had to be done. She also knew she didn't have to be in on the doing. She could have stayed at Armand's place and phoned Dolores or gone to Lucille's club, or gotten a lesson in peculiar plants from Lisa.

"Monkshood," she recalled, sidetracked. "Foxglove and henbane." Mary had mentioned those names, and later Lisa had talked about flowers called white false hellebore and mountain laurel. Eden remembered enough from her college botany classes to know that all those plants were poisonous.

Lisa hadn't shot her on the roof of her apartment building, but someone with a working knowledge of plants might have broken into her greenhouse, stolen the necessary leaves and doctored a bullet.

The thought fizzled out. People didn't need to go to those lengths for poison these days. Suppliers were listed on the Internet. New Orleans alone would have dozens of sources that a potential murderer could tap into.

But why poison a bullet? Because the shooter hadn't intended to kill her? Perhaps the shot had been a warning.

It was a complicated thought, one for which she had no answer. Thankfully, it was unlikely that poisoned bullets had anything to do with the loan shark Armand planned to confront.

A stop at the gym revealed that Cruz and his current best boxer had left thirty minutes ago. A bald man with a flat nose volunteered the information before Armand finished asking the question. He seemed relieved when, after a few moments alone, Armand turned away.

"Old friend of yours?" Eden assumed.

"We've met. Cruz and Jackson are at the cemetery."

"Looking for corpses to punch?"

"The boxer runs, Eden. Cruz times him. It's called building stamina." He took her hand, and they returned to the street. "What were you saying earlier about foxglove and henbane?"

"Nothing much. Madam Kafkha showed Lisa how to make a natural talisman against curses."

"Poison to ward off poison?"

"Plants with toxic properties aren't always bad, you know. Deadly on one hand, but digitalis—heart medication—is derived from foxglove, and alkaloids from white false hellebore are used to counteract hypertension. Agrimony's an anti-inflammatory, and I think even belladonna has some positive use in connection with ulcers."

"Your point is?"

"No point, just thinking out loud."

"About toxic plants."

"About lots of things, Armand. Like why, for example, someone would steal then abandon a statue in Lisa's back alley."

"That could be an attempted frame, *chère*."

"A pitiful attempt if you ask me. What kind of idiot would steal something like that right after committing a murder? Wouldn't a killer's first thought be to escape? Nick a watch or wallet maybe, but a ninety-pound statue? Seems unlikely to me."

Clouds scudded across the moon as they approached the cemetery gates. The street appeared to darken, but Eden saw Armand shrug. "It is unlikely, but then a good deal about this case makes no sense. He used his head to indicate a group of night mourners. "From voodoo to vampires."

The group, some thirty strong, wore drapey black clothes, high boots and makeup that gleamed white under the street lamps.

"Do you see Cruz or his boxer?" Eden asked.

"I see a man standing under a tree with two other men a short distance behind."

Eden surveyed the tall man with the paunch. He wore a pale blue suit over a black T-shirt, an earring in his left ear and his gray-brown hair in a slick ponytail.

"Why do I think pimp when I look at him?"

"Probably because loaning money is only one of many businesses he's into." Halting, Armand turned her to face him. "Do me a favor tonight, okay? Walk to that bench beside the cemetery entrance and wait for me there."

She jerked free, vexed. "I will, but only because I'm not

looking to get killed. I'm also not five years old, as your tone of voice implies.''

''I wasn't—''

''Talk to Cruz,'' she said. ''I'll mingle with the vampires and try not to get shot, strangled or stabbed.''

While he didn't look pleased, neither did he argue. Eden watched him walk toward the loan shark before she turned and headed for the bench—which was no longer empty, but it didn't matter. She would stand beside the open gate and keep one eye on Armand and the other on the vampire couple currently making out in plain sight.

Too edgy to stand still, she circled. More than would-be vampires drifted through the gates. A group of mourners, carrying all manner of objects from boxes to lilies to what looked like an armful of dried bones, trudged past. Some kind of voodoo ritual must be taking place inside. Madame Kafkha had told Lucille about a voodoo priest who'd died recently. Maybe these people had come to honor his passing.

Someone stopped a carriage at the curb. Eden couldn't see Armand or Cruz. With clouds obscuring the moon and tree branches blowing across the lamplights, she couldn't see much of anything.

Restless, she continued to walk. The voodoo mourners filed along in an eerie procession. One of them, an old man, raised his head and smiled at her. She smiled back, though it felt closer to a grimace. She kept seeing green glass eyes in a doll's scorched face.

Closing her own eyes, she tried to erase the images. It didn't work. Then Armand's features worked themselves into the mix.

''Damn,'' she breathed and turned toward the street. The procession was gone. Only their shuffling footsteps remained.

And a shadow that covered her from behind.

TWENTY MINUTES with Steven Cruz revealed several things about the loan shark. One, he'd had recent dealings with Robert Weir; two, those dealings had been terminated seventy-two hours ago; three, Cruz was only aware of Maxwell Burgoyne as a name not a customer and so had no reason to want the man dead; and four, he needed to bathe in something other than cologne.

"Ask around," Cruz said with a shrug. "Burgoyne was nothing to me. I loaned his partner cash, I was reimbursed in cash, plus interest. I don't trade lives for money."

"Do you know how Robert Weir came by this payback?"

"Scored at the racetrack's what I heard." Another shrug. "Burgoyne left him squat in his will. I have better friends on the police force."

Armand didn't doubt it. He wasn't sure he believed all that Cruz had told him, but enough of it rang true that he eased off.

He didn't like the fact that someone had parked a funeral carriage at the cemetery entrance, blocking his view of Eden, and the smell of unwashed body doused with cologne was giving him a headache. He'd run Cruz through the computer again tonight and see if he'd missed something in the cross-match with Maxwell Burgoyne, but he doubted it.

That didn't leave much, he reflected as he moved away. If Weir hadn't offed Burgoyne as part of a debt payment, his motive came down to one of hatred, and Weir hadn't struck Armand as the type of person to plot a murder based on emotion. Prod, needle and annoy, yes, but for a man like Robert Weir, murder for profit was likely to be the bottom line.

His thoughts circled back to Lisa and from her to Mary who could, if she put her mind to it and her makeup on properly, closely resemble her sisters. Then there was Lucille, also similar in appearance to Eden and Lisa.

He needed to talk to Robert Weir again, from the standpoint of an eyewitness.

Armand knew Eden hadn't gone to the cemetery bench. He'd seen the vampire couple making out while he'd talked to Cruz. She'd waited at the gate instead, and...

His blood chilled. She wasn't there. Not at the gate, not standing inside it.

"Eden!" He jogged to the entrance and shouted her name.

A man spoke up from the base of the wall. "If you mean the pretty lady, she got taken in."

"Who took her?"

"Didn't see a face."

"Man or woman?"

"Couldn't tell. Your lady seemed dazed."

"Which way did they go?"

The man gave the bone he'd been playing with a spin. "Eloise says left." He grinned. "I'm eighty-three, don't you know? My friend died last week. I wanted to go with the others and say goodbye, but Eloise said no way. Bad vibes inside tonight."

Bad vibes outside, too. Cursing, Armand went left. And prayed that, whoever the hell Eloise was, she had her directions straight.

IT WAS THE ODDEST FEELING to float, to know it, yet be unable to fight. Eden remembered a hand, gloved and holding a cloth. It had come out of the darkness to cover her mouth and nose. But only long enough to make her woozy.

She couldn't think—except she knew her feet were moving, and it wasn't Armand gripping her arm from behind. She should scream, but even that seemed beyond her right now. Easier to walk—or float—and watch the pretty headstones, tombs and crosses drift past.

Death was a big deal in New Orleans. Celebrated, ritualized, guided and toured. She needed to put an X on Marie Laveau's wall. She'd promised Dolores. This was the wrong way, though.

The lights from the street dimmed, and the moon hid behind the clouds. Alarm bells clanged in her mind.

"Armand…" she murmured.

The hand shook her. Her head snapped up and her eyes widened. For a moment, the cemetery came clear.

"Where are we going?" She tried to think.

Something clicked in her memory. She saw Armand's face,

heard his voice. "Walk to the bench by the cemetery and wait..."

She breathed in the night air. Deeply. Unobtrusively.

Who was behind her?

Maybe her muscles tensed. Maybe when she stumbled over a jut of old stone wall, she caught the person off guard. In any case, the hand tightened briefly, dragged downward on her for a moment, then released.

Before she could run, something—it felt like a shoulder—jammed into her spine. She would have fallen into a headstone if she hadn't planted her palms to stop her fall.

She heard a grunt and music in the air. Horns. Mournful blues.

A fist connected with her ribs. She honed in and kicked at what looked like a vampire in a black overcoat.

More grunts erupted. Her head ached. A layer of fog remained.

She needed a weapon. Her eyes landed on a large glass vase. Tipping out the dead flowers, she concentrated on her target.

Two crosses wobbled in her line of vision. Two stone crosses, two potted palms, two people in black coats.

Not vampires, not voodoo mourners. Probably not two people, either. Panting from the exertion of trying to focus, she swung the vase.

She heard it shatter, but couldn't stay upright. A body hit the ground. She heard footsteps and a moan, but didn't have the strength to look.

She needed to breathe, to uncoil and defog. She wanted Armand, but still couldn't use her voice.

On her knees, she brought her head up and forced her eyes open. No way was the person she'd hit going to escape. Armand said she'd picked up a shadow. Tonight that shadow would be named.

THE MAN—and Eden could tell by his profile it was a man—moved. She had the remnants of the jar in her hand and would have used it on him if he'd attempted to stand. Fortunately, she heard Armand calling to her and breathed a sigh of relief.

"Over here," she managed to call back. "I think I got him."

The man groaned. She responded by raising the broken jar. "Eden!"

Armand's hands gripped her arms, drawing her upright so he could look into her eyes. "Are you hurt?"

"Dizzy," she said and gestured at the fallen man. "He used something. I only inhaled a little."

Armand's eyes slid from her face to the man on the ground. "You hit him?"

"Guess so. I thought I missed at first, but I got lucky."

He tipped her chin up. "You sure you're all right?"

Nodding, she leaned forward on her knees. Her head was clearing, together with the attacker's features. "I've never seen him before, have you?"

The man's eyelids fluttered. He struggled to roll over. "Who hit me?"

"She did." With a final inspection of Eden's face, Armand released her and planted a knee in the small of the man's back. "I think you want to stay put, until we establish who you are and who you work for. It's all right," he said to Eden. "Set the jar down and relax. He's not going anywhere."

The spinning sensation subsided. Eden had a headache, but she could think now, more or less.

On her heels, she studied the man. "Why do you want to kill me?"

"I..."

Armand dug his knee in deeper. "No lies. I'm not in the mood."

"Can I turn over? Please?"

He didn't sound like a killer. His movements were awkward, and he winced as he ran his fingers over the lump on his skull.

Armand surveyed him close up. "What's your name?"

"Rick Lane." He rearranged himself with difficulty on the dirt path. "I haven't been trying to kill you, Ms. Bennett, I've been trying—though not terribly successfully, I'm afraid—to prevent you from being killed.'' He glanced from Armand to her and continued. "Someone's after you. I don't know who," he added before she could ask. "It's like I'm chasing a shadow. I catch a glimpse now and then. I watch you, I see something. I know it's not good, but I can't seem to outthink whoever it is.''

"Who hired you to watch me?" Although it could only be one of three people and the first two were less likely than the third. "Dolores?"

"She wanted to—"

"Keep me safe from the family curse." God knew why Eden wanted to laugh. Maybe it was belated hysteria. Letting her head fall back, she regarded the cloud-dusted stars. "I should have expected she'd do something like this.''

"Your mind doesn't run along devious lines." Armand said. "It's not a fault." He returned his gaze to Rick Lane. "You followed Eden's shadow tonight?"

"I did. We tussled right here. But, well…" He touched the lump on his head.

Eden continued to stare at the stars, a wry smile curving her lips. "Sorry about that. Was it a man?"

"I couldn't tell."

She'd anticipated that answer, as, apparently, had Armand. "Balaclava?" he asked.

"Or a ski mask. Black. I'm really sorry, Ms. Bennett. I'm a private investigator. Legwork's not my forte. My partner usually does it, but he's laid up. Things have been tight lately. We needed the money, so I tried to fill in." He raised hopeful brows at Armand. "I got most of a license plate number and the make of a car I've seen twice when Ms. Bennett's been attacked. It's a dark-green Chevy with a bent front plate and an after market brake light in the rear window with a melted casing."

"Give me the number." Armand helped Eden to her feet. "I'll run it tonight. In the meantime, I'll check your story with Dolores Boyer."

The P.I. regarded Eden from the ground. "Your grand-mother hired my partner and me because we were born in the bayou. She knew we'd understand about curses and how they work."

"They work because people who believe make them work, consciously or subconsciously."

"You should know better than that by now, ma'am. Your grandmother's a smart woman with a razor-sharp mind. If she believes, that should tell you something."

It told her she needed to have another talk with Dolores. Beyond that, Eden didn't want to delve.

But she felt better now, and curiosity won out over aggra-vation. "Does your car have a gash low on the passenger side?"

The man appeared startled, then flustered. "Uh…"

"I'll take that as a yes. What about blue-tinted headlights?"

He flinched, and she sighed. Another yes.

"I never meant to scare you, only to watch and help if help was needed."

He'd done both, but she didn't hold it against him. Dolores had done the hiring. And Dolores was, as Eden well knew, a force to be reckoned with once she set her mind to something.

Armand rubbed her arms from behind. "Let's go home." He took the license number the P.I. scribbled for him and tucked it in his pocket. "You need to rest, and I need to go over a number of things. Next time you see this shadow," he told the investigator who was still on the ground, "either catch him or call me."

The man climbed to his feet and started out of the cemetery ahead of them.

Eden wasn't surprised to discover he limped.

Chapter Sixteen

If he told her the truth now, he'd lose her. Armand was as certain of that as he was of his father's unstinting belief that deceiving her was the right thing to do. Only the end result mattered; the how was unimportant.

It was important to Armand.

Maxwell Burgoyne was dead. Ditto his lawyer. Why? He had no answers, only speculation. The murderer could be Lucille, Mary or Lisa. It could be Robert Weir. But the motives were thin for all of them.

With one exception.

Armand hated adding deviousness to deceit, but he had to know the truth. Lucille was a wealthy woman. She'd maintained certain business affiliations with Maxwell over the years. Not partnerships, more a number of loose ties which had profited her as they had the companies whose boards Maxwell had chaired.

Companies Maxwell hadn't owned outright or, as far as Armand could determine, had much say in the operating of. Burgoyne had profited to be sure, yet the power had remained tantalizingly beyond his grasp.

Armand pictured a carrot on a stick, with Maxwell chasing it and Robert Weir content, despite his gambling bent, to pick up the leftover bits of peel. That peel would have amounted to a tidy sum over the years, and Weir struck Armand as a shrewd and patient man.

With a headache throbbing at the base of his skull and Eden in the forefront of his mind, he took a long drink of beer. Ignoring the wind outside, he accessed the state files on his computer. Dolores's investigator had gotten most of a local license plate number. The third digit was missing and he hadn't been entirely sure of the first—possibly an eight, maybe a nine—but it was a start.

Armand brooded while the computer searched. The darkness in the room shifted with the rising wind. The shadow of a broken cross plastered itself across the wall to his left.

As omens went, it didn't feel good, but what did he care about omens when his thoughts were full of more disturbing images—of Eden in black lace underwear, a counterpoint to the silk slip she'd worn last night. Of her soaking in a tubful of perfumed bubbles, lavender, he decided because he'd caught that scent on her skin more than once.

She would be naked under those bubbles, wet and warm. A rueful smile crossed his lips as he closed his eyes and let the fantasy unfold.

The computer beeped. Cracking an eyelid, he checked it. Still searching.

Reality wanted to intrude. Armand sighed and rested his head against the chair back. He should accept that reality and admit he had no right to go to her under a cloud of lies. Want her, yes; fantasize about her, absolutely; care for her more than he had any other woman in his life... He paused there, not so much uncertain as stunned. The answer was a simple, mind-blowing yes. And it brought a release of breath coupled with a soft "Damn," as he rolled the cold beer bottle across his forehead. This was not a thing he'd needed to discover.

But it was done now, he realized while he sat in his home which had once been a church, in a city known for its sinners and its wicked ways.

He was a sinner. Not a wicked man, but not a saint, either.

Without moving his head, he let his eyes rise to the ceiling. No, most definitely not a saint.

EDEN COULDN'T SIT. She couldn't possibly sleep. She was wound up inside, unsure of what she wanted, even more uncertain of what she wanted to do.

Armand had brought her aspirin and tea earlier. He'd hovered in the awkward way men did, kissed her and, assured that she was as comfortable as he could make her, abandoned her for his computer.

It had been a grudging abandonment, though; she'd seen that when he'd paused to look at her from the threshold. It hadn't lessened the ache of desire inside, but it had helped her frazzled emotions to know he wanted her, too.

Arms folded and tapping her elbows with restless palms, she circled the tiny room. Wind howled through the cracks in the casement windows. It smelled like a bayou rainstorm.

No problem, she reflected. The storm brewing outside merely matched the one in her.

She wanted to make love with Armand—but she really should be thinking about her sisters, Lucille and Dolores. Robert Weir as well, although she couldn't see that leading anywhere except back to where this nightmare had begun. With Maxwell Burgoyne's murder.

It was funny, she mused as a bolt of lightning sliced through the sky, how life played out. If Maxwell hadn't died, she wouldn't have met Armand.

Dangerous line of thought, but true. Of course, if Lisa hadn't persisted in trying to find Maxwell, he wouldn't have died, Eden wouldn't have been forced to lie, and again, no Armand.

The branches of an old oak tree scraped the window. When Eden looked she saw her reflection in the glass. Another person might have mistaken her for Lisa. But mistaken her for Lucille or, as Armand had suggested, Mary? It seemed like a stretch to Eden. Unless the person in question wore extremely thick glasses.

The bed stood opposite the window. Eden sat down crosslegged, hugged a pillow to her chest and let the questions come.

Why had Lisa been so desperate to know her biological

family, in particular a father, supposedly dead, who'd never showed the slightest interest in knowing her? The first time she'd met him she hadn't liked him, so why had she pushed for a second meeting? What had Maxwell said to make her leave the restaurant after the salad course?

On a less charitable note, why couldn't Maxwell have died of natural causes instead of a blow to the skull? That would have simplified everything. He'd had a heart condition, probably popped pills three times a day. A miss here or there, a sudden attack in a deserted garden cemetery and, bam, no more problem.

It was a cold thought. Eden had never met the man. Her character sketch was based on hearsay. Unfortunately all she'd heard were negative comments.

Rain began to pelt the window. The drops sounded large and hard.

Was she being hard, Eden wondered, because she could find no scrap of compassion for a man whose sperm had given her life? Surely some part of her should care.

"Some part," she echoed, watching as the rain forged crooked lines from pane to sill. Yet all she felt was scratchy and hot, and that had nothing to do with Maxwell.

Tossing the pillow aside, she resumed her troubled pacing. The room was a cage. She needed to breathe, to walk, if she was lucky, to tire herself out so she could sleep and stop dwelling on Armand LaMorte.

"No cops." She said it out loud and in a tone so determined her voice shook. But anger wasn't the problem. It was all frustration. And fear.

"Hell." This time she breathed the word.

The wind gusted up. Behind it, the first peal of thunder rumbled through the sky.

Eden massaged her temples as she circled. The lights flickered but held. "Don't need that," she remarked. Not with the memory of a knockout drug and a hazy picture of Dolores's voodoo collection swimming in her head.

The air had grown hot and stuffy. Eden placed a hand on

her stomach and struggled to breathe. She needed space. She'd go crazy if she stayed cooped up here. Surely Armand would be asleep at—she glanced at the bedside clock—2:13 a.m.

Something banged, probably a loose shutter, and she jumped. "That's it." She strode to the door, yanked it open—and slammed face first into Armand's naked chest.

She resisted an urge to leap backward and hissed at him instead. "Why are you there? I come from a family of weak hearts, you know."

A slow, sexy smile touched his mouth. "The hearts are only weak on one side, Eden, and you favor your biological mother."

"Outwardly. It could be a very different story inside."

"And you could be stalling until you figure out where you can run that you won't feel cornered."

Her expression remained calm. Every other part of her trembled.

"I'm a grown woman, Armand. I don't need to run. I can say no easily enough."

His smile widened ever so slightly. He came into the room, forcing her to back up. "You could also say yes."

She could do that far more easily.

Music drifted up the staircase. Retro forties blues. Not her usual style, but it fit the moment.

"You're quiet now." His steady advance kept her backing up. "Why is that?"

"I'm thinking. Look, you're still a…"

"Don't say cop. Not tonight."

Her nerves hitched when she bumped into the wall, but her eyes never left his.

He stroked her face from cheek to throat. "Let me show you how much you can be wanted."

Her ex had wanted her once, Eden thought, but that was a distant memory and, as arguments went, not as potent as it had been in the past.

She set her hands flat on his chest, felt the heat of his skin and shivered in spite of herself. "I do want you, Armand. I have since I met you. But there's a crazy person out there, and a curse, and when they're gone, if I'm still alive, you'll move on to a new case, and…''

He silenced her by crushing his mouth to hers.

It took only that one quick action for every one of her arguments to dissolve. Heat surged past the barriers she'd erected over the years. Where she'd floated dazed through the cemetery before, now sensation coursed through her. It sideswiped reason and left no room for logic.

The scent of storm, church and man washed over her. Armand's taste was unique, and he kissed very, very well. Thoroughly, too. She'd been suffocating before he came to her, but it was nothing compared to how she felt now.

''Damn!'' She tore her mouth away. ''You don't do things in steps, do you?''

''Not this.'' He ran his thumb over one erect nipple. Even beneath a layer of black lace, the shock made her gasp.

He smiled against her hair. ''You were leaving your room when you ran into me, *chère*. Do you always wander around other people's homes with so little on?''

The hand he slid between her thighs made her groan. His statement made her laugh. ''I'm Eden, remember? This is an old church, there's a garden outside with at least two fruit trees on the perimeter. You should expect some form of temptation, don't you think?''

''Ah.'' He nibbled his way down her neck. ''So this black Irish lace is your version of an apple, then.''

''Could be.'' She cocked her head. ''Are you tempted?''

''Are you dead?''

Because she'd have to be not to notice how aroused he was and how hot his skin had grown beneath her fingers.

She tugged on his already unfastened waistband, unzipped his jeans as his mouth covered hers again. He really could kiss.

Thought and sensation jumbled together in a glorious ball. Right then she'd have been hard-pressed to recall her name, let alone the reasons why they shouldn't make love.

Setting his hands beneath her elbows, he lifted her up so

her breasts rubbed against his chest. When he raised her higher, she took the final step and jumped him. With her mouth still locked on his, she wrapped her legs around his hips, tangled her fingers in his hair and fisted them.

One thing she wouldn't do, she promised herself, was regret this. She wanted him, would have him. And she'd accept any and all consequences.

He made it to the bed, she didn't know how. She felt the mattress underneath her, but only for a moment. Then he shifted so she was on top of him.

No alarm bells sounded, or if they did, Eden was too absorbed to notice. She straddled him while he unhooked her bra and she worked on his jeans.

She was hungry, needful, impatient. When he brought her mouth back to his, she imagined what a starving person must feel. She couldn't get enough of him. It was a race of sorts, except she was rushing to a place she'd never been before and would probably never go again.

No, she wouldn't think that way. Armand's hands were on her, and she was hot and ready. Tonight was all that mattered. Tomorrow would unfold—however.

She managed to get his pants off and took hold of him. But before she could do anything more, he rolled her gently onto her back and lifted his head to stare down at her.

"You have to be sure you want this, that you want me."

She brushed the hair from his cheek. "I want you, Armand, you and this. I've been living in limbo for too long. I don't want to end up like…" She stopped herself before she spoke Lisa's name. "I don't want to live in denial."

"You won't."

"I could." She glanced away. "All too easily."

He nipped her bottom lip. "Not tonight, Eden. Not with me."

More shivers started up, but there was no fear in them, no hesitation. It was all anticipation and desire.

He moved slowly now, although she knew by the tension

in his muscles and the light in his eyes that it cost him to do so.

He had protection, which both touched and amused her. "Pretty sure of yourself, aren't you?" she teased.

"Just hopeful. With you, only hopeful."

He began to move, a lazy river rhythm. Smiling against his neck, Eden shook her head. "Not slow, Armand. Not tonight. This is New Orleans. Take my breath away."

He smiled back, and she felt it. "Like this?" he asked and slid his fingers inside her.

She hadn't expected it, was more than ready but simply hadn't thought he would respond so quickly. A gasp and a shaky, "Yes…like that," was pretty much all she managed before she surrendered to sensation and allowed it to overtake her.

He carried her on delightful little waves, up and down, then up again, higher than she'd ever been before.

Her nails dug into his shoulders as she arched to meet him. Take her breath away? He did that long before she could take him inside her. He stroked and caressed her, kissed her face, her throat, the soft underside of her breasts. He made love to her even as he discovered her.

Her own hands were greedy in their exploration. No cops… She must have been crazy to think that. No one else had ever filled her so completely, or made her want to give so much in return.

The colors in her head bled together. She shuddered when he finally entered her, then rose to meet that exquisite initial thrust.

Crazy for a while perhaps, but no more. As he exploded deep within her, she felt the last barrier fall away.

Armand dropped his head to her shoulder, murmured words she couldn't hear. Right then it was all she could do to breathe. Numb, she ran her hands over his sweat-slick skin, breathed out, then in, then out again in a rush.

No way back from this one, a distant part of her realized. She'd crossed the line tonight.

No ifs, though. When Armand rolled away far enough that she could move, she levered up on one elbow, pushed the hair from her face and whispered a soft, "Wow!"

He tugged her down and tight up against him. With his eyes closed, he smiled. "You're a true New Orleans woman."

She ran her finger over a small scar on his shoulder. "And that means?"

"You're gorgeous, seductive, mysterious." He kissed her gently, soundly. "Amazing."

"But I still don't believe in voodoo."

"Don't want to believe. There's a difference."

She fought off a tremor, realized the thunder was close enough now to rattle the windows. "Not one I want to analyze."

Half-lidded, he ran his gaze over her face. "Is there more than this one night for us, Eden?"

Because she refused to spoil the mood, she let humor spark her eyes as she stroked his hair. "That depends on more things than either of us can control. So…" She drew the word out, gave his bottom lip a playful bite. "What I think we should do—" she slid her hand over his stomach, then lower until he sucked in a quick breath "—is make the most of the time we have and see what the light of day brings."

Not voodoo, she hoped. Not anything bad.

Yet deep inside, she prayed for this to be the longest night of her life.

THINGS WERE NOT GOING WELL in Lucille Chaney's opinion. Instead of pushing for weekly family dinners, Lisa was sequestering herself into her garden. Mary appeared to be delving in pornographic photography and Eden had moved into a church. A disused church with rickety doors, large windows and a graveyard on the side.

In her office chair with the lights off, the storm gone and the first hint of dawn tinting the eastern sky, she regarded the tip of a fresh syringe. And wondered. How did one deal with a mounting threat in a way that was at once unsuspicious and permanent?

The phone rang at her elbow. She debated, before picking up.

"Why are you in your office at five-thirty in the morning?"

Relief loosened the knots in her neck. "Scheduling boon-doggles at the club, *Maman*. You of all people should under-stand such problems."

"I'm up to my eyeballs in them these days." Dolores paused. "Dali Kafkha says the curse is full at work."

Lucille snorted. "The woman possesses less than half of her marbles. I spoke to her. She gave me guesses."

"She gave you the willies."

"Nonsense," Lucille scoffed, but a tendril of fear feathered along her spine. "Worse than death is her prediction, and she won't be budged. I say she's wrong."

"You think Eden will die?"

"I think the curse is an old rhyme intended to frighten be-lievers like you."

"You can say that to me when your ancestor—"

"This isn't about ancestors, Dolores. It's about human na-ture. Mistakes. Regrets. Recompense. About family, yes, but not so far back as you would go."

"We'll never agree on this," Dolores retorted, "so I won't argue with you. I have a new problem. Can you come here tonight?"

"I planned to visit Eden."

"This involves Eden and a so-called private investigator who botched his job."

Lucille's cheeks paled. "What time?"

"Seven o'clock."

"I'll be there."

When Dolores hung up, Lucille pinched the bridge of her nose. God help her, if she had a time machine, she'd go back thirty years and change—her hand fell away—what? Alter one thing, alter it all. Wishes were for young children and old fools. She would deal with what was.

Picking up the syringe, she removed a bottle from her desk drawer, inserted the needle and drew the liquid inside until the vial was full.

FROM ARMAND'S POINT OF VIEW, the night passed in a heart-beat. He woke at dawn to find Eden curled against him. His face was buried in her hair, his limbs tangled with hers. He could happily have awakened that way every morning, but it wouldn't happen like that. It wouldn't. He'd lied to her, then made love to her. False pretenses, she'd call it, and she'd be right. He should have told her everything days—no, a week—ago.

Was he in love? he wondered. Because the question felt like a slap, and his mind shied away from it, he had a pretty good idea of the answer. But again, what could he do? What would she let him do?

Not her burden, he thought and disentangled himself with care. "Sleep," he whispered when she stirred. "I have work to do."

He wished he could make amends as easily. And when his cell phone rang, as he'd expected it would, he wished he'd never heard the name Maxwell Burgoyne.

HE BREWED COFFEE and left a rose on the pillow next to her. Eden appreciated one as much as the other because no day started well without caffeine. As for the rose—she hadn't stopped smiling since she'd woken up.

Life was getting complicated, but in this case she didn't mind at all. What to do about it was a tougher question. How much was she willing to admit to herself? How much could she admit to Armand?

She considered that and him while she showered and dressed.

It was a glorious late summer day, and she chose a sage linen dress with high-heeled sandals from the clothes she'd packed. A little glamour never hurt, although she'd rather be working. Armand had promised she'd be back drilling and filling by Monday, and Eden planned to hold him to it.

Her friend Justine phoned as she was putting the rose in water. She had the list Eden wanted and ninety minutes free at lunchtime.

They met on Canal Street on the fringe of the Quarter, and joined the late summer tourists for a stroll past shops and restaurants.

"Any more close calls?" Justine demanded while she fished in her purse.

"Nothing worth mentioning."

"Hmm, sounds evasive. How's Lisa?"

Eden lifted her face to the breeze. "Still not herself. She's repotting in her greenhouse to boost her spirits."

"She needs a man. You should get Mary to lend her one. It's weird, Eden. You've got a sister who dates a different guy every night, most of them mindless mounds of muscle but guys all the same, and another who's celibate. Doesn't Lisa ever have, you know, urges?"

"She likes plants. It's enough for her." Yet even as she said that, Eden knew she should have a better answer. That she didn't seemed to bear out Lucille's assertion that she'd never taken the time to know her sisters. "I'll talk to her," she said. "Maybe she feels awkward around men."

"We'll call her picky then. Actually, Mary could take lessons there. She was out with some guy the other night who had cauliflower ears and a permanently dazed expression on his face. You know, like he'd been punched one too many times in a barroom brawl."

Eden glanced in the direction of the St. Louis Cemetery. "Or a boxing ring," she mused out loud.

"Ah, here it is. One list of phone numbers. I didn't do names because my supervisor has an annoying habit of popping up when you least expect it. She thinks we're into chat rooms instead of working, so she sneaks around trying to catch us."

Eden unfolded the papers. "Set up mirrors," she suggested.

"If you place them in strategic spots on your desk, you can..."

Justine zipped her purse. "Something wrong?"

Eden stared at the recurring number. "This is Maxwell Burgoyne's account, right?"

"Doubled-checked, kid. When I give out illegal info, I get it right."

Eden read and reread the sheet. There was no mistake. She spotted a restaurant table a few feet away and sank into an empty chair. "I don't believe it."

"What?" Baffled, Justine peered over her shoulder. "Do you recognize one of the listings?"

"Yes." She went over each digit, and it still came out the same.

It took only a few seconds for shock to give way to anger. Eden's head rose, and her eyes stared northward.

Toward the bayou.

Toward Dolores's home.

Chapter Seventeen

She displayed her voodoo artifacts everywhere. On the porch, in the living room, in the kitchen, on the walls. A stick doll with painted green eyes sat beside a stack of envelopes. Chicken bones, feathers and polished stones littered the sideboard.

Eden stalked back and forth across the main room. Dolores wasn't here, but she'd show. Eventually she'd have to.

Punching numbers on her cell phone, Eden tried Lucille again—and was told again to leave a message on her voice mail.

She knew she should calm down, but she didn't want to. Maxwell had called Dolores's home number thirty-two times during the month prior to his death. That was an average of one call per day. And there was only one possible explanation.

Eden paced, spun and paced some more. The stick doll next to the envelopes watched her. She'd half thought—no, she'd hoped—that Dali Kafkha would turn out to be Maxwell's mother. Dali, or one of a handful of other possibilities. But not Dolores. Please God, not one of the few people she'd truly believed she could trust.

She thought of Maxwell's will, of MamaDees Molasses and Sugar products. Mama D's. D for Dolores. She wondered vaguely how she could have missed something so obvious.

The clomp of thick rubber boots on the porch heralded her

grandmother's return. Eden hadn't heard the truck; Dolores must have been down in the bayou.

"Eden." She managed to look surprised, apprehensive and pleased all at once. She set a fish basket down outside and scraped her boots. "If you've come to scold me about my private investigator, I'm ahead of you. I spoke to him last night and to your handsome police detective this morning." Eden didn't pull away when Dolores took her hands. "I see by your expression you're annoyed. But you know." She released her to shake a stern finger. "I only did it to keep you safe. The curse is on you, pretty girl. Full at work according to Dali Kafkha."

"Because of Maxwell's death."

"It was the catalyst, as I've said."

"Believing as you do, don't you think it's more likely that the curse was responsible for Maxwell's death because he was in fact the eldest born to eldest grown?"

Her grandmother, indeed the entire house, went still. Even the crickets outside seemed to stop chirping.

"You had an older brother who died many years ago," Eden ventured. "He was the eldest born in your family, but you were the eldest grown. And while Lucille may also have had a brother who died young, his death had nothing to do with any curse. And nothing to do with you in the end, because he wasn't your son any more than Lucille is your daughter."

They both heard a car engine outside and both chose to ignore it.

Dolores's lips thinned, but to her credit, she offered no denial. Meeting Eden's glare, she asked simply, "How did you find out?"

"I did some investigative work of my own. It was simple really. Maxwell—your son—telephoned your home every day for the last month of his life. Mama D., founder and principal shareholder of MamaDees Molasses and Sugar Mills, mother-in-law to Lucille at one time, but never her mother." Eden's eyes glittered with temper. "Tell me, Dolores, did you dream up the lie, or was it a joint venture?"

Dolores held the glare. "I devised it. Lucille resisted, but I persuaded her that my pretending to be your maternal grandmother was best for her daughters. Maxwell wanted no part of the children he'd sired. I did. We decided to cut him out and link ourselves instead."

Eden didn't know whether to shout or laugh. She supposed either one would be a release. When she spied a familiar figure on the porch, laughter temporarily won out.

"What, is this the night every week when you get together to create new plots and make sure the old ones are running smoothly?"

"There's no need for sarcasm." Dolores's voice held a warning Eden had heard many times.

Frustrated, furious and half-afraid she might say something she'd regret, Eden marched to the far end of the room. "How could you do this?" she demanded, turning. Her question included Lucille, who took one look at the pair and headed straight for the liquor cabinet.

"Don't make things worse, Lucille," Dolores snapped, although her eyes remained on Eden.

"They can be worse?" But Lucille only splashed the bottom of a small glass before recapping the sherry bottle. "I knew it would be you who exposed our secret." She toasted Eden and took a delicate sip. "Oh, I have missed that." One sleek brow arched. "Do your sisters know?"

"Not yet."

"I don't suppose you'd consider not mentioning it to them."

Now Eden's laugh was one of disbelief. "You can't possibly expect me to condone this charade. To what end?"

"Simplicity," Dolores said. "It benefits no one to learn the truth. I am your biological grandmother, that's a fact. Whether paternal or maternal is irrelevant to me, and likely to you as well. But will it be to them? Or will one or both of your sisters draw away knowing that I am Maxwell's mother, his flesh and blood?"

Eden made an agitated circle at the back of the room. "It won't matter to Mary."

"No," Lucille agreed. "She hates me, Dolores, but still likes you, so it stands to reason she won't hold Maxwell against you."

"What about Lisa?" Dolores countered. "Her feelings are vastly different from Mary's. She's fond of Lucille, but she hasn't a scrap of love for Maxwell's memory."

Eden wanted to kick something. She walked it off instead. "How is it that you can turn your lies around so I'm the one who feels guilty? They deserve to know the truth. Lisa's going through a bad time, but she's far too generous to hold your son against you."

Lucille ran a finger around the rim of her glass. "You know that, do you, the same way you know why she's been behaving so strangely lately? Why she's been pushing all of us away when it was her who brought us together in the first place?"

"Lucille…"

"I'm not going for guilt here, Eden. Yes, Dolores and I lied. Was it wrong of us to do so? Perhaps. But it's done, and neither of us profited from the deception. Believe it or not, we love you very much. Every decision we made, whether in tandem or separately, was fully considered before it was executed. I would not," she added without a scrap of remorse, "have been a good single mother."

Maybe it had to do with her feelings for Armand. Or maybe she simply understood how difficult some decisions could be. Whatever the case, Eden's anger began to subside. That didn't mean she thought Lucille and Dolores had done the right thing, but part of her could see the situation from their perspective.

"Walk a mile," she said and finally stopped pacing. "My mother preached that concept throughout my childhood. I suppose this is the first opportunity I've had to practice it." She stopped next to the sideboard with its voodoo trappings and other paraphernalia. "Why didn't you tell us after a few years had passed?"

Dolores gave her head a single, emphatic shake. "If Lisa had known Maxwell was my son and still alive, she would have tried to contact him that much sooner."

"But she discovered he was alive anyway, so your attempt to protect her failed, as you must have anticipated it would. Big secrets always come out, Dolores, usually at the worst possible moments."

"Amen to that." Lucille dipped a finger into her glass and licked the tip. "So are we square then?"

"Mary and Lisa should hear the truth." Eden was adamant on that point. "I don't want the burden of keeping this from them. It's too important."

"They can know," Dolores agreed, "when the time is right."

"Now is—"

"Not the right time." Setting her fists on her hips, Dolores glared. "You scoff at voodoo, but remember, Maxwell is dead. My son." She pinched her thin forearm. "My flesh and blood. The curse fell on him as the eldest born, the only born. But as such he was also the eldest grown, and you were the first child he sired."

To Eden's surprise, Lucille came to stand beside her. "You place too much weight on the past, *Maman*. Even magic can be diluted by time. New genes enter the pool. No, wait." She held up a hand. "That was the wrong thing to say. But violent storms play themselves out, why not curses as well?"

Dolores waved her off. "You want to equate our curse with a force of nature? Call it unpredictable then, but it's no summer storm. It's a volcano, dormant for years, until one day, bam, a powerful eruption."

Eden sighed. "All I want to do is tell Lisa and Mary that Maxwell was your son. How did volcanoes get into the picture?"

Dolores tapped her foot. "There have been attempts made on your life, yes?"

"A few," Eden agreed.

"All of which occurred after Maxwell's death."

"His murder."

"And now someone wants to murder you."

"Apparently."

"Why?"

Exasperated, and more than a little shaken by the steel in her grandmother's tone, Eden folded her own arms. "I don't know why, and neither do the police."

"Maybe it's an attempt to divert suspicion." Lucille gave Eden's hair an uncharacteristic stroke. "As things stood, Lisa was to have been accused of the murder. But then you appeared, and it didn't go down that way. Suddenly, there were two of you, and the witness was nearsighted. The police had to investigate the crime more thoroughly. Nerves set in. The authorities needed to be kept off balance. Everyone did. Answer? Smoke screen. How can a solution be found when there is no logic to be had?"

Eden disagreed. "I think there is logic, Lucille. Not visible now, but waiting to be unveiled. Like any big secret," she added, darting a quick glance at Dolores.

She set her hip on the telephone table. The stick doll wobbled and tipped nose down onto the envelopes. Outgoing envelopes, Eden noticed, as there were no postmarks.

"Do you know if Maxwell had any specific enemies?" she asked Dolores.

Her grandmother appeared startled for a moment, but recovered and raised her eyes to fix Eden with a firm stare. "There were several but none with any guts. It was the curse that killed him. Now we can argue this and get nowhere, or we can go into the kitchen and eat one of the blueberry pies I baked today. You choose."

Lucille chuckled. "You baked in the midst of all this turmoil?"

"It eases my mind. Eden?"

Well—could it hurt, really? And while devouring pie, she would make her point that much clearer and stronger. Mary and Lisa needed to know about Maxwell.

Eden doubted she would have paid much attention to the stack of envelopes if the casual act of straightening the toppled doll hadn't drawn a faltering step and a murmur of concern from Dolores.

"What?" She glanced at her hand on the doll. "It isn't broken."

That's when she saw it. The legal-sized envelope at the top of the stack. There was a business stamp in the upper left corner, D.B. Inc., another clue she'd missed over the years. However, it was the mailing address that riveted her attention.

"J.C.—" she spun the envelope around "—LaMorte?" Her head snapped up. Her heart slammed in her chest. "What," she demanded in a low voice, "is this?"

Thin-lipped, Dolores let the arm she'd stretched out drop to her side. "Not as bad as you're thinking."

Lucille gave a small, wry laugh. "Oh, I imagine it probably is." She held up a hand when Eden rounded on her. "Don't look at me. Whatever this story entails, I had no part in it."

"LaMorte." Eden began to shake. That didn't bode well for her state of temper, which was considerable when aroused. "J. C. LaMorte. Bayou address. Company stamp in the corner. Is this a pension check," she demanded, "or payment for some other service rendered?"

Dolores's right eye gave a tiny twitch. "J.C. worked for one of my companies, the sugar mill to be exact. He was there during a brief period of time when Maxwell had a hand in the running of things. Maxwell wasn't suited to operational management. He and J.C. butted heads. Maxwell wanted J.C. gone and the result was a plan of sabotage—botched, fortunately, but it resulted in a spinal injury for J.C. He continued as foreman after Maxwell was replaced, but he worked in a wheelchair from that time on. It's a point of pride that I compensate him each month for the loss of use of his lower limbs."

Eden resisted an urge to tear the envelope to pieces. "I see. Well, that's one question answered. Now tell me, how does Armand fit into the picture? Because I just know he does."

This time when Lucille splashed sherry into her glass, she filled it. "You might as well oblige the girl, Dolores. Once trapped, I see little point in gnawing off an appendage to escape when you'll simply bleed to death afterward."

"You're not helping, Lucille." Dolores speared Eden with a sudden stare. "You care about Armand, yes?"

She would hold her temper, Eden promised herself, and not shout or make an ugly scene. "My feelings are my business, and changeable as I've learned from experience."

"Feelings were not supposed to be an issue." Dolores set her lips. "You weren't supposed to become involved."

"So this is what—my fault now?"

"There's no fault, only unfortunate circumstances."

"Armand works for you, doesn't he? Cop by day, liar by night?"

"Are you going to be reasonable about this, pretty girl?"

"Don't call me that," Eden warned. "I want to know what your connection to Armand is, Dolores."

After a moment's hesitation, Dolores gestured sideways. "Sit then, and I'll tell you everything. About what Armand LaMorte is—and what he is not."

HE WASN'T SATISFIED. With Al's help, Armand had been running license plate numbers for the past two hours. Dolores's investigator, he concluded as he leaned over Al's shoulder to alter one of the letters, had the eyesight of a bat.

"Try H instead of A," Al suggested.

"I did. Maybe the D's an O."

"The six could be an eight."

"Or a five."

"It's a damned wild goose chase if you ask me." Al pushed away from his cramped desk. "And a blot on both our records if we get caught conspiring."

Armand continued to rearrange letters and numbers. "The blot'll be mine, Al. You can't say no to me."

"Yeah, but I can report you—should have reported you the moment you popped back into my life. Try S instead of Z."

"I did. The vehicle's a white Lincoln, registered to a cosmetic surgeon named LeBrun."

"I need coffee." Al stretched and patted his belly. "You

want some?'' Armand made a preoccupied sound, and with a gruff, ''Keep the blinds down,'' Al left.

Lane had said the car in question was a dark-green Chevy, but was he sure or just going by general size and shape? Armand sat back and thought. When the door burst open, his mind was on license plates. It took him a moment to adjust and recognize the silhouette on the threshold as Eden and not the figure eight he'd drawn in his mind.

Even as he got to his feet, his eyes narrowed. The shadows made it difficult to see her face, but he swore he felt sparks pelting him.

''What is it, *chère?*'' he asked with caution.

It took her three strides to reach him, and when she did, her hand snaked out too swiftly for him to avoid the blow. Not that he would have in any case, but the force behind it had him closing his eyes and lowering his head as he braced his knuckles on the desktop.

''You know,'' he said simply.

''I do. FBI, Armand?'' Her voice was a hiss. ''You lied to me. You said you were a cop, and I believed you.''

''I *was* a cop, Eden, for six years.''

''And a bastard for thirty-six.''

She wouldn't listen. He knew fury when he saw it, felt it when it struck him. Still, he needed to try.

He made a careful circle of the overflowing desk. ''Will you listen to me?''

For an answer, she sucked in a breath and stepped back. Her fists, he noted, were clenched at her sides.

On the threshold, Al halted midstride, two coffee cups in his hands. ''Not a good time, right?''

The look Eden bestowed on him contained only marginally less venom than the one she shot Armand.

''Eden…'' he tried again.

But she whipped up her hands and stepped away from both of them. ''Don't,'' she warned softly. ''Just—don't.''

Armand let her go. No way would she be reasoned with

right now. Maybe not ever if the expression in her eyes had been any indication.

Al made an awkward attempt to clear his throat. "I don't suppose I can help with this. Maybe time…" He regarded the empty corridor. "Or not."

Every emotion Armand possessed sealed itself off. It was a defense mechanism; he recognized it from when his mother had died. Don't think, don't feel. Keep busy. Do.

"Mandy?"

"Let it go, Al."

"Yeah, sure." Al handed him one of the steaming cups and resumed his seat at the desk. "So what say we try Q instead of D or O?"

Armand's gaze traveled to the empty hallway. There was only one thing he could do for her now, only one thing she would let him do and only because she couldn't stop him.

No matter what the cost, he would discover who was trying to kill her.

A RED HAZE TINGED THE CITY. Or maybe it was only her vision. Eden drove too fast on streets that were narrow and slick with a light sprinkling of rain.

More thunder had been promised for that night. Good. She'd welcome the fury of a storm. It wouldn't lessen the pain of Dolores's lies or, God help her, Armand's betrayal, but it would suit her mood down to the ground.

She wasn't going to cry, she told herself as New Orleans passed by in a blur. Not yet anyway. For the moment, her eyes were perfectly dry—almost painfully so—her hands steady on the steering wheel. And it only hurt a little when she breathed.

A sob climbed into her throat. She swallowed it and concentrated on the red haze. He'd lied to her. He'd led her to believe he was a cop. He'd made her think he cared.

"Damn you, LaMorte." She turned right with no thought for her destination, just so long as he wasn't there when she arrived.

Her breath came in spasms. A favor, that's what she'd been

to him. He'd agreed to watch her because his father had asked him to, as a special favor for a special friend. Good old Mama D herself, who'd gotten to know J.C. after the accident that had left his lower body paralyzed.

"Armand's FBI," Dolores had explained as if that justified something. "I wanted the best watching over you. I suspected my private investigator wouldn't be up to the task."

She'd been right there. The word *bungler* sprang to mind, but Eden hadn't said it to Dolores. She might be angry, but she wasn't cruel.

Her cell phone rang. She wanted to ignore it, would have, except she spied Lisa's telephone number on the screen.

She pushed Talk. "What is it, Lisa?"

"It's Mary."

Eden could barely hear her. She checked the battery, then shook the phone. "Where are you?"

"In the bathroom, and stop shouting. I can't talk any louder, or she'll hear."

"What's wrong?"

"That's a really good question. I came in, went to the fridge, pulled out some tired old greens and made myself a salad. Suddenly Lisa appeared and freaked. She knocked a bottle of French vinaigrette out of my hand, grabbed the greens and dumped them in the garbage. Then she started yelling at me not to drive anywhere. I think she actually swiped my car keys."

"Where is she now?"

"In the kitchen, stripping down flowers. I can't get past her to sneak out."

It had to be Maxwell's death affecting her. They'd met at a restaurant and eaten salad. He'd left in his car. The next thing Lisa knew, he'd been bludgeoned to death and she'd been under suspicion for the crime.

Guilt wormed its way through Eden's system. She hadn't talked to Lisa enough about this, had no true idea of how, or even if, she'd been coping.

"Is she calm now?" she asked Mary.

"She's not throwing dishes around if that means anything. Look, can you come? This is one teeny tiny bathroom, and I've discovered I'm totally claustrophobic."

In her car with pain weighing her down and thoughts of Armand threatening to make her either dissolve into tears or go for his throat, Eden understood her sister's plight.

In a twisted sort of way, she also felt she finally understood what it was to have sisters. Blood sisters, both of whom needed something she'd seldom provided. Support.

It might be late. It might be a feeble attempt given her emotional state. It might not help at all. But it was past time she made the effort.

"Fifteen minutes, Mary," she promised and turned toward St. Charles Avenue. She put from her mind the niggling fear that neither Dolores's private investigator nor Armand were there to back her up. Lucky for her, curses weren't real.

Too bad, she thought with a faint chill, murderers were.

Chapter Eighteen

"It's for a talisman, not to eat."

Lisa was flinging leaves and flower petals from counter to sink when Eden arrived. She assumed Mary was still locked in the bathroom.

"Lisa?" she tried from the doorway. Her sister's head swiveled. Her fingers continued to work. She grabbed a mortar and a pestle and began to crush something brown and wilted. Eden frowned. "What are you doing?"

Lisa swiped a hand across one cheek, leaving a smear of gooey green. "Helping you. Eldest born." She waved an arm at the garbage. "She was going to eat it. Foxglove, henbane, nettle. I said, let me make the meals, Mary, veggies and salads, but she never listens. People don't listen. They get drunk, and they say things and do things, but they don't listen. It's like suddenly they don't speak English. They laugh, oh yes, they do that, but their ears stop working and I think their brains must, too. White orchids, Eden. Pin them on and off we go. But no one mentions reimbursement. I know they don't, because I—" she poked herself in the chest "—listen."

Since she hadn't understood any part of Lisa's tirade, Eden had no idea what to say. Where had all of that come from—and why?

"Freaky, huh?" Mary tapped her shoulder and made her jump.

"What started this?" she whispered.

"I told you. I was hungry. Next time I'm going to McDonald's."

Lisa tossed hairy roots into the sink. "Frigid, that's what he said. Oh, but he'd fix that. And what did she say afterward? One of life's trials. Get over it."

Eden moved forward, uncertain and frankly a little apprehensive. "Are you talking about your mother, Lisa?"

"Men are weak, women are strong." Lisa's voice roughened. "Men just have the muscle to back their weaknesses up. Move on."

"I swear she's growing more than flowers in her greenhouses," Mary remarked under her breath.

Eden glimpsed tears on Lisa's cheeks, and her movements were jerky.

"Did someone hurt you?" she asked.

"White orchids. I should have known. It's a sign." She turned, flowers in one hand, leaves in the other. "I threw them out both times, you know. Still, though—" she lowered her eyes "—it isn't the flowers' fault."

Eden watched her closely. "Who brought you white orchids, Lisa?"

"Tear the leaves, grind the petals." Lisa regarded her balled hands. "I'm bruising them, aren't I? Flowers bruise so easily. You'll need more than one talisman, Eden. I'll make three." She shook her head. "I shouldn't have thrown the orchids away. It wasn't their fault. I didn't tell Lucille that part."

"Lucille?" Eden made a cautious advance. "You talked to her about—" she spread her fingers "—this?"

Lisa smiled. "I had to talk to someone, didn't I? Mary was busy, and you were working late." The smile faded. "My mother couldn't help." She sighed. "I wish Lucille wouldn't call her a bitch. Tough isn't bitchy, it's just—tough."

"I think we've gone way beyond *The Twilight Zone*," Mary muttered.

"Call Lucille," Eden returned in an undertone.

Lisa blinked. "Armand didn't give you orchids, did he?"

The pain wanted to crash in, but Eden beat it back. "No, he didn't." Roses, yes, but not orchids.

Lisa's mouth trembled. "I didn't hit him, you know. I wouldn't bludgeon someone for giving me an orchid."

Using Eden's phone, Mary tried Lucille's cell. "Oh great," she snarled. "Party unavailable. Try the club?"

Eden nodded. She touched Lisa's arm, felt her instinctive jerk of reaction. "You can make me a talisman later, okay? Let's go outside and talk."

"Not about orchids."

"Promise."

With her fingernails, Lisa pinched off the tips of the leaves she clutched. "Does Lucille think I'm weak?" she asked.

"Like she should talk?" Mary jabbed the End button. "The system," she mimicked, "is currently overloaded. I'm to call again later." She glared at the black cloudbank outside. "Must be satellite interference."

"Try the house phone," Eden suggested.

"You should talk to Lucille," Lisa said, "before Armand gives you an orchid—or did you say he already had."

"No, he hasn't given me an orchid."

"Well, if he does, don't go out with him again. The orchid's the tip-off, Eden. Lucille knows. How do you pay a man back who gives you an orchid?"

Eden glanced at the thickening clouds. She needed to talk to Lucille, she decided. "Watch Lisa." she said to Mary.

Lisa's shoulders hunched. "I shouldn't have burdened Lucille with my thoughts. I probably babbled." She returned to the counter, discarded the leaves and petals and let her head droop. "It isn't like I don't give back. I always give back. He was wrong to say that."

Mary edged away. "She's getting weird again. Here, take your cell and call while you drive. I don't care if it's unsafe." She followed Eden from the room. "Why go to Lucille, I wonder?"

"She told us why." Eden pocketed the cell. "We weren't available."

"Yeah, but Lucille? Come on, Eden. She'd have been better off with creepy Madame Kafkha."

"Or Dolores."

"Exactly. So why choose Lady Dracula?"

"Why choose anyone?" Eden retorted. "What happened to her?"

Mary shrugged. "Someone gave her a white orchid, and it scared her."

"An orchid did that?"

"Pissed her off then."

"Why?"

"Because..." Mary faltered, shrugged again. "Because."

Hadn't Armand said that once?

Not going to think about him, Eden reminded herself. She rummaged for her car keys. "Watch her, okay? And keep trying Lucille's number. Whatever's upsetting Lisa, she obviously knows about it. I'll phone you from the club."

She left a disgruntled Mary on the front porch, slid into her car and headed for the Quarter.

The clouds were rolling in fast. They looked dark and angry, the way Eden felt. Except she felt guilty as well, and incredibly sad. Fearful, too, though she didn't want to go there right now.

Armand's face tried to pop into her head. She almost let it. But damn the man, he'd lied to her. A big lie, bigger in her mind than any of Dolores's.

Pushing on her temple, she refocused, brought Lisa's image in, shoved his out.

Something was very wrong. Lisa's thoughts had been leap-frogging between the past and the present. In both cases, white orchids appeared to have been involved. Lisa had dated a boy in high school, then hardly dated at all after that. Had the boy tried to hurt her? A jolt ran through Eden's system. Had he succeeded?

Digging in her pocket, she retrieved her cell. She punched the gas and dialed Lucille's number again.

ARMAND WAS TEMPTED to grab the computer and shake the answers out of it. Hours of searching had produced no results. No dark-green Chevy matched any of the plates he'd entered, and none of the registered plate owners had any apparent connection to this case.

Al bailed at dinnertime, claiming a peptic ulcer as his excuse. "Gotta feed it regularly and with care. I'll bring you back a burger and fries."

Great care there, Armand thought with mild humor.

He continued to work letters and numbers. He didn't let himself think about Eden. He thought briefly of his father but not in a favorable way. Yes, he loved the old man, but J.C.'s methods for getting his way needed work.

Swallowing a mouthful of cold coffee, Armand regarded the monitor. He heard thunder outside and realized it had grown prematurely dark. Not good, he decided. He'd been at this too long and with no payback at all.

His only consolation was that Dolores had instructed her investigator to keep watching Eden. So far there'd been no frantic phone calls, ergo, she must be safe.

He checked the battery level on his cell just to be sure, then substituted two for eight and L for D.

The name that flashed up had his fingers freezing on the keyboard. He scrolled down to the vehicle model. It wasn't a green Chevy, but it didn't matter. This was the first match that made sense.

He saw it in his head—black electrical tape. Tape could be used to alter plate numbers. Remove the plates from one vehicle, tape them, put them on another. Hell, he'd been a bad boy once. Bad enough to know the tricks.

Except in this case, instead of a boy, he was dealing with a murderer.

Armand scanned quickly to the address. Bonnebel Place. He didn't recognize the street name, but he'd find it. And when he did, he'd also find the answers he needed to blow this nightmare apart.

Leaving a message for Al, he checked his weapons. Both were loaded and ready and so—he shot a dark look northward—was he.

"SHE CAME AND WENT, SUGAR." Lucille's assistant spoke to Eden from the base of the staircase. "I don't expect she'll be too long or she'd have told me."

"Thanks, Ty." Eden debated. Wait or leave? She was here, halfway up the stairs, and Ty was right. Lucille would have said something if she'd planned to leave her club for the night.

Besides, where else could she go? Back to her apartment? Not likely. And no way would she return to Armand's. She'd get Mary to retrieve her cat and her clothes.

Because tears threatened, Eden called up a fresh surge of anger. How could he have lied to her, knowing what she'd been through with her ex? The only explanation was that he simply didn't care. Unfortunately she'd allowed herself to care far too much.

Lucille wasn't expecting visitors. As Eden's eyes adjusted to the low light, she saw papers strewn across the desk, drawers partly open and an oil painting pulled away from the wall.

Rubbing her chilled arms, she wandered through the room. Like the bedrooms in Armand's converted church, the space felt tight and confined. Muggy.

She glanced out the window. The clouds were black with thunder and swollen with rain. They boiled and bunched and held the threat of serious violence.

Why hadn't he told her the truth?

Mired in misery, Eden almost missed the faint creak of door hinges behind her. When it registered, and she turned, she did a startled double take and immediately rushed forward.

"Lisa! What are you doing here? Where's Mary?"

Her sister's dark hair dripped onto Lucille's carpet. She was soaked and shivering as she held out a soggy cloth bag. "You forgot your talisman."

Eden thought Lisa looked as close to a zombie as she ever wanted to see. There was little inflection in her voice and absolutely no expression on her face.

Without touching—Lisa flinched when she made a move to do so—Eden took the bag and guided her to the sofa. "Did you follow me?" she asked.

"I heard you tell Mary where you were going. It's okay, though. I threw the bad stuff out and put a date loaf where she can see it. She'll eat that when she comes out."

Eden found a blanket in the closet. "Do you want some water?"

Lisa didn't answer. She shoved a finger down her tank top. "You should wear the bag near your heart. Life's blood pumps from the source." She glanced around, perhaps in search of a plant to tend. "Who do you think bludgeoned Maxwell?"

Eden started to suggest Armand's father, but stopped herself. That was bitterness talking, and she didn't want it to take root.

"I wish I knew," she replied instead. A pitcher and four glasses sat on a table behind Lucille's desk. She poured water into one of them and took it to her sister. As she passed the blotter one of the papers fluttered to the carpet. Eden gave the water to Lisa, then turned and retrieved the paper.

Columns of numbers stared at her. Current investments, she noted. She replaced the page, then cocked her head so she could see the others. Two of the banks involved were Swiss. Many of the totals exceeded six digits.

"Now that's interesting." She spared a thought for Lucille's privacy, but dismissed it when she recalled how many lies she and her sisters had been told.

Lisa found a rubber plant to fuss over while Eden rifled though Lucille's files. Debits, credits, assets, liabilities, principal, interest accrued, term deposits, the list went on. Lucille had been a busy little investor over the years.

Not to mention successful. The numbers were impressive, and grew larger as time went on. Except for two, no three, accounts and a mutual fund which had been drained. Recently drained, Eden realized, noting the date.

She picked up the pertinent reports. These couldn't be payments to Dolores's friend J.C.—easier to think of him that way than as Armand's father—and none of Lucille's New Orleans-based businesses were losing money. If anything she'd made a bigger profit this year than last. Eden's brows came together in a puzzled frown. "So why the closeout?" she wondered.

"Too dry," Lisa clucked. "I said keep it watered, Lucille. Why doesn't anyone listen to me?"

"She listens, Lisa." Eden continued to scan the reports. "Plants just aren't high on her priority list." She extracted the most recent printout. Why cash in a three hundred and fifty thousand dollar fund that hadn't been stock market based?"

Something cinched in Eden's stomach. Her gaze traveled to the window. "What are you into, Lucille?"

The question died when her eyes landed on a partly open drawer. The cellophane packet inside was foggy, but even that couldn't obscure the object it contained.

Eden stared for a full ten seconds before she moved. She was too familiar with hypodermic needles not to recognize one when she saw it.

"Plant food," Lisa announced from the far side of the desk.

Eden's fingers closed instinctively around the packet. "What?" She raised her head.

"Fertilizer. What have you got there?"

"Nothing." Eden slid her hand into her jacket pocket and dropped the needle inside. "A pen."

"Not a plant spike?"

"I don't think Lucille has any of those, Lisa."

"She should. I gave her a bunch of stuff last month."

Eden closed the drawer, heard the lock click. "We'll ask her when she gets here, okay?"

"If she gets here."

"She will." A thousand thoughts raced through Eden's mind. Syringe, rat poison, lamp cord, falling planter, liquidation of bonds, dead people...

She pushed away from the desk, ignoring Lisa's start of surprise. "She wouldn't hurt me. Wouldn't hurt any of us. Give us up for adoption, yes, but not harm us."

Lisa watched from the side of the desk. "Are you all right, Eden? You seem funny all of a sudden."

"I'm fine. We should put these papers back the way they were."

Lisa tucked one file under another. "Do you think anyone Maxwell knew was nice?"

"I don't know who he knew," Eden drummed her fingers on the blotter. "Maybe the properties Lucille inherited were mortgaged and she wants to pay them off. But that doesn't explain the hypodermic needle."

"He reminds Mary of a mole," Lisa said. "She thinks he wears too much cologne."

Eden scooped the hair from hair her face. "She can't be a drug addict—can she?"

In a rare move, Lisa dropped to her knees and wrapped her fingers around Eden's forearm. "Why did he say I hit Maxwell on the head? I'd never hit anyone, Eden, not ever."

Eden started to pat her hand, then zoned back in. "Wears too much cologne," she repeated. Armand had said that about the loan shark he'd met. "Were you talking about Steven Cruz a minute ago?"

"Who?"

"Steven—never mind."

"I meant Robert Weir." Lisa indicated a file. "Lucille left a Post-it note. 'Robert—4:45.'"

Eden read the scribble she'd missed before. "Robert..." She tested the name, the history, the possibilities both absurd and not.

Lucille had known Robert Weir for many years, almost as long as she'd known Maxwell. She'd said she would handle him at the reading of Maxwell's will. How? Using what as leverage?

"He inherited an old office sofa," she recalled. "I thought Maxwell was just being a heartless jerk."

Lisa stiffened. "Maxwell *was* heartless. That's why someone hit him."

"Hit him." Eden regarded her sister in speculation. "Then blamed you."

"What are you saying, Eden? That Robert Weir hit Maxwell? Because he gained nothing by doing it."

"That we know of. But what if he set it up with someone else, someone who did stand to benefit."

"You mean like Maxwell's anonymous mother?"

Guilt pangs assailed her, but now wasn't the time to divulge Dolores's lies.

Thunder rumbled a distant warning. What *did* she mean? Eden wondered. Lucille had inherited two properties, valuable yes, but surely not worth killing for. She'd given her daughters up for adoption...

Eden collapsed back into the chair. That couldn't be the answer. She fixated on the file. "What's in there, do you think?"

Lightning momentarily illuminated the room, casting shadows across the floor from the lacquered cabinets. Because her gaze was diverted, Eden didn't react to the faint creak of hinges behind her until another, more sinister shadow fell across the desk.

She felt a knife blade prick the skin under her chin, and in her peripheral vision saw the barrel of a revolver being pressed to the side of Lisa's neck.

Lisa froze. Only her fingernails digging painfully into Eden's arm betrayed her alarm.

"Good girls," a voice purred in Eden's left ear. "Different, yet alike in so many vital ways. Ah-ah. None of that, Eden. Move even the tiniest bit, and both you and your pretty sister will be swimming in your own blood. You don't want that, and neither do I..." The mouth drew close enough to move Eden's hair as its owner added a wickedly amused, "Yet."

Chapter Nineteen

Armand located the street. He found the house. He even discovered the car, tarped and tucked behind the carport. There were no plates on the front or rear bumpers and no one home to answer his questions.

This was the link, though; it had to be. Borrowed and altered plates attached to a car recently purchased, either at auction or through a private cash sale, would keep anyone who saw them guessing long enough for almost any plan to succeed.

It involved money somehow, Armand reflected as he yanked out his vibrating cell and answered. It had to.

Dolores's investigator came onto the static-filled line. He sounded woozy, and Armand's stomach clenched. "I followed Eden to Lucille's club, started to go inside. Something hit me. Woke up in an alley. Bum stole my wallet."

Armand abandoned the tarped car and ran for his truck. "Where's Eden, Lane?"

"Lost her. Bystander saw two women and a man get into a dark car. Could be them."

"Did you look inside the club?"

"Just woke up, man. Raining knife blades in the Quarter. Seeing double. Possible concussion."

Armand swore and cut him off. He hit Al's number as he floored it back toward the river. When he got his ex-partner's voice mail, he growled, "He's got her, Al. He's got both of them."

"Mandy?" Al picked up. "Who's got her?"

A wall of rain swept over the Explorer. Jagged forks of lightning like the tongue of a serpent snaked to the ground. They were followed by an earsplitting peal of thunder that made the floorboards vibrate.

Al shouted above it. "Mandy, what do you know?"

Armand swerved around a slower vehicle. "I know a damned office sofa isn't worth killing two people over, and it sure as hell isn't worth Eden's life, but that's who's behind this. He removed and altered the license plates from his ex-wife's car, and now he's taken Eden. It's Burgoyne's partner, Al. It's Robert Weir."

HE FORCED THEM DOWN the fire escape at gunpoint and into the alley. He held Lisa's arm and shoved the revolver into her rib cage.

"You know the deal, Eden," he mocked. "One wrong move, yadda, yadda."

Ahead of him, Eden said nothing. She had her purse and the syringe from Lucille's desk. As they descended, she popped the cellophane and snuck the needle into her bag. The procaine samples Phoebe had given her last week were still there. She fumbled one of the vials free, slid the needle inside and drew the liquid up. Then she pocketed the syringe.

For whatever good it might do.

She snatched her hand out when he used the gun to push her toward a dark-green sedan. The ground was slippery with rain, the sky so black it felt like full night.

"Drive," he ordered and set his mouth at the side of Lisa's head. "Little sister and I will ride in the back. Key's under the floor mat."

He released the locks, muscled Lisa inside and regarded Eden over the streaming roof. "I'll shoot her if I have to, Eden. You've done plenty to annoy me already." His lips moved into a cold smile. "You'd be unwise to test me further."

Eden stared back at the face of a man she'd barely spoken to, yet whose name had become an aggravating regularity in her life since Maxwell's death. Robert Weir. Partner, witness. Murderer.

"No glasses today?" she asked, though her heart was beating double time.

"Contacts." He gave Lisa's arm a twist that had her stifling a yelp. "Get in, start the car and drive north as I instruct. And don't bother looking for that useless investigator. I disposed of him while you were snooping through Lucille's files." He brought the revolver up as Eden opened her mouth. "In," he repeated. "Now."

Swallowing her terror, Eden obeyed. The investigator was gone, and Armand... She closed her eyes, clenched her teeth.

Robert would kill them, she had no doubt of it. He'd do it regardless, but that much sooner if she forced his hand.

Because her own hands threatened to shake, she gripped the steering wheel tighter. She saw his expression in the mirror, smug and condescending where once he'd struck her as rather timid. But really, how could anyone be timid who'd worked alongside Maxwell Burgoyne for thirty years?

"Turn right at the crossroad," Robert ordered.

She saw it approaching and glanced back. Lisa's features resembled marble. She stared at her lap while the ends of her hair trembled and dripped.

As angry as it made Eden to see that, this time anger couldn't block the fear. He would kill them, what choice did he have? Why else would he be taking them north?

To the bayou...

Eden shuddered and couldn't stop. No one would find them there, even if they knew where to look.

Only a few vehicles were visible through the swirling rain. There were no blue-tinted headlights, and there was no Armand. There was only mind-numbing fear and a man with a gun wedged against Lisa's neck.

Yet for all they'd discovered, Eden still had no idea why.

"Look, I can't tell you what's going on, okay?" Lucille's assistant spread his fingers in perplexity. "People coming and going, and not through the regular doors. First Eden arrives, then Lisa. They go up, then poof, they vanish. Lucille comes, says they're gone. Got a funny expression on her face. I'm trying to tell her about one of our musicians who's retiring and moving back to his hometown in Alabama, and all she says is how so many things in life end where they began. Then off she flies. Where? I ask. Back where it began, she says. So go figure, man, and when you do, you tell me what's what and who's where, because I'm totally muddled."

Armand processed the bemused offering. "Did a man go up to Lucille's office?" he asked.

"Not that I saw. Could've, though. Three ways up, not counting the fire escape, and I only got one pair of eyes."

Weir had taken them, apparently without a struggle. That meant he had a gun.

He ran to his truck, grabbed his cell and punched Al's number.

"I'm playing a hunch," he shouted above the thunder. The line hissed and crackled. "Back where it began, Al. He's either taken them to Montesse where the curse began or out to Concordia where Burgoyne was murdered. Weir's not into curses. I'm guessing it's Concordia."

"Say again, Mandy?" Al sounded a million miles away. "What about curses?"

Swearing in French, Armand started the engine and gunned it. "Concordia," he said in a normal tone, then dropped the phone onto the seat beside him and shot onto the rain-soaked street.

He'd been talking to air. The line was dead.

He tied their hands behind their backs and with a flick of his gun ordered them to walk.

Darkness had fallen. Wind whipped through trees heavily draped with Spanish moss. The swaying curtains resembled ebony ghosts, shackled and wailing at unwelcome intruders.

The silhouette of a plantation house stood before them. Half of it was in ruins, the other half might be livable, but Eden couldn't tell with the rain and only a flashlight to guide them.

Nausea churned in her stomach. She'd never been here before, but this had to be Concordia, the estate on which Maxwell had been bludgeoned. Robert was taking them past the ruined portion of the house, likely to the garden and on— Eden's breath hitched—to the graveyard.

Thunder, rain and wind made talking impossible. They trudged through overgrown weeds and bushes to a narrow path. Once there, Robert jerked his gun toward a walkway that ended at a decrepit stone outbuilding.

"Inside," he ordered.

It took all of Eden's strength to shoulder the door open. She pushed in, heard the skitter of dry leaves and immediately spied the raised tombs.

This wasn't an outbuilding, it was a crypt, with no windows, no vents and no way out except through the door, which Robert Weir had levered closed and now leaned against.

"He's going to shoot us, isn't he?" Lisa whispered. Although her voice wobbled, there were no tears.

Shoot or bludgeon, Eden thought and gave a grim nod. She watched as Robert lit a pair of kerosene lanterns on the floor.

"You planned this whole thing, didn't you?" she asked, amazed at her steady tone. A thread of desperation crept in. "Why?"

His face, wet from the rain, shone in the lamplight. "I do what necessity dictates, Eden. Your father left me a sofa. There's irony in that, I won't deny it, but value? It's a worthless relic from a time I scarcely remember."

With her back to one of the coffins, Eden found a rough corner and began to scrape her roped wrists against it.

"Should I know what you're talking about?" She held his gaze, prayed he wouldn't notice what she was doing.

His chuckle sounded hollow and dry, like the leaves underfoot. "It's history, nothing more. But you should know I'm not the raging bastard Maxwell was."

Eden couldn't help it. Her gaze chilled. "You've tried to kill me more than once, Mr. Weir. I think that you qualify."

"Eden..."

She disregarded Lisa's warning. "You've grabbed and threatened me so many times, I've lost count. And I still don't know why."

"Money," he said simply. "I need it, don't have it, deserve it."

It surprised Eden, as she continued to rub her bound wrists across the cornerstone, that his gun hand appeared unsteady. Or was that a trick of the lamplight?

Drawing a handkerchief from his jacket pocket, he wiped his damp face. "It could have been different." He ran the cloth around his neck. "I have a daughter myself. I love her. I'm not like Maxwell. I wouldn't harm my own or anyone else's child." His smile transformed from rueful to bloodless in the time it took Eden to blink. "Sadly, dear Eden and Lisa, it appears I have no choice."

ARMAND SKIDDED TO A STOP in front of the Concordia plantation house. She was here, they all were. The green sedan with the altered plates was parked just inside the gate, not quite obscured from view by a cluster of moss-cloaked oak trees. Where had Weir taken them though? Inside or out?

Back where it began...

No lights glowed inside the restored wing of the house. It would be locked in any case. The current owners lived in New Orleans, the previous one had died a month ago. The estate sale had been postponed after Maxwell's death. That meant the house contained a number of valuable antiques, and that spelled alarm system to Armand.

He circled the house with his Magnum drawn and his eyes and ears alert for anything out of the ordinary—although he had to admit the constant thunderbolts made his task doubly difficult.

He knew where the garden was, knew the exact spot where Maxwell Burgoyne had died. Glancing up, he left the path and slogged through a patch of weeds and mud to the water. He smelled the swamp, teeming with life, rife with death.

He felt Eden's presence here. Didn't believe in such things as a rule, but felt her all the same.

"Hold on," he said under his breath. "Just hold on."

Thunder reverberated overhead. Armand glanced back, saw the lightning—and then something else, something that resembled a car.

He frowned. He knew that car. It was long, sleek and sultry, very much like its owner.

Sparing the vehicle one last look, he moved deeper into the garden, closer to Eden. And checked his mounting fear as another piece of the nightmare puzzle slithered into place.

EDEN ENDEAVORED to keep him talking. She didn't like the sweat on his forehead and upper lip, and she didn't trust the gleam in his eyes.

"Why did you hit him?" she asked as the foundations of the crypt trembled. "Weren't you taking an awful risk under the circumstances?"

Robert dabbed his upper lip. "I didn't hit him, Eden, so there was no risk to me whatsoever."

Her ropes felt looser. "If you didn't do it, who did?"

Robert didn't answer immediately. "Where are you?" he muttered. He eased the door open and peered out. "I used the circumstances of Maxwell's death to my advantage." Agitation marked his voice. "I'm not a killer of innocents." He shouted through the opening, "But I can become one very quickly."

"You tried to kill me," Eden reminded him.

He gave her an irritated look. "Those were warnings, not true attempts."

"Strychnine wasn't a true attempt?"

"I was only going to prick you." He brought his wrist up, squinted at his watch. "Late, always late. Unless…" His head swiveled, and Eden spied a glint of fury in his eyes.

She twisted on the ropes, scraping them harder against the corner.

Robert's gaze circled the crypt. "Maybe you are here." He stared into the darkened recesses above. "Maybe you have a counterplan. Are you watching me, is that it? You always were a good schemer, weren't you? You understood my intentions before I spelled them out."

"He had no heart, you know," Lisa announced out of nowhere.

Eden nudged her ankle to quiet her.

Lisa ignored the gesture. "He was cold and unfeeling, and he gave me a white orchid."

Robert scowled. "What's she talking about?"

"Nothing." Eden struggled with the frayed rope. "Maxwell disappointed her."

"Of course he did. Bastard didn't have a decent bone in his body. Damnit—" he spun back to the door "—where are you?"

Bad to worse, was all Eden could think. Beside her, Lisa continued to mumble about orchids and weak hearts.

"That's it." Before Eden realized what was happening, Robert had grasped her arm and yanked her away from the coffin. He stuffed the gun into the crook of her neck and dragged her to the partly open door. Using his foot, he widened the opening.

"I'll kill her," he shouted into the darkness. "I'll put a bullet in her and drop her right where Maxwell fell. Minus the statue of course."

"You—" Eden's teeth gnashed as he jammed the gun harder against her neck. "You stole the statue that was here and planted it in Lisa's back alley."

"Confusion tactic. Incriminating evidence. Proof of nothing. Move."

Her heart tripped. "Where?"

"Where I say."

She stumbled on the wet ground. Rain pelted down, and when it came, the thunder was deafening.

Eden fought with the rope. Ten feet from the crypt door, a lightning bolt sizzled through the sky.

The rope broke.

She must have alerted him because he paused to shake her. "What is it?"

"I slipped."

"Keep moving."

He shifted the gun to her throat. He was beside her more or less. His breath came in spurts and from the way he squeezed her arm, like ripe fruit, she suspected his anxiety was swiftly turning to rage. Or hysteria. In any case, the gun he'd poked into her throat was lodged against her windpipe, making breathing as difficult as walking.

She wondered vaguely if Lisa would stay put or run. She willed her sister to run—but where? Robert had the car keys, and the highway would be tricky to access in this deluge.

"I know you're here," Robert shouted again. "Do you care so little for your own flesh and blood that you'd see her dead? Does your money mean so much to you?"

Despite the fear that clawed at her, Eden had his accomplice narrowed down to Dolores or Lucille. She went with Lucille simply because Robert had come into her office and it was her bank accounts that had been drained.

Wind moaned through the trees. She smelled the bayou, mud and slime and sluggish creature life. She thought of Armand and swallowed a sob. How could such a horrible nightmare possibly end well?

No. She sucked in a bolstering breath. She wouldn't think like that. It would end well. She just needed to stay calm and not panic. Think, watch, act.

"Come out now!" Visibly distressed, Robert thrust Eden off the path and into a crooked headstone.

Eden couldn't be certain with the wind blowing the tree branches every which way, but she thought she glimpsed a shadow, slippery swift, duck past.

Keeping one arm behind her back, she eased the other around and dipped her fingers into her pocket. The syringe was still there, the plunger still drawn back. Offering a quick prayer, she palmed it and drew her hand out.

Robert was working himself into a frenzy. He rammed the barrel of his revolver against her temple and cocked the hammer.

"Fine," he shouted. "You want her dead, she's dead. But remember, it's you who killed her."

Now or not at all, Eden thought. She wrenched her head to the side, shoved her elbow into his solar plexus and managed—she didn't know how—to jam the needle into his right forearm. With her own arm, she knocked the gun away. Unfortunately it wasn't far enough. It hit the raised headstone and rebounded to land at his feet.

Eden swore. Drawing her arm back, she gave him a right hook to the jaw.

His head snapped sideways. He bared his teeth. His left hand clipped across her cheek. In heels on the slick terrain, she lost her footing and went down.

The gun was her first thought, breathing her second as something solid and heavy slammed into her spine, pinning her against the wet stone.

She caught a flash of dark hair and another much larger gun. There was a thud and a grunt and finally a hiss that made her think of a highly disturbed snake.

Gasping for air, Eden turned in time to see Armand glance at her. Robert, his numb right arm cradled against his chest, lowered his head and charged.

"Armand!" she cried.

He avoided the blow, but Eden realized through a haze that bringing his attacker down wasn't Robert's goal. He was diving for his gun. And, left-handed, he got it.

A sheet of Spanish moss detached itself from a cypress tree and blew through the graveyard. As if willed by Robert, it wrapped itself around Armand's shoulder and cost him valuable seconds of reaction time while he untangled himself.

Eden scrambled to her feet. She'd lost her shoes in the mud, but that only made moving easier. "Armand!" she shouted again as, from the edge of the garden, Robert took aim.

Armand spun and fired. The revolver in Robert's hands zinged off into the darkness. Startled, but aided by the elements and close cover, he sprang backward and vanished into the foliage.

Still holding his Magnum, Armand seized Eden by both arms. "Are you hurt?"

"No." Other than her heart—and her lungs which hadn't returned to full capacity yet.

A sudden dreadful thought struck her. She clutched his soaked shirt. "Lisa! Armand, Robert's heading for the crypt!"

Armand uttered a soft curse and set her behind him. "I know you won't stay here, but at least stay behind me. Which way?"

"Along this path."

She had to shout the direction in his ear. The wind swept through the trees on the heels of a thunderclap that seemed to be directly above them.

But even thunder couldn't block out every sound. In the lull that followed the final rumbling note, Eden heard a shot. It came from the direction of the crypt.

Ignoring the pebbles and twigs underfoot, she ran with Armand toward the stone structure.

Had Robert been carrying a second gun? It was the only explanation she could think of. Oh, God, had he used it on Lisa?

Armand burst into the clearing ten feet from the crypt, then halted so abruptly that Eden plowed into him.

"What—?" The question stalled as her brain scrambled to make sense of the scene before her.

The crypt door stood open. Her sister was inside, huddled against the raised tomb.

Robert lay on the stone walkway, faceup, his eyes open and glazed. Disbelief registered on his features. Blood flowed from a bullet wound in his chest.

To the left of the crypt stood Lucille. She had a revolver in her right hand.

Chapter Twenty

Robert wasn't dead. Close, but he had enough life—and spite—left in him to tell Armand where the weapon that had ended Maxwell's life was hidden. Where he'd hidden it after Lucille had used it to strike his partner down.

Her fingerprints would be on it, Robert promised. That had been his hold over her, one of two instruments of blackmail.

The other had been Lucille's daughters, first Lisa, whom he had cleverly identified as Maxwell's murderer, and later Eden, upon whom he had leveled all manner of threats in an attempt to keep Lucille in line. His goal? To ensure the payments that he'd demanded in return for his complicity in Maxwell's murder continued to flow.

If Eden thought she'd been living a nightmare before, it was mild compared to how she felt now.

Robert died en route to the hospital. Lucille offered no resistance, no excuses and no defense for her actions. Although she was still smarting by what she viewed as Armand's betrayal of her trust, Eden admired the way he dealt with Lucille, both at Concordia and, later, when she was remanded into police custody.

He'd been a cop once as Dolores said. He was known in the department. Indeed, his ex-partner Al had helped him pull the deception off.

Which didn't endear Al to Eden, although again, she found it difficult to condemn the man for his loyalty to an old friend.

Unfortunately Lisa came out of the ordeal in a state far worse than the one she'd been in before.

"Maxwell had no heart," she said to Eden in the crypt. "Lucille shouldn't pay the price for his death. He gave me an orchid. He said he had a heart condition. He ate the salad. All bad things, Eden. I knew he was a terrible man, but how was I supposed to know he lied, that he had no heart to stop? Maybe I should have guessed. He ate the salad, then walked away. Time, I thought, time would make it work. Madame Kafkha says digitalis comes from foxglove leaves. It should have worked. But Lucille hit him, so now I'll never know."

She said all of this to her sister, but Armand heard and he understood the true horror of it. He'd have to be a fool not to, and whatever else Armand LaMorte might be, he was no fool.

Neither was Lucille who took up a protective stance next to Lisa. She regarded Eden and Armand with an expression so cool and detached it was spooky.

"You heard none of that, so think nothing more of it. I killed Maxwell Burgoyne. Why? Because he deserved to die. Because my resentment of him festered over the years to the point where I simply lost it. Call it a crime of passion. Call it temporary insanity. Call it an opportunity seized and executed in a moment of uncontrolled rage. Call it what you choose, but call me the murderer because I did the deed."

Lucille had bludgeoned Maxwell, yes, but for Eden, taking in Lisa's tortured eyes, her repeated whispers about salads and heart problems and now the heart medication digitalis being a derivative of foxglove leaves, the gut-wrenching question remained.

Who had really murdered Maxwell Burgoyne?

Chapter Twenty-One

"How is Lisa?"

Lucille asked the question through a cloud of cigarette smoke. Eden waited until it cleared before responding.

"She needs professional help and time to come to terms with what she did, and why."

Across the table in the police interrogation room, Lucille shrugged. "She did nothing. It was all me. I killed Maxwell and Robert."

"But Robert killed your lawyer."

"Not a killer of innocents," Lucille repeated Robert's words. "Always a justification with that man. True, Franklin Boule was no innocent, but he didn't deserve to die simply because he suspected to whom my money was being funneled."

Eden studied her across the stainless steel table. She couldn't think of Lucille as a murderer, no matter how many times Lucille herself said it. No matter what the courts might ultimately decide.

"Was Robert clever?" she asked.

Lucille drew again on her cigarette. She'd given up smoking a year ago, but had started again after her arrest three days earlier. Eden didn't blame her.

"I'd call him an opportunist myself. He's one of those people who slips and slides through life, always taking the path of least resistance, yet with an eye to the greatest profit. I thought that a clever thing when I met him, but of course my vision had been adversely affected by Maxwell, who didn't possess a single clever brain cell.''

"Maxwell made money."

"Thanks to Dolores's savvy. He played on the fact that he was her son, her only child, a child in line to be the victim of a family curse."

"Death or worse. It's quite a prophecy."

Lucille tapped an ash. "You don't believe in curses. *La morte* was for you as Dali Kafkha said."

Eden's stomach muscles tightened. "Don't go there, Lucille."

"Armand LaMorte, Eden, not death as you assumed."

"Lucille…"

"You'll be fine. I've always known that. Even as a child, you had very definite ideas about things. I wish—" she released a long breath "—I could say the same for Lisa."

The door behind Eden opened.

"Hello, Armand." Lucille kept her tone affable and her eyes on her daughter's face. "I was told we could converse off the record."

"I'm off duty, Lucille, and officially not listening."

"Eden?"

She stole a quick look at the shadows beside her. Damn, but it hurt to see him. It hurt even more to have finally realized why the cut ran so deep.

"I'm okay with it." She fixed her gaze on Lucille and her mind on the matter at hand. "Foxglove," she said. "The leaves are used to make digitalis. Maxwell took digitalis for a congenital heart problem. Ingesting too much of the drug is as dangerous, or possibly more so, as ingesting too little. Lisa added foxglove leaves to his salad the second time they met. Why?"

Lucille took a drag from her cigarette. "He tried to hurt her the first time. Didn't succeed, but he was drunk—often the case, I'm afraid—and he got rough with her in his car. He tore her dress, bruised her, frightened her badly. He'd have done more if he could have. Fortunately, you showed her how to throw a punch a few years ago, and she got lucky, hit him in the Adam's apple.''

"And the white orchid she mentioned?''

"Maxwell gave it to her when he picked her up that first night. Someone else did the same thing many years ago.''

"The boy she dated in high school.''

"He expected more than a good-night kiss at the door in return. Again, Lisa got frightened. Again, the boy got rough.''

"But he didn't—you know. Did he?''

"She fought him off. Still, he forced her to the ground before she managed it.''

"Do you think he hurt her more than she admitted?''

"Possibly." Lucille lit another cigarette. "That'll be for the shrinks to discover. My concern was over Maxwell's treatment of her, and the response I was afraid she planned to make.''

Armand spoke from the shadows. "She told you she was meeting him a second time.''

"She did.''

"And you suspected she was disturbed enough to try and kill him?''

"I knew she was. I spoke to her after the first meeting. She was raving, hopping between present and past. I've been around, Armand. I recognize an unbalanced mind when I see one. I hoped the fever would pass. When it didn't, I knew what I had to do.''

Protect, Eden thought, but didn't say it aloud. Something in Lucille's manner told her it wasn't a word she wanted uttered.

"Robert witnessed the murder," Armand continued. Eden felt his eyes slide over her but didn't look. "He devised a plan that would benefit both of you, but himself most of all. Did you realize his intention from the start?''

"I figured it out when he emerged from his hole and named Lisa as the murderer. He accused her, perhaps thinking that Eden might step forward to cloud the issue. It was the way he thought.''

"Twisted.'' Eden surmised.

"Devious," Lucille corrected. "Weaselly, as I said."

"What if I hadn't come forward? I'm not the one who thought of it, Lucille. I wish I could say I did, but it was Mary who pushed me into it."

"We'll never know how it would have gone otherwise, will we? You did what you did, Eden, and now it's done."

"Did you know Lisa had poisoned Maxwell with fox-glove?" Armand asked.

Lucille crossed her legs. "Her garden is vast, and she'd been conversing with Dali Kafkha about a curse-related talisman for Eden so, yes, I suppose I did know, if not consciously, then just below the surface." Lucille leaned forward, a faint twinkle in her eye. "I'm sure someone's mentioned to you that poison is frequently a woman's weapon."

Eden puzzled out her expression. "You sacrificed yourself for Lisa."

Lucille chuckled. "Nothing quite so dramatic. Robert forced my hand. I didn't plan to get caught. I owed you something for giving you away, but I never intended to go to the guillotine in Lisa's stead."

A thought occurred to Eden. "Boyer or Burgoyne, Lucille? Which name is real?"

"Dolores is a Boyer. Maxwell was born as such. He took the name Burgoyne from an obscure branch of his family tree. A married-in uncle who had ties to some thirties-style Chicago gangster. Maxwell thought it sounded glamorous."

Eden studied her thin face. "What about the syringes?"

"You saw them in my desk drawer, stole one. Good tactic, by the way. Robert stole one, too, as I'm sure you've realized."

"He filled his with strychnine."

"Another maneuver designed to confuse. Strychnine in the syringe—rat poison in Lisa's greenhouse. Stop examining me, Eden. I'm not dying. I'm diabetic, have been for several years. Six months ago, I graduated from pills to injections. It's not pleasant, but I'm coping."

"And now?"

Lucille moved a shoulder. "We'll see how it goes. Life is a series of surprises. Take care of Lisa and don't let Dolores badger you about that stupid curse. As I see it, you've nothing to fear." Her eyes slanted up to Armand's shadowed face. "Does she?"

Eden braced herself to look. It would get easier, she decided, when she didn't have to see him anymore.

While she dealt with the pain and depression of that thought, Armand replied, "You're descended from Eva Dumont, aren't you, Lucille?"

Eden snapped her head around. "But it was Eva who placed the curse on her father and his mistress."

"Through whom Maxwell was descended." Lucille inhaled smoke. "I married Maxwell. I bore you. You have the blood of both the cursed and the curse giver in your veins. My hope is that Eva's blood will win out."

"Chaney," Eden murmured.

"I guess you could say a lot of us search for a hint of glamor in our backgrounds. Mine comes from an embittered witch who blamed her father for everything that was wrong in her life."

"Not true?" Eden asked.

"Who knows?"

Reaching across the table, Lucille gripped her daughter's hands and held tight. The gesture was so rare it brought unexpected tears to Eden's eyes.

"You'll be fine. With help, so will Lisa. The law won't touch her. The blow I inflicted ended Maxwell's life. Lisa is under the care of a psychiatrist who will testify as to her injured state of mind. It's done. I want you to promise me you'll move forward." She glanced at Armand, then back. "Always move forward, Eden."

"I don't know what to do, Lucille. I don't know what I want." Eden sensed rather than saw Armand leave. She heard the door open and close clearly enough.

The tears that had threatened earlier spilled onto her cheeks. Lucille made a soft sound of sympathy. And for the first time in her life, Eden laid her forehead on their joined hands and let her natural mother comfort her.

DUSK WAS SETTLING, when she reached the bayou. Dolores wasn't home, so she sat on the back porch and waited. She breathed in the scent of the swamp and welcomed the heat. Maybe it would chase the chill from her bones. She didn't hold out much hope of anything helping the ache in her heart or the sadness spawned by the visits she'd paid to Lucille, Lisa and Mary.

Poor Lisa did not want to be in the hospital. Who would tend to her plants? Not Mary. As usual, their youngest sister was doing her utmost to ignore her problems, although she had brought Lisa a three-pound box of chocolates shaped like tulips and roses that morning. For Mary it was a definite step.

As for Lucille—Eden released a heartfelt breath. God knew where that would go. But her mother had a friend who was an excellent defense attorney. He was a bear of a man with a walrus mustache, a big laugh and a courtroom demeanor that tended to shred the opposition. So given the circumstances, she supposed there was hope in that area as well.

Armand was another matter.

Surveying the singed voodoo doll she'd removed from the front porch cabinet, Eden ran her thumb over the filmy green eyes until they shone. She held it up, let the arms and legs dangle.

"Burned but not destroyed. Maybe we have something in common, after all." She smoothed the ratty hair with her index finger. "Why do men always lie?"

"Possibly because they're forced to?"

She hadn't heard the man approach. She should have since he was on crutches and solidly built, but the rubber tips and her own preoccupation had made her oblivious.

Plunking the doll on the railing, she stood. "You're Armand's father."

"J. C. LaMorte." Balancing easily, he extended a big hand. "You'll be Eden. I've seen pictures. Dolores talks about you nonstop. All three of you, but you most of all on account of the curse.''

Eden eyed the steps. "Can you...?"

"No problem, missy." He hoisted himself up and over to Dolores's porch chair. Eden took the crutches and set them aside.

His smile was huge, nothing like his son's. As if reading her mind, he chuckled. "Armand takes after his mother. Beautiful woman. Like your mama is. Like you are." He gave her a thorough once-over. "I can see why he fell for you."

Her heart stuttered for several beats, before resuming its normal pace. "Armand watched out for me as a favor to Dolores. There was nothing more to it than that. I was simply a favor to him."

"Uh-huh." J.C. studied her half-lidded. "Dolores said you were smart. She didn't mention pigheaded."

Eden almost laughed, then realized she should probably be offended. "Most people think I'm logical."

"Don't see it myself. He's stuck on you, you know. Has been pretty much from the start. Didn't want any part of the lies we pushed on him. He did it for me in the end, but only because I guilted him into it. Raised him alone, no legs, gave up on my dream of six months in Rio so he could go to the best college and so on. Parent's prerogative. I milked it."

"He knew about Dolores's private investigator, didn't he?"

"We told him, yes."

"Armand chased him the night I almost got strangled."

"He didn't know it was Lane at first. By the time he realized the truth, it was too late."

"And that night at the church?"

"He went after Weir in the graveyard. It was Lane who knocked you down in the garden. Guess he figured it was better to tackle you than let you get involved, maybe take a bullet in your other arm. Armand meant well, missy. He only ever wanted to keep you safe."

She softened but wasn't prepared to give all the way. "He

could have told me the truth and still done what you wanted
him to.''

"Uh-huh? And you'd have let that go, would you? 'Hey
there, Eden. I'm an FBI agent doing a favor for your gran.
Gonna stick to you like glue in case the curse that's got her
chewing nails is real.' Hah. You'd have told him to shove off,
then you'd have stormed out here and given Dolores hell.''

"I don't give hell. I'm a very tolerant person.''

"Who doesn't believe in curses.''

"I'm not dead, am I? And nothing worse than death has
happened to me.'' Unless you counted Armand's deception,
which was his burden, not hers, even if it was her heart that
had been wounded.

J.C. shook his head. "Pigheaded, like your grandma. Where
is she, by the way?''

"Fishing. She likes her alone time.''

Eden heard footsteps on the path. She knew they weren't
Dolores's.

Armand looked cross when she spied him. His jeans were
faded and torn at both knees. His sleeveless T-shirt had seen
better days, and his boots looked older than him.

Mild annoyance became full-blown suspicion when he saw
his father. "What are you doing here?'' He glanced at Eden.
"Together.''

J.C. motioned for his crutches. "Myself, I'm leaving. I'll
wait for Dolores inside.'' He held up a hand. "Won't eaves-
drop, and that's a promise. I like her, Armand. She'll give you
the hell you need, and damned if she isn't just as pretty as
your mama.''

He left with a wink and a casual, "He's good with teenagers
and old people. Needs work with women.''

Eden watched him go. As before, she had to choke back a
gurgle of laugher, a surprisingly difficult feat since nothing
about the situation was particularly funny.

On the porch, Armand leaned against the rail and watched
his father's receding back. "Lucille's defense attorney arrived
from Miami yesterday.''

"I met him. I like him." She plucked the voodoo doll from the post and fussed with its limbs. "I like your father, too. I shouldn't, all things considered, but I do."

"He's colorful," Armand agreed.

She knew he was staring at her, couldn't bring herself to meet his dark eyes. They were too direct, they saw too much—and they were so damn gorgeous.

"He said he forced you to lie. Is that true?"

"He asked me to lie. I could have told him to stuff his favor. I wanted to tell you, but I didn't."

"So that makes you—what?"

He pushed off from the rail. "You tell me. A bastard? A jerk? A coward?"

"I was going for good son myself."

"Not so good. I didn't do what he wanted because he asked me to. I did it out of a sense of guilt."

"Yes, he mentioned that. Used it deliberately, he said. Parent to child. I'm thinking—" she set the doll down and faced him for the first time "—it's an awfully powerful weapon to pull out. I'm thinking I might have done the same thing in your position."

He moved closer, but it was a cautious advance.

"Are you also thinking you might forgive me?"

"I'm working on it." The barest hint of amusement sparked her eyes. "How did you know about Lucille's relationship to Eva Dumont?"

"I have access to many files. When we found the name Chaney on Eva's headstone, I ran Lucille's family tree."

She cocked her head, touched her tongue to her upper lip. "So, do you figure Eva's blood will keep me safe from Maxwell's curse?"

"If it doesn't, it'll still need to get past me in order to harm you."

He was inches away and not quite touching her, and somehow Eden couldn't get any air into her lungs. That had to be a promising sign, didn't it?

Reaching out a hand, he snagged the belt loop of her jeans

and tugged her toward him. With his other hand, he brought her fingers to his lips and kissed them. His eyes never left hers.

"I love you, Eden," he said and stripped away the last layers of resentment from her heart. "I won't lie to you again, not for J.C., or for anyone."

She regarded him through her lashes before asking, "Are you any good with gardens?"

He smiled. "Are you stalling?"

"Let's say I'm burdened with a little guilt of my own." She pressed her hands flat against his chest. "Are you?"

"I'm passable. Why?"

"Will you take care of Lisa's plants for me?"

"I might." He ran his lips over her brow, her cheek, her jaw and sent a shiver through her entire body. "If you say the magic words."

"I don't believe in magic, Armand. Or, well—" Sliding her arms around his neck, she let sensation take over. "Maybe I could be convinced. Would those words be I forgive you, I trust you, or I love you?"

"What do you think, *chère?*"

"I think—" her eyes sparkled up at him "—I love you. My mother taught me how to forgive, but we're going to have to work on the trust thing."

"For how long?"

"Kiss me, and I'll let you know."

"You are going to give me hell, aren't you?"

"It's in my blood," she agreed as he lowered his head. "Both sides. No more shadows, Armand, no more lies."

"No more curses."

No more voodoo, she thought, and while the green-eyed doll watched, she pulled his mouth down onto hers.

Epilogue

Lucille had written everything down and sealed it in an envelope. She had received permission to give the envelope to Dolores. All she had to do was hand it over.

Across the table, Dolores snapped her fingers. "You listening, Lucille? Bad enough poor Lisa's in a state. You gotta hold tight, for all our sakes."

"I'm holding, *Maman.*" Her gaze strayed to the wall. "Did I ever tell you why Maxwell left Robert that old office sofa?"

"No."

Lucille brought her eyes into sharp focus. "We made love on it, Robert and me."

"Ah. Well, I figured something like that. Maxwell found out, I suppose, took his petty revenge in his will."

"Maxwell never forgave me for that night, or Robert either, apparently. I thought he might divorce me then and there, but he didn't. He waited through the birth of three daughters before he left."

"His loss that he never cared about them, or you." Dolores toyed with her bracelets. "I still got big worries over Eden. That curse won't just up and blow away because she doesn't believe." She reached for Lucille's hand. "I don't want to lose her to it. Eva's blood's not enough. I'm going to visit Dali Kafkha tonight, see what potions she can brew up to help us."

"You do that," Lucille murmured. She glanced up. "I think you have to leave now. We're being signaled."

Dolores stood. "You'll take care, yes?"

"I always do. Think twice, act once, that's me."

She waited until Dolores was gone before retrieving the envelope from her lap. No point in giving it to anyone, she thought as she tore it into pieces. What good could come of it? Eden didn't believe in the curse, and Dolores's sense of victory would increase each time she believed she'd thwarted it.

Lucille's mind shifted gears. Sex on an old office sofa... It hadn't been a memorable event, merely one of those why-the-hell-not moments, but, oh, the result nine months later. A beautiful daughter born. An eight-month daughter, she told Maxwell, but she'd known the truth. Eden had been a full-term baby, conceived on a burgundy leather couch, after business hours and a little too much French wine.

There was irony all around in that.

The curse wasn't on Eden because she wasn't Maxwell's oldest child. That was Lisa's cross to bear. It always had been.

Dali Kafkha seemed to know the truth, but of course she couldn't prove it, and it was unlikely she would say anything to Dolores. No, Dali liked Eden. *La morte* was Eden's destiny. She'd seen Armand and probably realized the truth at that moment. Armand LaMorte.

It was Lisa who was the ill-fated voodoo child, the child with Carib blood and eyes of green, eldest born to eldest grown, condemned to bear her ancestor's pain. For deeds long past, Lisa, not Eden, would reap Eva Dumont's vengeance curse.

Of death.

Or worse.

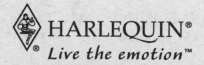

If you enjoyed what you just read,
then we've got an offer you can't resist!

Take 2 bestselling
love stories FREE!

Plus get a FREE surprise gift!

Clip this page and mail it to Harlequin Reader Service®

IN U.S.A.	IN CANADA
3010 Walden Ave.	P.O. Box 609
P.O. Box 1867	Fort Erie, Ontario
Buffalo, N.Y. 14240-1867	L2A 5X3

YES! Please send me 2 free Harlequin Intrigue® novels and my free surprise gift. After receiving them, if I don't wish to receive anymore, I can return the shipping statement marked cancel. If I don't cancel, I will receive 4 brand-new novels each month, before they're available in stores! In the U.S.A., bill me at the bargain price of $4.24 plus 25¢ shipping and handling per book and applicable sales tax, if any*. In Canada, bill me at the bargain price of $4.99 plus 25¢ shipping and handling per book and applicable taxes**. That's the complete price and a savings of at least 10% off the cover prices—what a great deal! I understand that accepting the 2 free books and gift places me under no obligation ever to buy any books. I can always return a shipment and cancel at any time. Even if I never buy another book from Harlequin, the 2 free books and gift are mine to keep forever.

181 HDN DZ7N
381 HDN DZ7P

Name	(PLEASE PRINT)	
Address	Apt.#	
City	State/Prov.	Zip/Postal Code

Not valid to current Harlequin Intrigue® subscribers.

Want to try two free books from another series?
Call 1-800-873-8635 or visit www.morefreebooks.com.

* Terms and prices subject to change without notice. Sales tax applicable in N.Y.
** Canadian residents will be charged applicable provincial taxes and GST.
All orders subject to approval. Offer limited to one per household.
® are registered trademarks owned and used by the trademark owner and or its licensee.

INT04R   ©2004 Harlequin Enterprises Limited

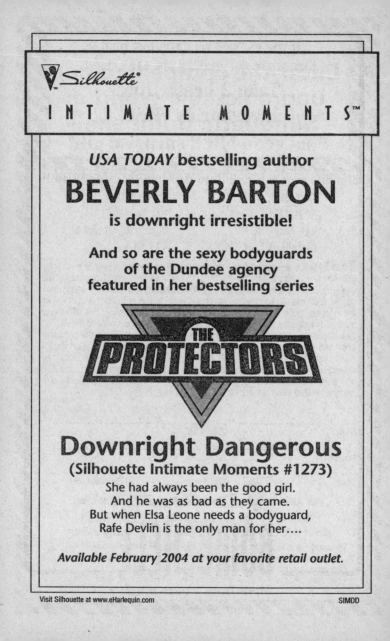

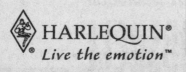